"*The Professor* is that rare combination of thrills, chills, and heart. Gripping from the first page to the last."

—Winston Groom, author of *Forrest Gump*

"Legal thrillers shouldn't be this much fun, and a new writer shouldn't be this good at crafting a great twisty story. If you enjoy Grisham as much as I do, you're going to love Bob Bailey."

—Brian Haig, author of *The Night Crew* and the Sean Drummond series

"Robert Bailey is a thriller writer to reckon with. His debut novel has a tight and twisty plot, vivid characters, and a pleasantly down-home sensibility that will remind some readers of adventures in Grisham-land. Luckily, Robert Bailey is an original, and his skill as a writer makes the Alabama setting all his own. *The Professor* marks the beginning of a very promising career."

—Mark Childress, author of *Georgia Bottoms* and *Crazy in Alabama*

"Taut, page turning, and smart, *The Professor* is a legal thriller that will keep readers up late as the twists and turns keep coming. Set in Alabama, it also includes that state's greatest icon, one Coach Bear Bryant. In fact, the Bear gets things going with the energy of an Alabama kickoff to Auburn. Robert Bailey knows his state, and he knows his law. He also knows how to write characters that are real, sympathetic, and surprising. If he keeps writing novels this good, he's got quite a literary career before him."

—Homer Hickam, author of *Rocket Boys/October Sky*, a *New York Times* number one bestseller

LEGACY
OF
LIES

ALSO BY ROBERT BAILEY

McMURTRIE AND DRAKE LEGAL THRILLERS

The Final Reckoning

The Last Trial

Between Black and White

The Professor

LEGACY
OF
LIES

A LEGAL THRILLER

ROBERT
BAILEY

THOMAS & MERCER

Text copyright © 2020 by Robert Bailey

Published by Thomas & Mercer, Seattle

www.apub.com

Amazon, the Amazon logo, and Thomas & Mercer are trademarks of Amazon.com, Inc., or its affiliates.

ISBN-13: 9781542004268
ISBN-10: 1542004268

Cover design by Shasti O'Leary Soudant

Printed in the United States of America

In memory of my friend Danny Ray Cobb

PART ONE

1

Frederick Alan "Butch" Renfroe began the day of his murder in a familiar but unlikely place. Before it closed in 2011, the Sundowners Club on Highway 64 was where Butch had liked to end his evening, not kick off the morning. Back then, after closing up his law office on the square at around five or six, he'd walk to Kathy's Tavern and drink enough George Dickel to catch a nice buzz. Then he'd drive out to the Sundowners, where he'd have a couple of more shots of George chased with several cold beers. After donating a handful of one-dollar bills to the stripper on the main stage, he'd round up one of his favorite girls for a lap dance or two. Every so often, on his birthday or some other special occasion, he'd splurge for a half hour in the VIP room upstairs.

Of course, his own enjoyment had never been the ultimate goal of his regular visits to the Sundowners. No, Butch had something else in mind as he'd gotten to know the dancers, the bartenders, the waitresses, the owner, and—most importantly—the customers during thirty-some-odd years of patronage.

Pimp was a dirty word in Butch's vernacular, and he didn't like to refer to himself or his partners in that way. *Running whores* was likewise distasteful, nor could Butch abide the terms *whorehouse, brothel,* or *bordello.*

Instead, Butch and his cohorts labeled their operation a ring or, to be more specific, "the ring." And for three decades, it produced a gravy train of money that lined their pockets.

But in October 2011, the owner of the Sundowners, Larry Tucker, was killed. All hell had broken loose. Part of the fallout was the condemnation of, for Butch's money, the best little strip club in southern Tennessee . . .

. . . and, with it, the end of the ring.

But sixteen months ago, in December 2013, a developer named Michael Zannick moved to Pulaski and began buying up land, buildings, and businesses. Everything started to change—and for the better.

Life was good, especially for Butch Renfroe, Zannick's handpicked corporate attorney. Butch had made nice commissions on each of his client's purchases. He had become the president of Zannick's start-up bank. And, as if all that weren't enough, his side hustle was back in business.

The Sundowners had reopened its doors, and "the ring 2.0," as one of his partners called it, was producing cash flow again.

Life was very good . . . until it wasn't. *And it doesn't get any worse than this,* Butch thought.

———

At this time of the morning, the Sundowners had none of the creature comforts that existed at night. No music. No booze. No scantily clad waitresses. And, finally, no exotic dancers. Indeed, illuminated by the stark glare of the sunlight peeking through the half-closed curtain that guarded the one window in the club, the pole on the main stage looked ridiculously out of place.

Butch was seated at a round table in the back of the building looking into the harsh hazel eyes of the club's manager, Finnegan Pusser. Finn, as he liked to be called, was no relation to Buford Pusser, the late sheriff of McNairy County, Tennessee, but he had something in common with the famous lawman. He liked to carry a two-by-four piece of lumber with him around the club to keep the patrons who were a bit too handsy at bay. Finn gripped the beating stick now with his right hand and glared across the table at Butch.

"Big day for you, Counselor." With his other hand, Finn fingered the handle on a cup of coffee but made no move to drink it. Butch gazed at the smoke coming off the hot mug and then, feeling sweat rings forming under his armpits, glanced around the renovated structure.

The layout was almost identical to how it had been when Larry ran things. The bar remained up front toward the entrance. Beyond that were three stages, each of which had a metal pole in the middle. Along one wall was a series of benches where men could get lap dances, and beyond the exit sign in back was a stairwell that would take patrons up to the VIP room. Adjacent to the opposite wall and sprinkled around all three stages were a number of tables with four chairs each.

Butch sucked in a quick breath and focused on the clock that hung above the bar next to a row of whiskey bottles. It was 7:30 a.m., and the club was vacant except for Butch and Finn.

"Did you hear what I said?" Finn asked.

Butch returned his gaze to the manager, who was now holding the stick up with the end pointed at the ceiling. "Yes . . . ," Butch began, ". . . but I don't think I'm going to be needed." The words sounded hollow even to him.

"You're wrong," Finn said. "And you know it."

"There's still a chance that Lou can change her mind. Lou—"

"—doesn't believe the General will budge, and neither does Mr. Zannick." Finn paused. "Lou is also cracking up. He drinks too much, and he's been beaten too many times by the prosecutor. He's become a liability."

"He's the best criminal defense attorney in town."

"So you say."

"No one has had more success defending cases in Giles County than Lou."

"You're wrong. There's a black man named Haynes that most of the town folks think is the best lawyer around."

Butch smirked. "Well, he ain't around anymore and hasn't been in years. And even if he was, there's no way that he would have represented Michael Zannick."

"Why's that?"

"Because Booker T. Rowe is Haynes's cousin." Butch licked his chapped lips and peered across the table at Finn. "You remember what we've done to Rowe, don't you?"

Finn didn't say anything, but his eyes flickered with recognition.

Butch took a deep breath. Though the floors, tables, and stages had been scrubbed clean this morning by a crew, he could still make out the faint smell of cheap beer and stripper perfume that was ever present during business hours. "Lou Horn was and is our best option. Besides . . ." He sighed and glanced at the sawdust floor. ". . . Lou has skin in the game just like me. He knows what's at stake."

For several seconds, the dark club was quiet. Butch could literally hear his heart beating as he gazed at the two-by-four, which Finn still held in an upright position.

"Assuming Lou fails, are you ready to do what you have to do?" Finn asked, smiling. His eyes held not a trace of humor.

"Yes," Butch said.

"You better," Finn said, standing from his chair and poking the end of the stick into Butch's stomach. "Unless you want to finish this day in the morgue." He gave the piece of lumber a firm jab, and Butch felt the wind go out of him. He sprawled forward and clutched his abdomen as his chin brushed against the rough wooden table.

As Finn walked away, Butch struggled to regain his breath and thought of what he must do if and when Lou failed. Then another realization hit him even harder than Finn Pusser's lumber stick.

"We're all going to fail," Butch whispered, closing his eyes and cursing his own stupidity as the inevitability of what was about to happen sank in.

I'm a dead man . . .

2

Lou Horn stuffed his hands in the pockets of his trousers and leaned his ample backside against the edge of the table. His stomach was queasy, so he dug out a pack of Tums and flipped one in his mouth. As he chewed the chalky antacid, he said a silent prayer that today's docket would be handled by the assistant prosecutor. Subconsciously, he glanced down at his watch. It was 8:25 a.m., and the docket call wasn't supposed to start until 9:00. Despite how early it was, the courtroom was crawling with defense lawyers, all vying for one last opportunity to be heard by the prosecutor before the judge took the bench. The gallery was a cacophony of nervous laughter, loud whispers, and the occasional sneeze or cough. The noise reminded Lou of the way a church congregation sounded before the music began and the preacher ascended the pulpit.

"Horn," Dick Selby said, approaching Lou and taking a place next to him. Dick was a short thin man who used to be bald on top but, a few years ago, had undergone a hair transplant. Now the top of his head looked like a cornfield, except instead of rows of the crop there were columns of curly hair lining his scalp. Some members of the bar called him "Pube Head" behind his back, but Dick didn't care. Lou figured that when your name was "Dick," it was hard to get too riled up by any other handle someone bestowed upon you.

"Dick, how are you?" Lou spoke without looking at the man as both gazed past the sea of their colleagues to the double doors that marked the exit and entrance to the courtroom.

"A lot better now," Dick said, his voice gruff.

"Why is that?"

"A little birdie just told me that Gloria was doing the docket today by herself."

Relief washed over Lou like a cool blanket. If that was true, then settlement of his case was possible. He couldn't suppress the smile that came to his lips. "Dick, you just made my—"

He stopped when he heard the double doors creak open. All conversation and laughter in the courtroom died in an instant. Seconds later, Gloria Sanchez walked through the opening rolling a large black briefcase behind her. Lou's smile widened as he heard the collective exhale of fifty lawyers who all knew their day was about to be much better. Gloria strode forward with a lean, her eyes locked on the prosecution table in front of her. She was an attractive young woman who Lou thought would be far prettier if she smiled more. Of course, when you worked for who Gloria did, the smiles were probably few and far between. He was about to approach her when he heard another sound that made his blood run cold. The clicking of high heels on hardwood.

Every head in the room turned again to the double doors, and Lou felt hot breath in his ear that smelled like coffee and bacon. "April Fools," Dick said, nudging Lou's elbow with his own and snickering.

Lou Horn felt the unmistakable twinge in his scrotum that he always absorbed every time he heard the echo of the General's footsteps. He wondered how many other men in this room had the same reaction and what the corresponding vibe was for the smattering of female defense attorneys. The General didn't cut anybody slack. If there was a dog in the room, Lou figured the animal would be whining and pissing a puddle on the floor.

"Shit," he said.

As the sound of the clicks grew louder and Lou saw her walk through the opening, Dick Selby muttered, "Have you ever figured out where she parks her broom?"

It was an old joke, and Lou didn't laugh. For once, he was more afraid of his client, who was expecting a settlement today, than he was of the woman striding down the aisle.

"Shit," he repeated.

———

Helen Evangeline Lewis relished the look of fear she saw in her colleagues' eyes. The familiar expression sent electricity through her bloodstream and, in truth, was the only feeling anymore that gave her a high. Better than alcohol. Better than sex, though it had been years since she had felt that sensation. To be respected was wonderful, but to be feared was divine. Part of the feeling was the power of her office. She was the district attorney general of the Twenty-Second Judicial Circuit, which comprised the counties of Giles, Maury, Lawrence, and Wayne. The lawyers in this courtroom represented clients whose futures could rest in her decision whether to deal or go to trial. But she knew that wasn't entirely it. The attorneys didn't just fear the office. They feared *her*.

She walked slowly, her back straight and her head completely still, just as her mother had taught her when she was a teenager entered in every beauty contest in southern Tennessee. She had never won a single event, though she had gotten third place in Ms. Teen Giles County. But the training in posture and stride had served another purpose: it had given her poise, confidence, and discipline, which she had later relied on to succeed in the male-dominated world of law.

The color of Helen's hair, which fell to her shoulders, was midnight black, and her skin was pale. She wore a black suit and matching high heels, with lips painted bright red. The outfit was her trademark, so to speak, and she figured there were few attorneys in Giles County who could remember her wearing anything different to court. She knew the clothes added to her aura, and oddly enough, it was her ex-husband, Butch, who had unwittingly suggested the look.

During their marriage, which had ended in divorce in 1995, he liked to watch NASCAR on Sunday afternoons. He even took Helen to the Talladega 500 in 1991. Butch's favorite driver was Dale Earnhardt, and it wasn't just the man's ability behind the wheel that made him a fan. "The Intimidator," as Earnhardt was known, drove a black stock car with a white number 3 outlined in red painted on the sides. His helmet, jumpsuit, and racing glasses were also black and white, which made him strike a formidable pose on the track. At the race in 'Dega, Butch got them a seat close to Earnhardt's pit crew. He said that the black car and uniform were the perfect complements to Earnhardt's fearless, almost reckless brand of racing and made him stand out among all the other sponsor-supported cars with their colorful, forgettable designs. "Brilliant marketing," her ex-husband marveled. The week after the race, Helen wore a black suit to work every day. Since then, it was the only color she had donned in the courtroom.

As she strode to the front, she let her eyes move over the swell of attorneys, a few of who were brave enough to issue a greeting. "General, how are you?" "Morning, General." Helen nodded, saying nothing, but she relished the military bearing that was an oddity of Tennessee law. In most jurisdictions in the United States, the district attorney bore no title. He or she was simply called by Mr., Ms., or Mrs. in the courtroom. If there was any reference beyond that, it was simply as "the prosecutor." But in the state of Tennessee, the district attorney was referred to as "General" during court proceedings. For Helen Lewis, who had been one of only a handful of women to graduate in her law school class of over one hundred at the University of Tennessee in 1978, to be referred to as "General" by the opposing attorney, who was almost always a man, was empowering.

When she stopped at the prosecution table, where Gloria Sanchez was removing file jackets from the briefcase, she caught the same look of trepidation in her young assistant's eyes as she had seen in the gaze of the defense attorneys whom she had just walked past. And though Helen knew that her look and title added to her intimidation factor, the final and most important piece was her attitude.

Helen Evangeline Lewis, for lack of a more sophisticated term, was mean. Not evil. Not bad. Mean. She had tried being nice and cordial early in her legal career, but the effort made her feel weak, and she found that her male counterparts did not take her seriously. Worst of all, she had lost cases she should have won and pled matters that should have gone to trial. When she thought of those days, it was hard not to be sick to her stomach.

"Docket sheet," Helen said, her voice sharp and clipped.

Gloria handed her a stapled packet filled with the names of the defendants who were on this week's trial agenda. Helen scanned the list for show. She had meticulously gone over the docket in her office for the past hour and knew exactly what she wanted to do with every case.

"General, can we talk?"

Helen recognized the voice without turning. She spoke while still gazing at the list of cases. "What do you want, Lou?"

"A second of your precious time," Lou said, not feigning his irritation.

She turned and bore her eyes into his, and the large, plump man whom she had waged battle against in this very courtroom for almost three decades held her gaze. "OK," she said.

"Zannick." Lou spoke the name as if it pained him to say it. "Can't we reach a resolution?"

"I've made my final offer."

"Ten years with no possibility of parole is worse than what he'll get if the jury convicts, General. Be reasonable, please."

"He raped a fifteen-year-old girl, Lou."

"He thought she was eighteen, and it was consensual. There are extenuating circumstances. Please—"

"No. The fact that Mr. Zannick is a wealthy playboy who's donated a truckload of money to Martin Methodist College isn't an extenuating circumstance."

"I'm not talking about that, General. The girl . . . *the victim* may have only been fifteen, but she was sexually promiscuous. I have witnesses who say she was giving out blow jobs for one hundred dollars a pop in the boys' locker room."

Helen glared at the defense lawyer, not believing what she'd just heard. "Lou, under the rape shield rule, evidence of a victim's other sexual behavior is strictly prohibited. Even if your witnesses were telling the truth, which I doubt, those facts don't come in, and you damn well know it."

Lou crossed his arms over his chest, undeterred. "I suppose not, but good luck finding any jurors who aren't aware of Amanda Burks's reputation at Giles County High. This is a small town, Helen. And while Mandy's sexual exploits might not come in, the fact that she waited a month to report the alleged crime will." He paused. "Do you really think a jury will believe anything she says?"

"Yes, I do. She was in *ninth grade*, Lou. The victim was a child, and Mr. Zannick, despite how he dresses and how much time he spends with college students, is a thirty-seven-year-old man."

Lou took a step closer and spoke in a low whine. "General, do you want the town to lose the Hoshima contract?"

Helen folded her arms but said nothing.

"According to my client, the paperwork has been finalized, and the only holdup is this charge. *Hoshima*, General. I know they aren't Toyota or Honda, but they are an up-and-comer in the automobile industry, and their plant will bring almost a thousand jobs to Giles County. Think about that for a second, would you? A thousand jobs."

"There isn't a power and influence exception to rape, Lou, and this isn't just a statutory charge. Your client used force and intimidation to have sex with the victim against her will."

"Her word against his."

"I'll take hers, and I believe a jury will too."

Lou held his mouth open, but no words came out.

"Are we done, Lou? There are a few others here who want to talk with me."

Lou Horn finally closed his mouth and licked his lips. "You're making a huge mistake."

Helen squinted at him. "I'm doing my job."

"If you convict Michael Zannick of rape, you won't have your job come November." He stepped closer to her. "The people of this town are tired of you and your strong-arm tactics, General. Pulaski is dying on the vine and needs the energy that an automobile plant would bring. Sack Glover understands that. Why can't you?"

Helen bristled at the mention of her opponent's name in the upcoming election. "All that man understands is taking care of those who are financing his campaign." She paused. "Like your client."

Lou smirked. "The parole board last Friday found him pretty persuasive." He leaned forward and spoke in a lower voice. "You put Ennis Petrie in prison for being part of a race crime that garnered national headlines. And yet, at the hearing, despite how hard you argued that Ennis didn't deserve parole and how you shamed the board at even considering the suggestion, they gave it to him anyway."

Helen set her jaw and steeled herself. She would remain calm. "You and I both know that if Bo Haynes had been there, the outcome would've been different."

"Woulda, shoulda, coulda," Lou snapped. "Let's suppose Bocephus Haynes had shown his face. I doubt the board would have thought much of what a twice-suspended lawyer with a criminal record felt about anything. All I know is that Ennis Petrie, former sheriff of this county, charter member of the Tennessee Knights of the Ku Klux Klan, and one of the ten men in 1966 who lynched Bo's father, or, to be technically correct, *stepfather* . . . is walking the streets of Pulaski again. And you want to know why? Because the board followed the hearing officer's recommendation and not your own." Now it was Lou who paused. "Remind me who the hearing officer was again, General?"

Helen glared at Lou, whose pale face had broken out in sweat. She ignored the question. "The rest of the cases on this docket are probably going to plea out or be continued. If Zannick doesn't take the deal I've offered, then we're teeing it up in a few hours."

Lou took a step back and squinted at her. "You're gonna regret this."

Before Helen could respond, Lou turned and walked away. Helen squeezed her hands into fists, reeling from the encounter. She'd tried cases against Lou Horn since the late 1980s, and, though their discussions had often been spirited, the crotchety defense lawyer had never insinuated that a decision might affect her political standing.

Dick Selby took his place in front of her. "General, you look nice today. I like your shoes."

Helen rolled her eyes, grateful for a return to the familiar. "I've worn the same brand of high heels for twenty years, Dick. If you're going to be such a serial ass-kisser, you could at least become good at it."

His face fell, and his slim shoulders sagged. "Can you do any better for me on Paulson? Maybe reckless driving and community service?"

"No, he has to plead to DUI. I can lower the fine to four hundred dollars, but once we start striking the jury, all offers are off the table, and I'll seek the maximum fine of fifteen hundred dollars as well as sixty days in jail. What says Mr. Paulson?"

Dick grimaced, but he didn't hesitate. "He'll take the deal."

3

The law firm of Frederick A. Renfroe, LLC, was located on West Madison Street a block from the courthouse. Three doors down from the office was the two-story square building where, on Christmas Eve of 1865, six Confederate veterans had formed the Ku Klux Klan. For decades, a plaque commemorating the founding of one of the world's foremost hate groups had been plastered to the front of the building, but in 1989, the owner had removed the monument and then welded it on backward. Now, all you could see when you passed by was a blank green-and-black slab.

Butch gazed out the window of his second-floor conference room, gripping tight to the cell phone he held in his right hand. From this position, he could barely make out the plaque. Occasionally, on what used to be called Robert E. Lee Day but now was celebrated in most of the country as Martin Luther King Jr. Day, Butch would see tourists walking aimlessly down Madison, clearly trying to find the plaque that no longer had any words on it. And just last week, some Klansmen marched around the square after news broke that Ennis Petrie had been granted parole. Some of the men had ambled down the sidewalk and had knelt in front of the plaque, and a few had even kissed the damn thing. Then Butch had stood in this spot and marveled at how there were people in this crazy world who still celebrated the exploits of the Klan and wore the white robes and hoods with pride.

Now, though Butch was looking out the same window, he saw nothing at all. If the Klan were marching below in full regalia, Butch would have stared right through them.

Though the air-conditioning was blowing full blast, beads of sweat had pooled on Butch's forehead and under his arms. With his left hand, he reached down and grabbed the pint of George Dickel he'd placed on the sill. The top was already off—he'd had several belts since coming in that morning—and he took another pull.

"Easy with that, Butch. What is it? Nine thirty in the morning?"

"Nine fifteen," Butch said and took another sip of whiskey. Then he turned around and looked down at the conference room table, where Terry Grimes was seated with his hands clasped in a tent position over his stomach. Terry wore a blue-and-white seersucker suit—the same one he had donned for the commercials he'd cut for Terry Grimes Ford/Buick, which was the largest dealership in town now that Walton Chevrolet had closed a few years back. In public, Terry almost always wore a coat and tie. A friendly seersucker for his TV spots, a navy or charcoal suit for the hearings he attended as a six-term county commissioner, and perhaps a sports coat and slacks for meetings of the numerous civic organizations and bank boards he served on. He was a clean-shaven man whose salt-and-pepper hair was thick and curly, and for as long as Butch had known him, Terry had been trim and fit. He worked out at the YMCA five times a week, didn't smoke, and never touched alcohol.

But despite these healthy habits, Terry Grimes did have one dubious and dangerous vice.

Which is why we're all sweating bullets now, Butch thought.

"Anything from Lou?" Terry asked, smiling up at Butch. One thing about Terry was that, regardless of his mood or stress level, the man had an almost permanent smile attached to his face. While Lou seemed to be buckling under the pressure of their predicament and Butch wasn't far behind, Terry's demeanor was unchanged. He looked like he was

16

waiting on the results of a horse race as opposed to information that could send him to jail for the rest of his life.

"No," Butch said, turning back to the window and beginning to feel the alcohol permeate his bloodstream. He pressed his forehead to the glass and closed his eyes.

———

The ring began on November 17, 1993.

As with many instruments of evil, it started innocently enough. Terry Grimes was celebrating his fortieth birthday, and Butch and Lou wanted to do something fun and memorable to mark the occasion. By that time, Butch's marriage was all but over, and Lou had been divorced for years. Meanwhile, Terry, ever the politician, maintained a delightful public image with his beautiful wife, Doris, a platinum blonde with Dolly Parton–size breasts, and their three golden-haired daughters, all of whom would one day be elected homecoming queen of Giles County High School. In November of 1993, Terry had just been elected to his first term as county commissioner and already served on the board of directors of almost every financial institution in Giles County. He had also become the owner of the local Ford dealership, which allowed him to buy a nice condominium in Orange Beach, Alabama, for his family.

But despite living what most would consider the American Dream, Terrence Robert Grimes had a weakness. Terry, for lack of a better term, was a pervert.

And Terry's two best friends, Butch Renfroe and Lou Horn, knew it. Hence, on the evening of Terry's fortieth trip around the sun, Butch and Lou set up a VIP room extravaganza for their pal at the Sundowners Club with several willing dancers. Though the girls were supposed to only fondle each other, once the whiskey started flowing, Terry found his pants around his ankles. When the show was over, Terry, ever the salesman, confided in his two friends that perhaps other hardworking men might like to enjoy the pleasures that he had experienced.

"For a reasonable price, of course."

———

Keeping his lids shut tight and gritting his teeth, Butch thought back on that infamous night. How could he possibly have known that a birthday present to a friend would evolve into a prostitution scheme that would spread out over eight counties and two states and last over twenty years, bringing in more than $5 million in cash?

Or that it would eventually involve the trafficking and sexual exploitation of minors?

But it had and did.

And now, after all that time, they were finally paying for their sins.

Butch opened his eyes when he heard heavy footsteps trudging up the stairs. He turned and waited, his stomach fluttering from nerves and dread. Below him, Terry Grimes crossed his legs, his hands still resting across his stomach, the picture of calm and cool.

Seconds later, Lou Horn stood in the doorway to the conference room. His face was ashen.

"Well?" Terry asked.

"No deal," Lou said, moving his gaze from Terry to Butch. "Trial begins this afternoon at one thirty." Lou staggered toward the table and grabbed the pint of George Dickel. After pausing for a couple of seconds to let out a raspy breath, he took a long swallow.

"What in the hell are you doing?" Butch asked, snatching the pint from Lou's sweaty hand. "You can't be drinking four hours before the start of trial. Are you crazy?"

"Easy, boy," Lou said, reaching for the pint. "I know exactly what I'm doing."

While Lou and Butch stared each other down, Terry stood from his chair and put his hands in his pockets. "If you have a plan, Lou, why don't you enlighten us?"

Lou's fingers clasped around the bottle, and Butch finally released his grip.

The defense lawyer took another long sip and sighed. Then he peered at Butch with hollow eyes. "Buying you some time."

4

At 10:30 a.m., Helen walked briskly out of the courtroom. Her prediction to Lou Horn had come to fruition. Of the twenty-eight cases on the docket other than Zannick's, all but four were resolved with a plea agreement, and the remainder were continued. Now, Judge Page was taking the pleas while Gloria Sanchez and each defendant's respective attorney stood by to answer any questions. Before beginning the process of officially entering the plea agreements, Page had assured Helen that the Zannick trial would start that afternoon at 1:30 p.m. sharp.

Helen felt her heartbeat racing as she headed down the hallway to her office. Some lawyers couldn't handle the pressure and intensity of criminal prosecution, but Helen Lewis lived for it.

The countless hours of preparation. The patience, persistence, and backbone required to handle the various personalities of witnesses, opposing lawyers, and judges. And the day-to-day hassle of settlement dockets and taking pleas.

It was a brutal grind, but the buzz she felt right now made everything worth it. Helen stopped when she reached the sign reading **DISTRICT ATTORNEY GENERAL**. She took a deep breath and straightened her suit.

In a rape trial, the most important witness was the victim. Making sure Amanda Burks was ready for what awaited her in the courtroom would be the difference between winning and losing. Over the course of the past six months, Helen had met with Mandy at least fifty times to go over her story and to prepare her both for the questions that Helen would ask on direct examination and, perhaps even more importantly, the accusations that Lou Horn would hurl on cross.

Now they were out of time. This would be their last session before trial.

Helen exhaled and opened the door to the office. Her secretary, Trish DeMonia, who was on the telephone, hung up the receiver after muttering a salutation under her breath. Then she pointed at Helen's private office. "They're both inside."

———

Mandy Burks sat in one of the two client chairs. She wore a violet sundress that hung to her ankles and was cut right below her neckline. A conservative look that would hopefully make her present to the jury as a young underage girl. Mandy had olive skin, brown hair, and brown eyes. Holding her hands in her lap and fidgeting in her chair, she was the picture of vulnerability and youth. Helen had to fight the urge to smile. *Perfect,* she thought, turning her focus to the other woman in the room.

Lona Burks was in her midthirties. She wore a black dress fit for a funeral, which was one of three outfits that Helen had picked for her to wear to court. Helen had also advised Lona to trim her hair, which had once hung below her shoulders. But even with the conservative hairdo and clothing, Lona Burks was still a striking woman with her hourglass figure. She would probably be considered beautiful if not for the crowns that littered her mouth, the product of years of tooth decay from methamphetamine abuse. Lona had kicked drugs and alcohol five years ago, which was around the same time she had quit her job as an exotic dancer at the Sundowners Club. Now she worked as a housekeeper for several families in town and mowed lawns on the weekend to make ends meet. Unfortunately, her sobriety and newfound employment had done nothing to improve her prior reputation in the community as a drug addict and stripper. Since she'd brought her daughter to the sheriff's office to report the rape last November, Lona had been worried and angry that Mandy wouldn't get a fair shake because of her mother's indiscretions. Now, Lona's knees knocked against each other, and she gripped her arms tight across her chest. She peered at Helen with eyes full of fear and anxiety. "You're sure it's going to happen."

Helen nodded. "We start in less than three hours."

Lona's eyes moistened. "Thank you, General. For not settling and for getting us this far. I . . ." She stopped talking as emotion finally got the better of her.

Helen glanced at Mandy, who continued to fidget and was now gazing at the floor.

"Lona, would you mind sitting out in the reception area while I go over Mandy's testimony with her?"

For a moment, Lona looked as if she might protest. But then, nodding and biting down on her trembling lower lip, she stood and planted a kiss on her daughter's cheek. "You listen good to General Lewis, OK?"

Mandy said nothing and continued to look at the carpet. After hugging Mandy's shoulder, Lona mouthed another *thank you* to Helen and opened the door. Once it shut behind her, Helen reached forward and took Mandy's hand.

"Look at me," Helen said.

Mandy did as she was told, but her eyes appeared vacant.

"Are you all right?"

Mandy shrugged. "Just nervous."

Helen gave her hand a squeeze and let go. "Me too."

Mandy raised her eyebrows.

"I am," Helen said. "But nerves can be good. They create energy and will keep us on our toes. We have to use that, you understand?"

"Yes, ma'am." Her eyes had drifted to the floor again, and her voice was so quiet that Helen barely heard her.

"Sit up straight with your eyes on me," Helen snapped.

Startled, Mandy pressed her back against the chair and peered at Helen. "I'm sorry, I'm just—"

"You're anxious. You're scared. You're doing something that a teenage girl should never ever have to do. I get it, Mandy. I understand, and I think a jury will too." Helen paused. "But you have to be strong. Do you understand?"

Mandy nodded. "Yes, ma'am," she squeaked.

"I didn't hear you."

"Yes, ma'am," Mandy barked, and her face had wrinkled into a defiant scowl.

Perfect, Helen thought again. Innocent. Vulnerable. But determined when her story is challenged. That was the dance they were about to do. The jury must sympathize with Mandy Burks, but they also, most importantly, must believe her.

"Good girl," Helen said, leaning back in her chair and crossing her legs. "Now let's run through it one last time."

———

The rape itself had taken less than two minutes.

Mandy went to a party at a mansion off Highway 31, just a mile or so from the high school. She'd been invited by her boyfriend, Jason Lightfoot, a senior at Giles County High and a starting linebacker on the football team. Jason had heard about the event from a friend of his who was a freshman at Martin Methodist.

Mandy hadn't even known who owned the house when she and Jason arrived at around two o'clock in the afternoon. The attendees were a mixture of college kids and grad students. There were kegs of free beer, and a couple of guys were passing around plates of green Jell-O laced with vodka.

Mandy wasn't sure how many Jell-O shots she'd done, but after a few, she was able to stomach the taste of beer. In addition to drinking, the afternoon was spent riding four-wheelers through a path in the wooded area behind the house, Jet Skiing in the man-made drainage lake, and finally swimming in the Olympic-size pool. By sunset, Mandy was drunk and asking Jason to take her home. But her boyfriend, who was also hammered, wanted to take one final ride on an ATV before dark. They got in a fight, and Jason went by himself on the trek while Mandy went inside the house to pee.

The downstairs bathroom was occupied, so she stumbled upstairs until she found one that wasn't. After doing her business, she opened the door and bumped into a man who was standing in the hallway. He was holding a blue drink in his hand, and the collision caused him to spill it all over Mandy's white cover-up. Mandy laughed and started to try to find the stairs, but the man stopped her and asked if she wanted to clean up. He had some things of his girlfriend's that she could borrow to wear.

Despite her drunkenness, Mandy could tell that the man was much older than she was. Nevertheless, he was cute, and Mandy, still mad at Jason for abandoning her, said, "OK."

He led her into a huge bedroom and told her that she could use the shower. By that point, Mandy felt sick. Her memory was hazy on some of the story, but she knew she had thrown up before getting in the shower. Once she turned the water on, she heard the glass door open and close. The only thing keeping her from passing out at this point was the water that pelted her forehead. Then she felt his soapy hands on her body. Touching her. She said no, but he didn't stop. He slid his finger inside her, and she tried to fight off his hand, but she kept losing her balance on the slippery tile floor. She elbowed him in the stomach and managed to climb out of the shower, but he caught her by the vanity. He straddled himself against her so that she couldn't move and pressed against her back until she was bent over the sink. She screamed "NO!" but his hand clasped over her mouth and muffled the sound.

And then . . .

———

"And then *what*, Mandy? What happened next?" In the small confines of her office, Helen could hear Mandy's choppy breathing pattern.

Mandy Burks bit her lower lip and peered straight ahead, her eyes and voice fierce with determination. "He raped me."

"How long did it last?"

Her face remained stoic. "A minute. Maybe two."

"Is the person who raped you in the courtroom today?"

Mandy nodded and pointed to her left, which would be the direction of the defense table from the witness stand once they were in the courtroom. "Yes. He's sitting right there. Michael Zannick."

Helen gave her a swift fist pump and cleared her throat. "Let the record reflect that the witness has identified the defendant."

For several seconds, there was silence in the office. Finally, Helen cleared her throat. "You know what's coming on cross?"

Mandy nodded.

"You were drunk on the night of October 2, 2014, isn't that correct?"

"Yes, I was."

"And you admittedly don't remember everything that happened that evening, correct?"

"That's correct, but I do remember being raped. I'll never forget that as long as I live."

Helen flashed a thumbs-up sign and continued. "Now, Ms. Burks, you didn't report what happened to you for over a month, isn't that correct?" Helen mimicked Lou's southern drawl.

"Yes, sir," Mandy said. "I wish I had come forward sooner, but I was embarrassed and scared."

"You were so embarrassed and scared that you waited thirty-six days from October 2, 2014, the night of the alleged rape, to November 7, 2014, to tell anyone about it."

Mandy set her jaw and looked straight ahead where the jury would be sitting. "I wasn't sure anyone would believe me and, yes . . . I was terrified. But, eventually, I realized that I didn't want Mr. Zannick to do what he did to me to anyone else."

Helen leaned back in her chair and extended both of her hands toward Mandy in a double thumbs-up gesture. "Great job. You may not get a sarcastic question like that at the end, but Lou is known for taking things too far. If he does, you shove that answer straight up his butt."

Mandy managed a tentative smile. "Yes, ma'am." Then, smiling, she added, "Thank you."

Helen returned the smile and walked around the desk. She squatted and grabbed both of Mandy's hands in her own. "Are you ready to put Michael Zannick where he belongs?"

"Yes, ma'am, I am."

5

In the reception area of the district attorney general's office, Helen exchanged hugs with Mandy and Lona and advised them both to get something to eat. "Two hours till go time," she said. "I need you both to be strong and alert."

"Will do," Lona said, escorting her daughter out of the office. As they were walking out the door, Gloria Sanchez brushed past them. She looked at Helen as she placed several file folders on her desk. "I've talked to Jason Lightfoot and the high school, and he can be here to testify with thirty minutes' notice."

"How do you feel about him?" Helen asked, not hiding the challenge in her voice.

"For what he brings to the case, I think he'll be fine. He corroborates Mandy's story up to him leaving to take the ATV out before sundown. When he returned, he'll say that he found her in the house, hugging her knees by the fireplace. When she saw him, she begged him to leave, and her eyes were red as if she'd been crying."

"How will he hold up on cross?"

Gloria sighed. "He'll admit he had been drinking, and so had Mandy. He obviously didn't see the rape, and Mandy never mentioned it to him, despite him asking her all the way home what was bothering her."

Helen rubbed the back of her neck, thinking about Mandy's reputation at Giles County High. She knew that Lou was right about one thing. Pulaski was a small town, and Mandy's exploits would precede her into court regardless of whether the jury was shown any evidence of it. "What does Lightfoot say about the blow job in the locker room mess?"

Gloria peered up at the ceiling. "He's never heard anything about that."

"And you think he's lying."

Gloria met her gaze. "I know he is."

"And why's that?"

"Because half the students I've talked to had heard that rumor. Mandy supposedly gave head to one of the Fitzgerald twins before the first home JV basketball game."

"The rumor started with the Sartain kid?"

Gloria nodded. "Joey Sartain. He's a freshman guard on the team who'd arrived early to the game to get some extra shooting in and saw Mandy blowing Doug Fitzgerald in the locker room. He took a picture on his phone and sent it to several of his friends on Snapchat."

"He didn't see any money exchange hands, though, right?"

"Correct. We're still not sure where that part of the story originated. Probably an embellishment as no one I've spoken to corroborates that detail."

"The Snapchat photograph disappeared after his friends opened it, right?"

"Yes, that's the way it works and why the kids like Snapchat so much."

Helen again worked the facts through in her mind. She was aware of all of this type of information already and knew that none of it would come into evidence. "You've seen the picture, right?"

Gloria nodded. "The school investigated the incident after a parent of one of Sartain's friends reported it. The school's IT person captured the photograph."

"All the image shows is Doug Fitzgerald's pleasure-soaked face and the back of the girl's head," Helen said.

"True."

"There's no way you can definitively identify Mandy from it."

"True again."

"But you think it's her."

Gloria cocked her head at Helen. "Don't you?"

Helen didn't answer the question, instead firing off another of her own. "The JV basketball game was about a month after the rape."

"Correct. The game was on November 3, 2014, and the rape happened on October 2." She paused and swatted a stray string of hair out of her eyes. "If it's true, General, and I believe that it is, why would Mandy Burks be engaging in oral sex in a public place so soon after such a traumatic experience?"

Helen glared at her young assistant and stepped toward her. "Rape affects women in different ways, Gloria. You'd be wise to not make any callous assumptions."

Gloria held her ground. "Just pointing out the potential prejudice. A reasonable person on the jury who's aware of this rumor might ask the same thing. He or she could also ask why Mandy waited until November 7 to report the rape, which was thirty-six days after the crime but only four days after the tryst with Fitzgerald at the ball game."

Helen cringed, knowing that Gloria was right. She decided to switch gears. "Why did Mandy and Lightfoot break up?"

"Mandy broke things off a week after the rape. Said she liked him but that they didn't have anything in common."

Helen gazed down at the hardwood floor and bit her lip. "Let's go back to the night of the rape. As far as we know, Zannick has no alibi for where he was when Mandy was in the house."

"None. It's a straight-up he-said-she-said."

For a moment, there was silence in the small space as the two women eyed each other. "Good work," Helen finally said.

"Thank you. General, can I ask you something?"

"Shoot."

Gloria darted her eyes at Trish, who looked down at her desk when Helen's gaze landed on her.

"Have you thought about pleading Zannick out to distribution of alcohol to minors and dropping the rape charges?"

Helen ground her teeth together. "No, I have not. We don't plea out rape cases in this office. We try them."

"I understand that," Gloria continued, holding Helen's eye. "But the defendant is a popular figure in town, and we don't have a witness to the rape. And given Mandy's reputation . . . we could lose, General."

"What's your point? Losing is always a risk." Helen took another step forward. "Why don't you spit out what you are really trying to say?"

Gloria sucked in a quick breath. "Do you want to risk losing a high-profile case so close to the election?"

Helen scowled at her chief deputy. "The *election* will never sway me from doing what's right. Mandy Burks deserves to be heard. You got that?"

Gloria's face turned crimson. "Yes, ma'am."

"Good. Do you have our requested jury instructions ready to go?"

"I need to tweak a couple of the patterns, and then I'll walk them down to the judge's chambers and give them to Clarice."

"All right, then get to it. I don't want any holdups once we start pretrial motions this afternoon. If everything goes smooth, we may have a jury in the box by the end of the day and might even squeeze in opening statements."

"That's not going to happen," a raspy voice said from the doorway.

Helen wheeled at the sound and saw an unwelcome visitor standing in the opening, holding a newspaper in his hand.

The Honorable Harold Page was a tall, skinny man with thin white hair and a bald spot on the back of his head. He eased into the room, nodding at Gloria and Trish and then propping himself on the edge of Trish's desk.

"Your Honor, what gives us the pleasure?" Helen asked, not bothering to keep the annoyance out of her voice.

Page folded the paper and stuck it into the crook of his armpit. "You're not going to like it," he said, and the frown on his face caused his eyebrows to crease. Page had been a circuit court judge in Giles County since Ronald Reagan was president, and most members of the bar didn't even know what he had done before taking the bench.

Helen did. The judge had been an assistant district attorney when she had joined the office in the early eighties. They had worked on a few cases together, and she had found him to be dim witted and dull. She also hadn't liked the way he would sometimes put his arm around her and let his hand drift a little too close to her backside. But Page was affable and had family connections littered throughout the town. He won election to the court in 1983 and had always been perceived as a prosecution-friendly judge.

Helen never liked the man and still didn't. If there was one quality in a human being that she detested above all else, it was laziness, and Harold Page was lazy. She suspected he was about to prove it again.

"I'm waiting with bated breath," Helen said. "What am I not going to like?"

"General, my judicial assistant just got off the phone with Sandra over in Lou Horn's office. Sandra told Clarice that Lou is vomiting in the bathroom. Not sure if it was something he ate or if he's come down with a bug." He stopped, and Helen gazed back at him with a cold stare.

"And?" she said.

"He's asked for a continuance until tomorrow morning."

"Faking a sickness to get more time is a rookie play, Harold," Helen said. "You've been doing this long enough to know that." Helen rather enjoyed calling Page by his first name, which she regularly did when they weren't in an official proceeding. Page had been on the bench so long, Helen figured his wife probably answered, "Yes, Your Honor," when he asked for sex after turning off the lights in their bedroom at

31

night. She knew that the informal address irritated him, and that was why she did it.

"We've both known Lou for an awful long time, *Helen*," Page said, also forgoing formality. Helen could tell that it pained him to do so. "Have you ever seen or heard of him telling a lie to get out of court?"

Helen hadn't, but she wouldn't give Page the satisfaction of agreeing with him. "He looked fine this morning," she said.

"Really? I thought he appeared a little pale."

Helen chuckled. "That's because he knows he's going to get his butt kicked. There were a lot of pale faces in court today."

Page sighed and pushed himself off the desk. "You may be right, but all the same, Lou's never lied to me before. I'm going to continue the trial until nine in the morning."

Helen gave him a tight smile, knowing that further argument would be fruitless. "Then I guess I'll see you tomorrow."

Page walked around Helen to the door and, after twisting the knob, paused in the opening and gazed at her over his shoulder. "Any chance y'all might settle? Seems like there would have to be room for a deal in this situation."

Helen shot a glance at Gloria, who was now sitting behind her desk. The assistant prosecutor crossed her arms and averted her eyes, making Helen wonder if the judge had planted the seed of a settlement with Gloria while pleas were being taken in the other cases. Helen gritted her teeth and turned back to His Honor. "Why is that, Harold? Because the defendant is rich and about to open an auto plant?"

The judge's jaw tightened. "I was thinking more about the victim and her mother. This trial will be torture for them and . . . could air a lot of dirty laundry."

Helen glared at Page, feeling sick to her stomach. "Not if the judge on the case follows the law."

Page's face flushed dark red, and he narrowed his eyes into slits. For a long three seconds, he said nothing. When he spoke, his voice was low and filled with menace. "Because of your many years in this office, I'm going to give you a mulligan this time, General." He paused and pointed a shaky index finger at her. "But if you *ever* make an insinuation like that toward me again, I'm going to hold you in contempt, and you'll spend the night in a jail cell. Do you understand?"

Helen maintained her glare and swallowed back the words she wanted to say. "Yes," she managed.

Page waited a half beat for an apology that wasn't coming before shaking his head. "I'll see you at nine tomorrow morning." Then he slammed the door behind him.

6

At 1:30 p.m., the exact time when the trial of Michael Zannick should have started, the courtroom was empty except for Helen, who sat in the back row of the jury. She had taken her heels off and was scratching her left calf with the stockinged toe of her right foot. The Zannick file lay on the chair next to her, and she had finished reviewing Sheriff Springfield's investigative report for at least the hundredth time. She took a sip of coffee from a Styrofoam cup. It tasted harsh and bitter. Exactly the way she felt.

Helen rose from her seat and began to pace the floor, digging her toes into the hardwood. She had dispatched Gloria to notify Mandy and Lona as well as to update their other witnesses on the change of schedule. Helen suspected that her young assistant was now in the office going over the pretrial motions and the witnesses whom Helen was going to let Gloria handle during the trial. Though the office of the district attorney general was out the double doors and down the hall, Helen preferred to work in the quiet of the empty courtroom away from the ever-ringing phone, the nagging emails, and the annoying drop-ins from defense attorneys.

But there was more to it than the elimination of distractions. She loved the circuit courtroom of the Giles County Courthouse. She thought of the area between these four walls as her church. Her cathedral. Her *home*, if you wanted to get it down where the goats could eat it. She gazed up at the old balcony, whose original purpose was to segregate black spectators from the whites and which now was more of a museum piece that Willa Michaels, the archives custodian, would show visitors during tours of the courthouse. So much history had transpired between these four walls. Some good. Some bad. Some downright ugly.

In that sense, the courtroom's past mirrored that of the town of Pulaski.

Helen never took for granted the importance of her position and the fact that during each trial she had a chance to create her own legacy, one carved in justice.

The lower gallery had four separate seating areas with six rows of wooden chairs that converged upon a railing that separated the judge, jury, and lawyers from the spectators. Beyond this barrier were the prosecution and defense tables and, between them, a box with a high-back chair inside, where witnesses were called to testify.

Helen ran a hand over the wooden armrest of the witness stand, thinking about Mandy Burks, who would be the first witness called by the state. After jury voir dire and opening statements, Helen knew that the jury would be chomping at the bit to hear from the victim, and she wouldn't make them wait.

"Feet hurt?"

Startled, Helen turned toward the voice, which sounded familiar. The lights in the gallery had been turned off, and Helen squinted into the darkness. After a couple of seconds, she saw the shadow of a man rise from a seat on the left side, about halfway back, and approach slowly. He had his hands in his pockets, and when he walked, each shoulder dipped slightly. Helen knew the stride without seeing the man's face, and she subconsciously gritted her teeth. "How long have you been here?"

"Not long," the man said, opening the small gate that separated the gallery from the bench and bar. "About five minutes." He paused and took a step closer. "I've always enjoyed watching you work."

Helen felt heat on her face. "Maybe because work has always been such a foreign concept to you."

He shrugged. "Maybe. But it might be because you're so damn sexy when you walk around the courtroom in your socks."

She rolled her eyes. "What do you want, Butch? I'm prepping for a trial." She turned away from him and walked back to the chair in the jury where she had placed her file.

"So I've heard," he said, following after her. "Michael Zannick, right?"

"Your buddy," Helen said, sitting down and pulling out a folder from the file. "Did Lou send you down here to try to get me to change my mind on the deal I offered?"

"No," Butch said. "I was actually hoping you would let me take you to dinner tonight. Maybe Legends? Or, if you're up for a short drive, we could go to Fayetteville and eat at Cahoots. Get a table in one of the old jail cells. You used to love that place, remember?"

Helen gazed up at him. Even at sixty-four years old, Butch still reminded Helen of a matinee idol with his athletic frame; thick, perfectly combed hair; and toothy grin. The only differences were that his once blond locks were now silver, and his blue eyes, which had always seemed to carry a hint of mischief, now contained the dull and permanently bloodshot afterglow of alcohol abuse. "Are you drunk?" she asked.

He scoffed and stuffed his hands back in his pockets. "I was feeling nostalgic and wanted to take my ex-wife to dinner. That's not a crime is it, General?" He forced a smile, and Helen noticed he was bouncing on the balls of his feet. *He's nervous,* she thought. "Or maybe you don't want to go to dinner because you're dating someone," Butch said, squinting down at her.

Helen felt a tingle of irritation, but she bit her lip to quell it. There was something wrong here. Since their divorce almost twenty years ago, Butch had kept his distance, occasionally calling her but never stopping in to see Helen at work. "Who I date is none of your business," she said, her voice measured.

"Have you seen anyone since . . . Professor McMurtrie?"

Helen felt a wave of sadness ripple through her. More than a year had passed since Tom McMurtrie had succumbed to lung cancer, but hearing his name was like a kick to the stomach. For a moment, she struggled to breathe. His loss had begun to resemble a wound that almost had started to heal and then, at the mention of a place, the recall of a memory, or sometimes even a whiff of aftershave, broke open, and the hurt was fresh and even more painful than before.

"Are you OK, Helen?"

Helen exhaled and bit her lip. She glared at her ex-husband, unwilling to show any weakness or vulnerability in front of him. "Why are you here?"

Butch took his hands out of his pockets and rubbed them together while gazing down at the floor. Then he walked around the front row of the jury and took a seat next to Helen in the back. "I'm in trouble," he whispered, still looking at the floor.

Helen's stomach tightened. "You need money?"

"It's more complicated than that." He shook his head and turned to look at her. The whites of his eyeballs were a forest of red fissures, and she smelled the familiar scent of bourbon masked by mouthwash on his breath. "I need you to dismiss the rape charge against Michael Zannick and plead him to a misdemeanor." He paused. "A slap on the wrist."

Helen shot to her feet. "Lou did send you."

"No," Butch said. "He didn't."

Helen picked up her file jacket and placed it under her arm. "Then Zannick did. You're in deep with that son of a bitch, aren't you?"

Butch didn't answer, his hollow eyes looking out toward the dark gallery.

"Answer me," Helen demanded, stepping closer to him. "You're Zannick's contract lawyer, right? If the deal between that rapist and Hoshima goes through, then you make a huge commission." She paused, and when he remained silent, she stuck her index finger in his chest. "Am I right?"

He gave a swift nod of his head and continued to gaze at the gallery. The scene reminded Helen of the many times Butch had come home drunk at night and she had laid into him while he sat at the kitchen table and gazed dull-eyed toward the den. The memory only angered her more.

"You listen to me, you selfish leech. There is no way in hell that I'm going to dismiss the charges against Michael Zannick. He raped a fifteen-year-old girl, and he's going to serve the maximum."

"I'm not here because of the deal with Hoshima." He paused. "Or my commission." He chuckled bitterly. "I wish that was it."

Helen cocked her head at him. "What then?"

Finally, he pulled himself to his feet, but he still didn't look at her, now peering at the floor. His mouth curved into a tired smile. "We should've had kids, you know. I think that would have done it."

"Done what?" she asked.

"Saved our marriage."

She scoffed. "You think a couple of rug rats would have stopped your boozing?"

He finally looked at her, and his eyes were now blood red. "They might've made you take a step back. Maybe paid a little more attention to what was going on at home instead of your all-powerful career."

She crossed her arms tight around her chest. How many times had she heard this same spiel over the years? In her ex-husband's mind, Helen should have spent their marriage revolving around his orbit. Being the good wife who had dinner prepared every night when he got home. Listening to him whine about his workday and stroking his ego if he still wasn't feeling ten feet tall and bulletproof.

Subordinating all her own hopes and dreams to his own.

Helen Lewis wasn't wired that way, and Butch should've known that going in. He hadn't met her at a church picnic. They had met during her first year and his third of law school in Knoxville. She had never wavered in her desire to one day be a prosecutor. Butch had always thought he could change her. *Soften* her, as he liked to call it, but it was he who'd ended up changing in the end.

"We tried to have kids," Helen finally said. "Remember? For three years, we tried. It wasn't in the cards, and you didn't want to adopt."

"You know that's not the whole story," he said.

"Is that why you came down here?" she asked, edging closer to him and catching another gust of mouthwash and George Dickel. "To rehash old grudges?"

"No," he rasped.

"Why then?"

He leaned forward and whispered into her ear. "Dismiss the charges against Zannick." He paused. "Please . . . do it for me."

"No," she said. "That entitled prick is guilty of raping Amanda Burks, and my job under the laws of the State of—"

"To hell with your job," Butch snapped, lashing out with an open palm at one of the jury chairs. "Everything is always about your job, *General*." When he spoke her title, spittle flew from his mouth, and his face flushed almost as red as his eyes. "The victim may have been only fifteen years old, but her mother is the easiest lay in Giles County, and based on what I've heard from the high school, little Mandy is following in Momma's footsteps. If that girl is a victim, then I'm a teetotaling priest."

Helen felt heat behind her eyes. "Whether Mandy Burks was sexually promiscuous or not has no relevance to the case, and I won't allow Lou to put her character on trial or play any victim-blaming games."

Butch sighed and then he smiled, but there was only sadness in his eyes. He walked toward the gate with his patented uneven stride. When he reached it, he spoke without turning around. "You're up for reelection in November, right?"

Helen felt her stomach tighten. She didn't answer the question.

"Someone finally has the balls to run against *the General*," Butch said, his voice rising to the rafters of the courtroom. He turned to face her. "Sack Glover was in my law school class. Did you know that?"

Helen did, but she held her tongue. She sensed that the point of this little charade was about to be made.

"Yeah, old Sack was never much of a student. And mediocre is probably the best description of him as a lawyer. You know that better than me." He paused. "But one thing I'll say about old Sack. He's a persistent bastard. Ever since he declared his intent to run against you, he's been burning up my cell phone trying to get me to disclose any dirt I might have on you. Were you aware of that?"

Helen wasn't, but the information didn't surprise her. She didn't respond.

"I have some dirt," he said, and Helen felt a cold tingle run up her arms. "Wouldn't you agree?"

"Butch—"

"Remember what you did your third year of law school?" he interrupted, rubbing his chin in mock thought. "I think it was around December or so of 1977, wasn't it? If that ever went public . . ." He trailed off and whistled. "It'd be the atomic bomb to your campaign and career."

Helen glared across the courtroom at him. Gooseflesh had broken out on her arms and the back of her neck, and her heart was pounding in her chest. She was dumbfounded, but shock was beginning to give way to white-hot anger. "*You wouldn't dare,*" Helen finally said, speaking through clenched teeth. "You promised. You *swore* that you would never speak of that to anybody. We both did." She gazed down at the hardwood floor and bit her lip, trying to stem the tears she felt forming in the corners of her eyes.

I won't cry, she told herself. *I will not let this son of a bitch make me cry.*

She was still peering at the floor a few seconds later when her ex-husband's black loafers came into view. He had walked back to her and now was only a foot away. When Butch spoke again, his voice was soft but firm.

"I know what I said, Helen, but desperate times call for desperate measures. This is a conservative county. How do you think the community will feel about what you did? With Sack's family and business connections, the only thing keeping you ahead in the polls is the common folk. You've always owned the grass roots of this county, and for good reason. You're a hard-boiled prosecutor and a former cop. And your record is pristine." He licked his lips. "But how do you think your supporters at the First Baptist Church will feel about what you did in December of '77? Think they'll still take up a collection for you and come out to the polls in droves? How about the men at the Elks Lodge that you've had curled around your finger for years? What about the deputies in the sheriff's office that all worship you?"

She finally raised her eyes. "And if I dismiss the charges against Zannick?"

He ran a finger over his closed mouth and flung an imaginary key over his shoulder. "My lips are sealed."

"You're blackmailing me. I ought to arrest you."

"You won't," Butch whispered. "If you haven't dismissed by the time opening statements begin tomorrow, I'm going to tell Sack everything. You hear me? And I've also drafted a press release for the *Pulaski Citizen* and all the local radio and TV stations, which I'll distribute the second you begin your opening." He paused. "Is prosecuting Zannick worth losing your whole career?"

He took several steps backward, squinting at her the entire time. Then he pivoted and headed for the gate. When he reached it, her voice stopped him.

"Frederick Alan Renfroe!" During their marriage, when Butch had thoroughly pissed her off, Helen would snap off his full name as if it were the final straw. The last warning whistle, so to speak.

He turned his head. "I'm sorry, Helen. I really am, but I have no choice."

"You're bluffing," she said, her voice a low growl. "You don't have the balls to blackmail me."

41

"I wish this was a bluff." He paused. "You have until opening statements begin."

"I'm going to kill you!" she screamed. "I swear to God, Butch, as Jesus Christ is my witness, I will kill you dead."

He smiled, and his eyes shot to a spot behind Helen before meeting her eye. "I love you too."

———

Once Butch had fled through the double doors, Helen clenched her fists and let out a scream. She wheeled toward the chair she had been sitting in toward the back of the jury, and that was when she saw the figure standing at the door to the judge's chambers.

Gloria Sanchez's face had gone pale, and her back was against the door.

"What are you doing?" Helen asked.

"I dropped off our requested jury charges and thought I'd see how things were going in here. Since the judge has taken the afternoon off, Clarice let me cut through his chambers." She paused. "Are you OK? Your hands are shaking."

Helen clasped her right hand in her left and then rubbed them both against her skirt. "I'm fine." She started to walk toward the double doors but then stopped and squinted back at Gloria. "How much of . . ." She waved a hand at the gallery. ". . . *that* did you see?"

Gloria shrugged. "A few seconds maybe. I had just walked in. Long enough to hear him tell you he loved you." She gave a nervous smile. "Who was that?"

Helen smirked. "An asshole of biblical proportions."

"Oh . . . I thought he might be your ex-husband."

"One and the same," Helen said, her stomach twisting into a knot as her mind drifted back to Butch's threat. *One and the same . . .*

7

Butch Renfroe's mother liked to say that her only son was "sorry."

Now, Gladys Renfroe didn't mean "sorry" in the sense that a person was apologetic or regretful but rather the lesser-known and undeniably southern definition of the word.

Useless. Wretched. Pitiful. If a person needed a picture to illustrate this meaning, Butch figured that a snapshot of himself would do the trick.

I'm a sorry son of a bitch, he thought, gazing at his reflection through the display window of Reeves Drugs on the Giles County Courthouse square.

His cell phone vibrated in his pocket, and he grabbed it without glancing at the screen. He knew who was calling just as sure as he knew that his ex-wife wouldn't be backed into a corner.

"Yeah," he answered.

"Did you deliver the message?"

"Yes."

"And?"

"She said she was going to kill me." Butch winced at himself through the glass.

For a good fifteen seconds, there was silence on the other end of the line. Then the voice, low and deliberate, responded. "Sounds like you're a dead man, then."

8

Helen held the revolver in both hands and pointed it at the target's forehead. Instinctively, she squeezed her left eye shut, and the index finger of her right hand hovered over the trigger until . . .

She fired without thinking. Once, twice. Three, four, five, six times. Then she lowered the .44 Magnum, whipped off her goggles, and walked forward until she could survey the results. The pattern wasn't her best. Two shots between the eyes, a couple on the chin, one on the left temple, and one just under the left nostril. Still, she had hit the face six times from twenty-five yards out. *Six kill shots,* she thought, nodding her head in satisfaction. That was good shooting under anyone's gauge.

She replaced the target sheet with a clean one and returned to her spot at the end of the range. At 8:00 p.m., she was the only person here, and in truth, the facility had been closed for almost an hour. But Doug Brinkley, the owner of the place, had been a friend ever since Helen's days as a deputy in the sheriff's office, and since he lived only a quarter mile from the range, he didn't mind opening it for her.

"Big trial tomorrow, huh?" Doug had asked after turning the lights on and giving her several target sheets.

Helen nodded, anxious to burn the stress of the day off.

"Well, I hope you put that bastard under the jail," Doug said. "I know what he's done for the town, but I don't like him. And I don't trust anyone from New York City."

The popular rumor was that Michael Zannick hailed from Manhattan, but his last address prior to Pulaski had actually been in

Boston. Regardless, Helen didn't correct her old friend. Instead, she simply said, "I'll do my best."

"Your best is usually more than enough," Doug said before giving her the key. "Stay as long as you want and then lock up. You can put the key in my mailbox on your way out."

Despite the anxiety she felt, she smiled, grateful for good people like Doug Brinkley whom she'd spent the last thirty years of her life earning the trust of.

What will Doug think if Butch drops the bomb tomorrow? Helen asked herself once she was alone in the facility. As she began to shoot—starting with twelve warm-up shots at three yards and gradually moving to twelve more at five, seven, ten, fifteen, and finally twenty-five yards before starting over at three again—more questions dogged her mind. *Will he still unlock the shooting range for me after hours? Will he even vote for me in November? Could thirty years of goodwill be erased by one awful mistake?* And then there was "the nut cutter," as she so eloquently labeled the most critical question in any case.

Am I willing to find out?

After an hour, Helen's face and neck gleamed with sweat, and her shoulders ached. She had completed three circuits and counted only a handful of misses. Despite wearing plugs, her ears still rang with the sound of the gunfire, but like always, she felt better. More in control of herself and her emotions.

When she was a young girl and only child, her father had taken her dove hunting every fall and deer hunting in the winters. By the time she was thirteen years old, she was a crack shot with a twelve gauge and not bad with a rifle. John Paul "J. P." Lewis had been a lieutenant in the Pulaski Police Department, and he worked six days a week. Since he was always working or sleeping, the only quality time Helen ever had with him was in a field or a deer stand. Though her mother abhorred the hunting excursions, thinking they made her daughter "too rough" and hurt her chances to compete in beauty pageants, Helen loved every minute of them. For her sixteenth birthday, her dad took her to a range and showed her how to shoot handguns. Then let her ride patrol with him that night, and she saw him arrest a drunk driver. J. P. Lewis wasn't a sophisticated man by any stretch, but he was a good man and had an important job that had helped keep the town safe.

What would Daddy have thought about what I did in law school? she wondered, cringing as she stuffed the snub-nose revolver in her pocket and headed for the door.

She turned off the lights to the warehouse and locked up. Then she walked toward her car—a government-issued black Crown Victoria. She'd stopped at home to change clothes after work and now wore faded jeans, a gray sweater, and a black cap with an orange *T* on the front. She had replaced the high heels with dark brown cowboy boots— "shitkickers," as her daddy would have called them.

As she started the vehicle and gazed out at the hilly landscape of Highway 64, which was lit by a full moon, she wished she could call Tom; if there was anyone in the world she could talk to about her current predicament, Tom McMurtrie would have been that person.

But cancer had taken Tom last year. Helen had no one she could speak with about her problem, so she did what she always did when she was under extreme stress. She didn't talk to anyone. She didn't pray. She didn't go for a long walk or run.

She'd fired her powerful revolver over and over again at the paper targets, and as the sound and smell of gunfire filled her eardrums and nostrils, she eventually realized there was only one fail-safe solution to her current situation.

Helen squeezed the steering wheel, wishing for all the world that there was another way. *But there isn't,* she thought, putting the Crown Vic in gear and involuntarily tapping the pocket of her jeans.

9

Butch lived in a two-bedroom house off East College Street about a half mile from downtown. At 9:30 p.m., he'd just showered and changed into boxer shorts, a navy bathrobe, and flip-flops. He poured himself a glass of Dickel over ice and plopped down on the couch in the small den, bringing the bottle with him so that a refill would be within easy reach.

Butch thought back to Finn Pusser's not-so-subtle threat at the Sundowners that morning. *Assuming Lou fails, are you ready to do what you have to do?*

Butch grabbed the remote and flipped channels on the tube until he found a basketball game. Sighing and caring nothing about either team on the television screen, he took a sip of whiskey and wrinkled his face as the liquor burned his throat going down. He'd done what he had to do, and the results were as predictable as Vanderbilt failing to contend for the SEC championship in football every year. Helen hadn't budged, and his time was almost up. If anything, Butch's actions today had only made things worse.

His cell phone lay on the wooden coffee table in front of him, and he snatched it. He'd missed no calls, text messages, or emails while he had been in the shower. He clicked on his texts and reviewed the two messages he'd sent Helen after leaving the courthouse. The first, an hour after their conversation in the courtroom, was short and sweet. Have you thought any about what I said? I'm probably going to the Hickory

House for dinner if you want to join and talk more. Please, Helen. Don't force my hand.

The second text, five hours later at 7:35 p.m., was even shorter. Well . . . it said.

Butch gazed at the television screen. "Well . . . I'm screwed," he whispered.

"Talking to yourself now?"

Butch turned his head toward the voice but didn't get up off the couch. He focused his eyes toward the kitchen, where there was a door that opened to the outside. "I thought I locked that door," he said, slurring his words ever so slightly.

The figure approached the couch. "I've done a lot of thinking about what you told me."

Butch raised his eyes. "And?"

"And there's only one way to fix our dilemma."

Butch exhaled and cocked his head at the figure. "I agree, but—" His words caught in his mouth when he saw the revolver in the person's right hand, rising until the barrel was pointed at him. *Where did that come from?* Butch wondered, blinking his eyes. The figure must have been holding the weapon the entire time, and Butch hadn't seen it in the dark. "What are you doing?"

"Solving the problem."

"*No,*" Butch whispered.

"Yes." The voice and the barrel of the gun remained steady. "I'm sorry, but this is the only way."

Butch Renfroe felt tears forming in his eyes. He leaned back against the couch and took a final sip of whiskey. On the TV, two players scrambled for a loose ball, and the referee blew the whistle. Butch thought of his mother and how unsurprised she would be at this end for him. All of that accumulated waste packaged into one perfect and fitting finale. "Just get on with it," Butch finally said.

He raised his glass again, but it never touched his lips.

10

Helen's body tingled with adrenaline as the twelve jurors who would decide the fate of Michael Zannick took their seats. She let out a deep breath, trying to calm her rapidly beating heart. She was always amped for the beginning of a trial, but today was different.

Helen hadn't slept a wink. She'd sat in the recliner in the den of her home and tried to think through all the various scenarios. Her instincts, which normally were tried and true, had failed her. Finally, as the sun began to rise, she'd showered, gotten dressed, and drunk several cups of coffee, but she'd been unable to eat anything. She'd driven to work, fully expecting officers to be waiting on her when she arrived, but they weren't. Even so, throughout jury selection, Helen had found herself distracted every time the double doors to the courtroom creaked open and closed, thinking each time that someone was going to come in with news about Butch.

Now it was go time. Regardless of what had happened last night or what the consequences of her actions might be, there was a rapist sitting across the courtroom from her who belonged in a prison cell.

Helen moved her eyes to the defense table, looking past Lou Horn to the defendant. Michael James Zannick wore a gray suit with a navy tie. With brown hair cut short and a slight build, nothing about the man's appearance stood out save for a surgically repaired cleft lip that had left a faint triangle-shaped scar just under his nostrils. Zannick could have easily covered the blemish with a mustache, but he was clean shaven. As Helen gazed at the man, she thought—not for the first time—that he didn't look like a sexual predator. Of course, neither did Ted Bundy.

As a career prosecutor, Helen knew that the most dangerous predators, like Zannick, were the ones you didn't see coming.

As if sensing her gaze, Zannick turned his head and looked at her. His expression was blank, but after running his index finger over his scar, he winked.

Helen felt her stomach tighten into a knot, but before she could react any further, she heard Judge Page's gravelly voice.

"General, is the state ready for opening statements?"

As if on autopilot, Helen stood. "Yes, Your Honor." While she walked toward the jury railing, she saw Clarice Hanson, Judge Page's judicial assistant, bust out of the doors of his chambers. Clarice approached the bench, where Page had risen from his seat. He leaned forward and listened to her whisper something in his ear. Then, just as Helen was about to address the jury, Harold Page's voice stopped her.

"Ladies and gentlemen of the jury, I'm sorry to have to do this, but we are going to need to take a recess. Sundance . . ." Page glanced at the bailiff, who had been within earshot of whatever Clarice had informed him.

"Members of the jury, please follow me," Sundance said. As he ushered them out, the bailiff stole a glance at Helen.

Ricardo Cassidy was only a couple of inches over five feet tall, but his upper and lower body were chiseled from years of weight lifting. His skin tone was almost orange from tanning bed use, and he dyed his hair platinum blond. Because of his hair and last name, Helen had taken to calling him Sundance from almost the minute they had been introduced, and the nickname had held over the years. Now everyone, even Harold Page, addressed the bailiff in this manner. As he looked at her, Sundance's normally tan face was even more ashen than Lou Horn's.

Once the jury had filed out, Judge Page, who'd remained standing, ushered the attorneys forward. "Counsel, let's talk in chambers," he said, the tension in his voice palpable. "You too, Hank," he said, pointing a finger at Sheriff Hank Springfield, who'd been sitting next to Helen at the prosecution table.

Helen's feet remained glued to the floor. She was still standing in the well of the courtroom, that place right in front of the jury, her customary spot for beginning an opening statement. All morning, she had been under the odd and ridiculous notion that if she could start her opening, everything would be OK. All that had happened last night after she'd left Doug Brinkley's gun range would go away. *So close,* she thought.

She felt a hand squeeze her arm, and she glanced at Gloria Sanchez, whose eyes were wide. "Any idea what this is about?" Gloria asked.

"No," Helen said.

Helen was the last person to enter Page's chambers. As she did, a uniformed deputy closed the door behind her. She blinked her eyes, noticing that two other officers were also in the room. Judge Page had already taken his robe off, and he and Hank were whispering back and forth. Remembering her place in these proceedings and steeling herself for whatever came next, Helen stepped forward and spoke in a sharp voice. "What's going on here, Harold?" She frowned at Page, knowing that everyone would expect her to be annoyed that her opening statement had been interrupted.

The judge grimaced and then turned to the sheriff. "Hank?"

Hank Springfield had been the sheriff of Giles County for the past two and a half years, rising to the top position when Ennis Petrie was sent to prison. Hank had an athletic, lanky build and in a former life had been the starting fullback for the Giles County Bobcats. Now, at just under forty years of age, his brown, curly hair was beginning to have some salt and pepper on the sides. Helen had always thought Hank was attractive in a boyish way. She also liked his eyes, which were sky blue. They pierced hers now with concern. "General, we received a 911 dispatch from Butch Renfroe's house off East College about fifteen minutes ago. A neighbor had gone to Butch's home to check on him when Butch hadn't shown for their morning workout and wasn't answering his cell phone." Hank paused, glancing at Judge Page before turning back to Helen. "Butch is dead."

Helen's knees shook and her legs felt wobbly. She grabbed the chair in front of her and sucked in a quick breath.

"General, are you OK?" Hank asked, touching her lightly on the elbow.

Helen blinked back tears and looked at him. "I'm fine."

"I need to go," he said. "It's a crime scene, and I should be there."

"Crime scene?" Helen managed.

He nodded. "He was shot several times." The sheriff paused. "His face and upper body were also badly beaten."

Helen gripped the chair and sucked in a ragged breath.

"General?"

"Go," she said. When he hadn't moved, she straightened her body. "*Go*," she repeated, speaking through clenched teeth. Then, as Hank shuffled out the door with the three deputies trailing on his heels, Helen looked at Page, who was now standing behind his large desk. "Judge, we'd ask for a short recess until . . ." She stopped, feeling tears again welling in her eyes, but she fought them off. ". . . until the sheriff's office can complete their initial investigation of the crime scene."

Page turned to Lou Horn, who'd sat down in one of the visitor chairs. "Any objection, Lou?"

The defense lawyer's face was ghost white as he brought a shaking hand to his lips. Slowly, he shook his head.

"OK," Page said, gazing at Lou with concerned eyes. "I'm going to adjourn with instructions to arrive back at nine tomorrow morning. By then . . ." He sighed. "Maybe we'll know the next step."

11

Helen left the courthouse ten minutes later, telling Trish that she didn't feel well and was going home. Once in her car, she pulled onto East College Street. As she passed the Dollar General, she saw several police cruisers turning left down Pecan Grove Drive toward Butch's home.

Helen felt her pulse quicken and turned into the parking lot of Carr & Erwin Funeral Home. She doubted Butch's body had arrived here yet, but by the end of the day, it would. Gripping the wheel, she fought back tears, knowing that time was in short supply.

She closed her eyes and forced herself to take several deep breaths. When she finally opened them, she unclicked the glove compartment. The revolver wasn't there.

Sweat beads percolated on Helen's neck and forehead as she gazed into the opening. All she saw was her car registration materials. She looked away and slowly began to count. A thousand one, a thousand two . . .

When she reached ten, she looked again. There was still no gun.

A guttural moan escaped Helen's lips. She slammed the glove box shut and again squeezed the steering wheel. She needed to be calm. *Think,* she told herself. *Think, damnit.*

"I'm going to be charged with murder," she said out loud, gazing over the wheel at the funeral home where her mother and father had both been laid to rest and where her ex-husband's service would be handled in the very near future. There wasn't a doubt in her mind over the proclamation she'd just made. The only question was how long it would take before she was brought in.

Gritting her teeth, she put the car in gear and headed out of town. When she reached the junction with Highway 64, she hung a left and drove east, passing Walton Farm, where she'd almost been killed three and a half years earlier and would have been if not for Tom McMurtrie. She soon reached Lincoln County. Once in Fayetteville, she turned south on Highway 231. *If I'm gone much more than a few hours, they might see this as fleeing,* she thought but didn't care.

For the first time in her adult life, Helen Evangeline Lewis felt strung out and at the end of her rope. And she needed help.

As she passed a green sign saying **WELCOME TO ALABAMA THE BEAUTIFUL**, she knew it went even deeper than that.

"*I need a lawyer,*" she whispered.

PART TWO

12

Suffice it to say, the men's room on the eighth floor of the Madison County Courthouse would never grace the pages of *Southern Living* magazine. The square-shaped box had one urinal, two stalls, and a sink. The walls were gray cinder blocks, and at four o'clock in the afternoon, the tile floor looked and felt grimy after a day's worth of use. The pungent odor of disinfectant permeated the tight space, but despite the heavy dose of cleaner, the restroom's lone occupant could still make out the faint whiff of dried urine in the air.

Bocephus Aurulius Haynes took in a shallow breath and gazed at himself in the mirror above the sink. His eyes were bloodshot, and the dark brown skin on his shaved scalp glistened with sweat, but otherwise he felt that he looked presentable considering the circumstances. Like his head, his face was clean shaven, and he wore a custom-tailored gray suit with a white shirt and red tie. At six foot four inches tall and weighing in at a shade over 240 pounds, Bo had a hard time finding clothes off the rack that fit. This suit normally made him feel good, but all he could sense now was anxiety. His mouth and throat tasted dry, and his heavily calloused palms were clammy. Bo turned on the sink faucet and ran his hands under the cold liquid, washing them and then rewashing them. He splashed water on his face and looked at himself again, gripping the porcelain sides of the sink and trying to steady his nerves.

He thought about all the verdicts he'd waited on during his twenty-five-plus years practicing law. In the personal injury arena, there had been wheels cases, premises liability, product malfunctions, and medical malpractice. On the criminal side of the fence, he'd run the gamut early in his career, defending murder cases all the way down to first-offense DUIs and other traffic violations. He'd even been the defendant himself in a capital murder case a few years ago, though that matter had never reached a verdict, and all charges were eventually dismissed.

But never in all the time he'd spent in courtrooms across the states of Tennessee and Alabama had he ever been as nervous as he was right now.

He heard the entrance door to the restroom swing open and then the sound of loafers trudging over the worn tile. "Bo, it's time," a sharp voice said. "The judge has reached his decision."

Bo squeezed the sides of the sink, and his heart began to pound in his chest. He turned to face his attorney. Burgess Cloud was a compact and trim man with curly brown hair and a pencil-thin mustache. He was widely regarded as the best domestic relations attorney in Huntsville, if not the whole state of Alabama.

"Already?" Bo asked, feeling a bit light headed. Judge Woodruff had asked the parties to hang around after the evidence had closed fifteen minutes ago, but Bo figured His Honor would have at least taken an hour to think about it.

"Yes," Burgess said, and Bo noticed that his lawyer's ruddy face had darkened.

"Awful fast," Bo said. "That good or bad?"

"We're about to find out," Burgess said.

The Honorable Lucas Baines Woodruff made a tent with his hands and peered over the bench. Woodruff was the dean of the Madison County judiciary, having served as a circuit court judge for almost thirty years. He was a political survivor, having been elected in the late '70s as a yellow dog Democrat and then, when it became obvious that no one could win an election in Alabama as a Democrat anymore, he switched parties on the eve of the 2006 election. In February 2015, he'd run unopposed in the Republican primary, and it was doubtful that any Democrat would be foolish enough to run against him come November. Woodruff was a balding man with two patches of white fuzz on the sides of his head. He wore bifocals to read, and now after clearing his throat, he lowered the glasses to the edge of his nose so that he could see the parties and their attorneys, all of whom were standing.

Bo sucked in a deep breath and stole a glance across the courtroom at the petitioner's table, where attorney Candy Hoffpower stood with her hands folded behind her back, eyes locked on to the judge. Her client, Bo's former father-in-law, stood next to her. Ezra Henderson had a full head of silver hair and a matching beard. Ezra's skin was milk-chocolate brown and mirrored that of his daughter, Jasmine.

Jazz . . . , Bo thought, seeing a vision of his deceased wife in his mind. It was always the same image. Jazz with a confused expression, reaching out toward him with blood on her fingers, her cream-colored dress stained red from the first gunshot and then, before Bo could clasp her by the hands, her head . . .

He closed his eyes, feeling shame, bitterness, and despair engulf him.

"Mr. Haynes," Judge Woodruff bellowed, his voice harsh and cold. Bo's eyes snapped open. "I have considered the evidence in Mr. Henderson's petition carefully, and I think, at least at this juncture, there is only one way that I can rule and be assured that I'm acting in the best interest of your daughter, Lila, who is fourteen years old." He paused, frowning at Bo with creased eyebrows. "Given your criminal record, your multiple suspensions from the practice of law, the fact that you currently do not have gainful employment, and finally that you are renting a farmhouse on the edge of the county that, in light of where Lila currently attends school, would not be a suitable residence, I'm going to award full custody of Lila Michelle Haynes to her grandparents, Mr. and Mrs. Ezra Henderson."

Bo felt heat on his cheeks and face but kept his expression neutral.

"As for your son, Thomas Jackson 'T. J.' Haynes, who is seventeen years of age, though I would certainly recommend that he also stay with the Hendersons, it is the court's decision to allow T. J. to decide where he wants to live." Woodruff stood and motioned with his hand to the back of the courtroom. "T. J., will you please approach the bench?"

Bo looked over his shoulder and watched his son stride down the aisle. Even under such dire conditions, Bo couldn't help but swell with pride as he watched his boy walk with poise and confidence toward the bench. T. J. was a junior at Huntsville High and had scholarship offers to play basketball at Vanderbilt, Middle Tennessee State, and Auburn. At six feet two and 180 pounds, he wasn't quite as tall or thick as his father, but T. J.'s sleek build was perfect for cutting around screens as a shooting guard.

"Have you made your decision, young man?" the judge asked, his tone a hair softer.

T. J. gazed over his shoulder at Bo, who gave him a firm nod.

For a moment, father and son stared at each other, but finally T. J. peered back up at the judge. "I want to live with my grandfather," T. J. said, his voice resigned.

"Very well," Woodruff said, wrinkling up his mouth in what must have constituted a smile for His Honor, though it looked to Bo more like a grimace. "You may return to your seat."

T. J. did as he was told but not before shooting his father a glance and ignoring the outstretched hand of Ezra Henderson.

"With respect to visitation," Judge Woodruff continued, his voice turning arctic again as he took off his spectacles and held them by the frames, "I agree with the schedule proposed by Ms. Hoffpower."

Every other weekend and holiday, Bo thought, gritting his teeth but again forcing his face to register no emotion.

"I have one final thing to say," Woodruff said, returning to his seat and letting out a deep sigh. "It is not without a good deal of anguish that I make this ruling today. Though I am finding against Mr. Haynes for the reasons already stated, it would be unjust and unfair not to recognize Mr. Haynes's long and distinguished career as a trial attorney in Pulaski, Tennessee, and the fact that Mr. Haynes's 'criminal record . . .'" He paused to make the quote symbol with the index and middle fingers of both hands. ". . . as well as his second suspension from the practice of law, both stem from a conviction for misdemeanor assault last year that arose during a confrontation with his deceased wife where he was attempting to keep her out of harm's way." Woodruff licked his lips and blinked his eyes. "Unfortunately, as we all know, Ms. Jasmine Haynes was murdered outside the Von Braun Center in December 2013. Since such time and up until the first of this year, the two children of the marriage, T. J. and Lila, have been living with Mr. and Mrs. Henderson with Mr. Haynes's apparent blessing as even you, Mr. Haynes, must have thought they were better off with their grandparents during such time. When you demanded that the children be returned, Mr. and Mrs. Henderson filed their petition with this court." Again, Judge Woodruff formed a tent with his hands. "Because of these unusual circumstances, it is this court's ruling that today's judgment is temporary and will be revisited in six months' time. If Mr. Haynes has established gainful employment, obtained a suitable residence in line with the children's school, and has had no further run-ins with the law, then the court may reconsider this order." He paused and smacked his lips. "Does everyone understand the ruling of this court?"

"Yes, Your Honor," Burgess Cloud said.

"Yes, Judge," Candy Hoffpower added, smiling up at the judge.

"Yes, Your Honor," Ezra Henderson's low growl of a voice uttered. "Thank you, sir." Ezra peered over at Bo, and Bo wasn't sure whether he saw triumph or rage in the older man's gaze. *He will never forgive me for Jazz's death,* Bo thought, scowling hard back at his former father-in-law. *And no punishment, not even taking my kids away from me, will ever be enough.*

"Mr. Haynes?" Judge Woodruff asked. "Do you understand?"

Bo opened his mouth to speak, but his throat was so dry the words wouldn't come. He coughed and swallowed hard. "Yes, Your Honor," he finally managed.

Woodruff nodded at him. "I wish you luck, sir. I hope you use the next six months to turn your life around."

13

The Voo Doo Lounge was a hideaway bar on the south side of the Madison County Courthouse square. Located on the basement floor under a Greek restaurant called Papou's, it was hard to find unless you were a local.

Burgess Cloud liked to have his posttrial powwows at the Voo Doo, and this time the location seemed appropriate. Bo sat next to his attorney on a stool at the rustic cherrywood bar and gazed into a glass of Jack Daniel's over ice. He had yet to take a sip.

"The ruling is only temporary," Burgess said, squeezing Bo's shoulder. "Now that you have your law license back, you can open up an office, and you'll be up and running in short order."

"We lost," Bo said, gaping at him. "You understand that, don't you? I was just stripped of legal custody of my kids."

"We did *not* lose," Burgess said, taking a sip from a pint glass of amber-colored beer. "A loss would have been a final judgment, but Woodruff qualified his ruling. You can get them back, Bo. You *will* get them back if . . . you follow the judge's instructions."

"Get a job, buy a house in town, and stay out of trouble," Bo mumbled, lifting his glass off the bar but then setting it back down.

"Yes," Burgess said, draining the rest of his beer in one long gulp. "Which, as you might remember, was exactly what I told you last month. If you had taken those steps on the front end as I'd recommended, today's decision might have been a full victory."

Bo gritted his teeth, knowing that his attorney was right but not appreciating the *I told you so* sentiments.

"Another beer, Mr. Cloud?" the bartender asked.

Burgess glanced up at the attendant and then over Bo's shoulder toward the front of the bar. Then he hopped off his stool and pulled a ten and a five out of his wallet. "No, I'm good, Pete. This ought to cover it." He placed the bills by his empty glass and leaned down and whispered into Bo's ear. "We didn't lose today, all right? Trust me. I've been doing this a few years. But in order to win in six months, I'm going to need your help. It's time to move forward, Bo."

Before he could respond, he saw his attorney pointing behind them. "You have a visitor." Burgess winked and gave Bo's shoulder another squeeze. "I'll call you next week to see how things are going."

Bo nodded at his attorney and then looked over his shoulder. He tensed when he saw who was heading his way.

T. J. Haynes walked with a forward lean and nodded at Burgess as they crossed paths. Then, without sitting, he peered down at his father.

"Why won't you let me live with you?" He slapped his hands against his sides. "I hate living with Mammy and Pops. Don't get me wrong. I love them and all, but I hate the way Pops blames you for everything, and I don't like the way they check up on my homework every night. I'm a junior in high school, for God's sake."

Bo squinted up at his son, who had his mother and grandfather's skin, but his father's black eyes. "I need you to look after your sister. I don't want you two to be separated. You're a team, you and Lila. This custody thing was all or nothing. I told you that before it started. If I lost, I wanted you to stay with her." Bo paused. "And don't be fretting about your homework being checked on. I'd be doing that at my house too, buster."

"It's not fair, Dad. The way everyone has blamed you for Momma's death. You tried to stop her from walking across that parking lot." T. J.'s lip began to quiver, and he looked away. Bo also turned from his son and again gazed at his untouched glass of sour mash whiskey.

"JimBone Wheeler killed Momma. Just like he murdered Uncle Rel and Detective Richey. Just like he tried to kill Professor McMurtrie and his grandson."

Bo nodded as his mind drifted back to the two weeks when James Robert "JimBone" Wheeler had escaped death row and went on his rampage to bring a reckoning on the Professor and everyone Bo's mentor held dear. Those events seemed like two lifetimes ago.

Rel . . . Wade . . . Jazz . . . all murdered. The Professor had survived Wheeler's onslaught, but now he was gone too.

And I have nothing, Bo thought, running a finger around the rim of his whiskey glass. *Not even my kids.*

"Dad?"

Bo gazed up at his son and gripped his forearm. "You just stay the course, all right? Put your grades first, go to class, and keep practicing."

T. J. nodded and then frowned. "The offer from Bama still hasn't come."

"It will," Bo said. He and Jazz had wanted their son to continue his hoop dreams in Tuscaloosa, where they both had lettered in sports. Bo had played linebacker on Coach Paul "Bear" Bryant's 1978 and '79 national championship football teams, and Jazz had been a sprinter on the track team. "It will," he repeated, squeezing his son's arm.

"Dad, are you going to be OK?"

"Don't you worry about me. You focus on yourself and Lila." Bo sighed. "And you mind your mammy and pops. I know I've been cross with them since your momma died, but Ezra and Juanita are good people, and they love you and your sister very much."

T. J. nodded, but again the teenager's lip began to quiver, and he bit down on it. "I'm worried about you, Dad. What are you gonna do?"

Bo forced a smile and then rose from the stool and gripped his son in a fierce hug. "I'll be fine."

When they pulled away from each other, T. J. didn't seem convinced. "What are you gonna do?" he repeated.

Bo ignored the question. "Give your sister a kiss from me, and I'll see you both next weekend, all right?"

T. J. started to protest, but Bo grabbed his arms and gave them a shake. "OK?"

Finally, T. J. nodded. "OK." He started to walk away and then looked back at Bo, who remained standing. "I love you, Dad."

"I love you too, son," Bo said, feeling an ache deep in his chest as he watched his boy leave the bar.

Bo plopped down on the stool. Exhaustion and depression began to consume him. He turned to the glass of Jack Daniel's and this time brought it to his lips, turning it back until the ice cubes collided with his teeth. The whiskey scalded his throat going down and burned his stomach.

And then Bocephus Haynes felt a wave of heat rush over him that had nothing to do with the alcohol he'd just consumed. Hate for himself, which he'd been able to quell during the custody trial, returned with a vengeance.

It's all my fault, he thought. *Jazz's death. Losing the kids. Everything.*

"Another, sir?" the bartender asked, removing the empty glass.

Bo glared up at him and nodded. *What are you gonna do?* T. J. had asked. Bo watched as another glass of Jack Daniel's over ice was placed in front of him.

"I'm going to get drunk," he whispered.

14

At 8:00 p.m., Bo stumbled up the stairs of the Voo Doo Lounge and out onto the sidewalk. For early April, the night felt humid and sticky, which typically meant that rain was on the horizon. Bo had parked his car a couple of blocks east of the courthouse and began to trudge that way. As he passed by a restaurant called Commerce Kitchen, he glanced inside the big glass window and saw Judge Lucas Woodruff eating dinner with a distinguished-looking silver-haired woman who Bo assumed was His Honor's wife. For a moment, Bo stopped and stared at the man who just hours earlier had decided that Bo wasn't fit to be his children's custodial parent. He wanted to go inside and tell *His Honor* what he really felt about him, but that would only bring him more problems.

As a cool mist began to fall, Bo took a step closer to the glass and remembered the judge's last words to him: *I wish you luck, sir. I hope you use the next six months to turn your life around.*

"Go to hell," Bo mumbled, but the words felt weak and stupid coming out of his mouth.

Inside the restaurant and oblivious to the large man staring at him outside the window, Woodruff lifted his fork to his mouth and laughed at something the woman said. If his custody ruling from a few hours earlier was bothering him, the judge was disguising his concern well.

As the rain began to pick up, Bo forced his legs to move down the sidewalk. Woodruff hadn't seen him. Hadn't even noticed him.

I feel invisible, Bo thought, passing by three twentysomething young men who likewise didn't bother to glance at him.

After walking another two blocks, Bo came to his white Toyota Sequoia. He clicked the electronic entry button and collapsed into the front seat. He was so tired. He started the car and gazed over the windshield for a long time, not seeing anything. The rain was now pouring, but he didn't turn on his wipers. He gazed forward, unable to see anything now, and wondered if he was staring at his future.

No light. No visibility. No path to take.

No life . . .

In the days after Jazz's murder, he'd considered suicide but hadn't been able to do it. He couldn't orphan his children.

Now they're gone anyway . . .

He sighed and placed his forehead on the steering wheel. "And they're better off," Bo said out loud, wrinkling his nose as the scent of the whiskey on his breath filled the close confines of the SUV.

Bo formed images of T. J. and Lila in his mind and held on to them like a lifeline, trying to remember Judge Woodruff's last comments and Burgess Cloud's upbeat outlook.

Six months, he thought. *If I can get my life in order in six months . . .*

He closed his eyes. When the pictures that formed behind his lids switched to Jazz in her bloodstained cream dress, he gritted his teeth and forced his thoughts back to his daughter.

Lila had been a shell of herself since her mother's death, and regardless of whether she lived with her grandparents or with Bo, she was going to continue to need psychological counseling, which she now attended three times a week. Her grades had slipped, and she had missed a number of days of school with a mystery stomach ailment that her psychologist thought was a result of the stress caused by trauma. As he thought back to the days after Jazz's murder and holding Lila in his arms while she cried, Bo finally broke down.

"I'm s-s-so sorry," he whispered, letting out a hollow sob. "So . . . sorry."

A few seconds later, the fatigue and alcohol finally did him in, and the world, like the view out his front windshield, went dark.

———

The sound of the car horn jarred him awake.

Bo's eyes shot open, and he pushed himself back against his seat. The blaring tone dissipated, and he blinked to get his bearings. He was still in his car, and if anything, the rain was coming down harder. His forehead stung from being stuck in place against the leather steering wheel. After rubbing his face with his hands, he glanced at the clock on the dash: 9:30 p.m.

He had passed out for over an hour, and it would probably have been longer if his arm hadn't inadvertently pressed against the horn. Peering around the almost barren parking lot, he saw no people and only one other car—a single-cab Dodge truck—besides his own. Beyond the lot, there were no people walking on the sidewalk nor any cars passing by on the adjacent road.

Lucky it's a rainy Tuesday, Bo thought, knowing that a clear weekend night would probably have attracted more people and hence more cops. He wasn't sure if he would have been arrested for passing out in his still-running car, but he was glad he wouldn't have the luxury of finding out.

He coughed, and his mouth tasted bitter. He rolled down the window and stuck his hand out, letting some of the rain gather in his palm. Then he splashed the water on his face.

The cool sensation of the raindrops sent a shiver down his body, but he felt better. He put the car in reverse and looked over his shoulder. Then, sighing, he returned the gearshift to "Park" and cut off the ignition.

He wasn't sure about passing out in a parked but running car, but he knew he could be arrested for driving under the influence of alcohol.

If I get a DUI, I can kiss T. J. and Lila goodbye forever . . .

Bo fumbled in his pocket for his cell phone, and after a couple of minutes, pulled up the Uber application. He requested a driver and was informed that one was on the way and would arrive at his location in fifteen minutes.

While he waited for the stranger who would drive him home, he gazed forward at the driving rain that continued to pelt the front windshield. Over the past sixteen months since his wife's brutal murder, Bo had felt many competing emotions. Anger. Despair. Depression. Fear. Anxiety. Frustration. All part of his daily cocktail of thoughts.

But now another vibe had infiltrated his being. To Bo, this one was worse than any combination of the others.

For the first time in his life, Bocephus Haynes felt utterly and completely lost.

15

The Uber driver introduced himself as Hooper. He was a heavyset man wearing a white button-down and jeans. Bo could barely see the man's face because it was covered with a crimson trucker cap with the words *Roll Tide* embroidered on the bill. Once Bo was seated in the back of the car, which was a tan Nissan Maxima, the driver turned to look at him. "Bocephus Haynes." After saying Bo's name, Hooper nodded as if he was sizing Bo up.

"That's right," Bo said.

"Middle linebacker. 1979 Bama team. Made a couple of tackles and a sack in the Sugar Bowl against Arkansas."

Bo forced a smile. It had been a while since he'd been recognized from his playing days, but it still happened from time to time, especially when he was in Alabama. "Good memory."

"You were a hell of a player," Hooper said, pulling out of the parking lot. "Preseason All-American in 1980 but blew out your knee in the first game that season, right?"

"Yep," Bo said. "Damn artificial turf at Legion Field."

"Too bad," Hooper said. "Hey, are you hungry?"

At this, Bo smiled. He was famished after having not eaten since lunch and was beginning to feel the first beginnings of a hangover. "I'm starved."

Thirty minutes later, Hooper pulled the Maxima up the driveway to Bo's rental house in Hazel Green. "Nice looking farm," Hooper said. "How long have you owned it?"

"Not mine," Bo muttered, chewing up the last of his burger and washing it down with a sip of Diet Coke. On the way home, they had stopped at a Krystal drive-through, which Hooper had described as "one of his old stomping grounds." Apparently, in the late 1980s, the kids from Huntsville High School had liked to loiter in the parking lots of Krystal, AmSouth Bank, and an old grocery store called Big Brothers, which were all within a half-mile radius on Whitesburg Drive. "Good times," Hooper had said with a hint of wistfulness in his voice. "Been a lot of places, but for my money, the girls at Huntsville High School in the late '80s were the hottest chicks that have ever breathed air."

Bo had smiled at the memory. He figured a lot of men remembered their own high school glory days in the same nostalgic manner. Hell, Bruce Springsteen had written a song about it. Sometimes he wished that he had been able to have a normal childhood, where he'd hung out with other teens in the backs of parking lots drinking Miller Lite out of the can and scoping girls, but alas, that hadn't been in the cards.

Normal wasn't a word that could ever be used to describe Bo's life.

"What's your friend's name?" Hooper asked as the car came to a stop in front of a carport. Despite the steady patter of rain, the rows of recently planted cotton could be seen from the glow cast by the full moon above.

"What?" Bo asked, wrinkling his face at the lone car parked under the covering. It was a black Crown Victoria with a Tennessee license plate. There was only one person in the world he knew who drove that type of vehicle.

"Your friend?"

When Bo still didn't answer, Hooper turned around and looked at him.

"You know, the guy who owns the farm. I wonder if I might know him."

Bo blinked his eyes and finally took them off the Crown Vic. Then he gazed out at the farmland. "His name was Tom McMurtrie. You probably heard of him. Played on Coach Bryant's '61 team and then taught Evidence at Alabama's law school for forty years."

Hooper opened his mouth in an aha manner. "I *have* heard of him." He gave his head a jerk. "No offense, Mr. Haynes, but that '61 team will always be the greatest."

Bo smiled. "None taken."

"You said his name *was* Tom McMurtrie. Is he—?"

"He died last year. Lung cancer."

"I'm sorry."

"Me too," Bo said, holding out a twenty-dollar bill to the driver.

Hooper smiled. "The bill was only eighteen dollars, and your card will be automatically charged."

"Keep it," Bo said, pressing the cash into the driver's hand. "I appreciate the ride and you stopping for food. What did you say you did during the daytime?"

"I didn't," Hooper said, reaching into a pouch on his dashboard and handing Bo a card.

Bo read it. "Hooper, Private Investigative Services." He smiled. "Just Hooper?"

He nodded. "Wanted to be different."

"What's your first name?"

"You assume Hooper is my last name?"

Bo smiled. "Isn't it?"

"I only tell that to folks who hire me," he said, putting the car in reverse. "Let me know if I can ever be of service."

"Will do," Bo said, sticking the card in his pocket. As he watched the Maxima ease down the driveway and turn right onto Highway 231,

Bo chuckled. He had enjoyed the chatty Uber driver's company more than anyone he'd been around in a while.

"Make a new friend?"

Bo wheeled at the sound of the familiar voice, the sharpness of which had cut through the air and the rain like a machete.

"General?" Bo asked, squinting into the carport.

"You're getting wet," she said, rising from the storage bin that she'd been sitting on in her customary black suit and heels. What wasn't customary was the six-pack of Miller High Life that lay next to her on the concrete. Two of the bottles were missing from the carton.

"Drinking alone?" Bo asked, walking under the cover of the port.

"No," Helen said. "Lee Roy's been keeping me company." She pointed to the corner of the carport, where a sixty-pound white-and-brown English bulldog lay on a fluffy khaki pillow snoring. "Haven't you, boy?" Helen asked.

Lee Roy wagged his stubby tail and grunted. Then he went back to snoring.

"Yeah, he's a barrel of laughs," Bo said, smirking at the animal. Bo had inherited Lee Roy from the Professor. Despite the dog's current state of being, he'd been a good and faithful companion.

"Here," Helen said, grabbing one of the beer bottles and handing it to him. "Join me."

Bo took it and popped the top. After a long sip, he grimaced. "Drinking the good stuff, I see."

She snickered. "Our mutual friend Powell liked these. Thought I'd give them a try."

Bo smiled. Powell Conrad was the district attorney of Tuscaloosa County and an old friend. *Whom I haven't seen since the Professor died,* Bo thought, shaking his head and taking another sip of beer. He leaned against the hood of the Crown Vic and gazed down at Helen. "What brings you out here in the middle of the night, General?"

"Ennis Petrie was granted parole," Helen said, grabbing a bottle from the carton and opening it.

Bo gripped the beer bottle tight and gazed down at the cement. "I know. There was a blurb about it in Sunday's paper."

Helen smiled. "You still read the newspaper?"

Bo smirked. "The online edition. When will he be released?"

"Already has," Helen said. She took a sip of beer and then sighed. "Last Friday, a few hours after the ruling. Look, I'm sorry I didn't call. I just didn't want to bother you with the child-custody dispute still going on."

Bo shook his head. "I'm sorry I wasn't at the hearing."

Helen plopped back down on the storage bin. "How did the custody trial go?"

"I lost," Bo said, his voice soft. Rain now pounded the roof of the carport.

Helen grimaced but didn't say anything.

If he was honest with himself, Bo didn't think she looked all that surprised. *And why should she be?*

For at least a minute, Bo and Helen drank in silence, the only sound being the breathy hum of Lee Roy's snoring. Finally, Bo cleared his throat. "Did Booker T. show up at Ennis's hearing?"

Helen shook her head. "No. There was no family present. I tried to get him to come, but he's been hard to reach."

Bo cocked his head at her. "Really? What's going on with Booker T.?"

She squinted at him. "You don't know?"

"Know what?"

"He lost his farm. Bank foreclosed a couple months ago." She frowned. "I would have thought for sure you knew about that. I assumed he'd probably asked you for money."

Bo felt a pang of guilt in his chest. When was the last time he'd spoken to his cousin? Six months? A year? At Jazz's funeral? He sighed and took another pull from the bottle. The beer tasted sour and wasn't mixing all that well with the Krystal he'd just downed on the way home, but he drank it anyway.

"No?" Helen pressed.

"No," Bo said. "I haven't heard anything from him. Didn't even realize he was hurting for money." He paused. "What bank foreclosed on him?"

"Z Bank," Helen said, almost spitting the words out.

"Never heard of it," Bo said. "I would have thought Booker T. was dealing with FNB."

"He obviously should have. Z Bank is new. Opened last year by Michael Zannick. They've been giving a lot of folks short-term loans that the borrowers can't pay off and then foreclosing. I don't like it, but there's nothing I can do about it."

"Zannick," Bo said, snapping his fingers. "Didn't you mention him when I called last week to tell you I couldn't make Ennis's parole hearing?"

Helen nodded, and despite the darkness in the covered area, her face looked even paler than normal. "I did. Zannick's rape trial was supposed to start today."

Bo cocked his head. "Rape?"

"I charged him with the statutory and forcible rape of Amanda Burks, a fifteen-year-old student at Giles County High."

"That's right," Bo said, remembering. "You said *supposed* to start. Was the trial put off?"

Helen blinked up at Bo and then stood and walked to the edge of the carport. She knelt and stroked Lee Roy's back, and the dog's tail began to shake again. Then she straightened. "Yes," she finally said, her voice sounding farther away than where she was standing.

Bo took a last sip of beer and flung the bottle in the trash can next to the storage bin. Then he approached her. "General, mind telling me what's going on?" He reached into his pocket and pulled out his phone, looking at the time. "It's eleven at night, and you're here at my house.

You didn't call ahead, and I know you didn't come all the way to Hazel Green to tell me that Ennis Petrie was granted parole." He touched her shoulder. "What's up?"

When she didn't answer, Bo gently turned her around to face him. "General?"

This close, he saw that Helen's eyes were puffy from crying and that her makeup had smeared from tears. He'd never seen the head prosecutor of Giles County, Tennessee, look so vulnerable.

"I miss him, too, you know," she said, her voice awash with anguish. "I miss him every day." She made a fist with her right hand and punched at the air in front of Bo. "You had over twenty years with him as your teacher and friend. I barely had three, and he was sick for a lot of that." She pointed to the farm, where on the northern tip, a tombstone marked the grave of Tom McMurtrie. "And now he's dead, and we never . . ." She flung her hands up in the air and let them drop to her sides. "There was never a *we*. There was never an *us*. There was never a *something*."

Bo took a step backward and looked down at the concrete. "I'm sorry."

Helen scoffed and snatched a beer out of the carton. She popped the top and took a long sip, spilling some of the liquid down her neck. "You're sorry?" she whispered.

Bo continued to peer at the ground, feeling the heat from her eyes on him.

"Where the hell have you been?" Helen snapped. "Other than your call last week, I haven't heard from you in over a year. You don't keep up with your cousin. You don't keep up with me? Do you talk with Rick? Or Powell? Or any damn body?"

The answer to all those questions was no. Rick Drake had been Tom McMurtrie's partner. *And also my friend . . .*

Bo hadn't spoken to him since they'd all gathered here at the farm to pay their respects to the Professor last year. He likewise hadn't spoken with Powell or anyone else.

"I've been trying to get custody of my kids," Bo said.

"No, you haven't," Helen said. "Trying would involve some effort on your part. Getting a job to tide you over until your suspension lifted. Renting or buying a house closer to your kids so that you could show that you had a suitable home for them. Doing . . . *something*." She paused and punched his shoulder. "But all you've done is sit out here on this farm and feel sorry for yourself. Poor old Bo. Lost his wife. Lost his best friend. Gonna lose his—"

"That's enough," Bo said, feeling anger swell within him but also knowing that something was off here. "General, did you really come all the way out here to berate me on the state of my life?"

Fresh tears had now formed in her eyes, and she shook her head.

"What then?" Another thought struck him, and he cocked his head at her. "How long have you been here anyway?"

She blinked and wiped her eyes. More makeup smeared her cheeks. "I don't know. Six hours. At seven o'clock, I drove down to a place called Posey's and ate dinner. Got a six-pack at a gas station on my way back."

"General, tell me what's going on."

She coughed and let out a ragged breath. "Earlier this morning, my ex-husband, Butch, was found murdered at his home in Pulaski."

Bo creased his eyebrows. As a lawyer in Giles County for close to twenty-five years, Bo had crossed paths with Butch Renfroe a few times, but not often. Butch's arena was in the corporate and tax world, and Bo focused on litigation. "I'm . . . sorry," Bo said.

"I'm here because I need a lawyer."

Bo narrowed his gaze and took a step closer to her. "You need *a lawyer*?" Above them, the rain's constant patter on the roof had slackened, but a jolt of thunder rang out, causing Bo's chest and arms to tense. When Helen didn't respond, Bo asked the obvious follow-up question. "Why?"

Helen sighed. "Because I'm going to be arrested for Butch's murder."

16

At 11:00 p.m., the Giles County Sheriff's Office was a zoo of people, movement, and noise. It had been thirteen hours since dispatch had been notified of the death of local attorney Butch Renfroe, and all hands were still on deck. Murder was a rarity in Pulaski, and the intentional killing of a prominent professional was almost unheard of. Not since Andy Walton's brutal killing almost four years earlier had a homicide so captured the pulse of the town.

The phones hadn't stopped ringing all day, most of the calls being from press outlets across Tennessee, but there were also a few offers of help from the sheriff's offices and police departments of neighboring counties and towns.

Inside his private office, Sheriff Hank Springfield sipped scalding hot coffee from a Styrofoam cup and gazed out the glass walls to the hallway and the lobby beyond, where he counted at least four deputies fielding phone calls and completing paperwork. Hank sighed and spoke in a tired voice. "Run it down for me again," he said.

Sitting across the office from Hank in a high-backed worn-leather chair was Chief Deputy Sheriff Frances Storm. Frannie was a light-skinned black woman in her late twenties. At just over six feet tall and 140 pounds, she was thinner than when she had starred at David Lipscomb College as a power forward on the women's basketball team. After college and a brief stint in the WNBA, Frannie had returned home to Pulaski, where she'd started as a patrol officer in the Pulaski Police Department. When Hank became sheriff, he'd hired Frannie as a deputy, and she'd worked her way up to chief. There was no one in the department whom Hank trusted more.

"We've interviewed every neighbor of the victim's on Pecan Grove Drive. The woman who lives across the street from him, Bonita Spencer, said she saw a black Crown Victoria pull up on the curb outside Butch's house between 9:00 and 10:00 p.m. She couldn't remember the exact time. She also said she saw the victim's ex-wife . . ." Frannie paused. ". . . General Helen Lewis exit the vehicle and walk around the side of Butch's house. Bonita was putting away dishes at the time and didn't think much of seeing the car because she knew that Helen and Butch had been married once." Frannie smiled. "Bonita, who is eighty-two years old, said she figured that Helen was making a 'booty call,' which is what Bonita said she'd heard the kids around town call it."

Hank didn't smile. "Continue."

"About thirty minutes after seeing the Crown Vic park on the curb, while Bonita was turning out the lights and making sure all of the doors in her house were locked, she glanced out the window again and saw that the car was gone. She did find that strange, because she figured a booty call would have lasted longer than thirty minutes."

"Did she see any other vehicles stop at Butch's house?"

"No. The only other car she saw was a Ford truck, but it didn't stop."

"Do any of the other neighbors remember seeing or hearing anything suspicious?"

"No, but Terry Grimes, who lives three houses down from Butch, is the one who found him dead this morning and called the police. Grimes got worried when Butch failed to show up at the YMCA for their workout."

"How did Grimes get in the house?"

"He said the side door, which opens to the kitchen, was unlocked."

"Which is presumably the door the General came in the previous night."

"It is the door. We've matched her fingerprints to the knob."

"Any other prints on it?"

"Just the victim's and Grimes's."

"What about the rest of the house?"

"Dusted it clean. The only prints that we've found belong to Butch, Grimes, and the General."

"Go on."

"Autopsy from Melvin Ragland was done this afternoon at 2:00 p.m., and you and I were both present for it. Cause of death was two gunshot wounds, one to the sternum and the other to the head. Bullet fragments found in the victim's chest reveal that the murder weapon was a .44-caliber revolver. Based on the condition of the body, Ragland's preliminary conclusion for the time of death is between 9:00 p.m. and 12:00 a.m. Additionally, the victim's face, shoulders, and chest were covered with red-and-purple bruising, which Melvin concludes came from the gun. It is inconclusive whether these were made before or after the victim was shot."

"Pistol-whipped and shot execution-style," Hank muttered, taking another sip of coffee as a vision of Butch Renfroe's ruined corpse filled his mind.

"Looks like it."

"What about forensics?"

"Particles of blood, hair, and skin were found in the den where the body was discovered. Most of it was on the couch where the body was laying, but there were also small amounts of hair and blood on the carpet, a lampshade, and a coffee table." Frannie paused. "All of the DNA has been sent off to the crime lab in Nashville."

Hank sighed, thought about taking another sip of coffee, and then changed his mind. He turned from the window, where the officers in the lobby were still working away, and looked at his chief deputy. "What else?"

"According to our investigation and the statement of Mr. Grimes, who'd visited the victim's house on several occasions, the bedroom that Butch used as an office had a desk and a laptop computer." She paused. "The computer is gone."

"Prints?"

"Only two in that room."

"The General and the victim," he said, turning and looking at her.

She nodded, and her face was grave. "General Lewis's prints were found on the doorknob and the desk." Frannie approached the wall and stopped when she was a foot away from the sheriff. "Hank, when you take all of that and add in the victim's last two text messages combined with the press release . . ." She pointed at the lone piece of paper on Hank's desk. ". . . we have to do it." Her voice had softened to just above a whisper. "I know how much you respect her, but we have to do our job."

He groaned and leaned over his desk, looking close at the bond paper with the letterhead of "Frederick A. Renfroe, LLC" centered at the top. "We need a handwriting expert to examine the signature."

"Already in the works. I've placed a call to Paul Graham over in Lawrenceburg. He's the best in the area."

Hank nodded, impressed as always with the thoroughness of his chief deputy's work. "Remind me where the press release was found."

"In a hidden safe behind a portrait of General Neyland in the den. Our team cracked the combination in less than an hour."

Hank sighed. "What about the murder weapon?"

"There were no guns located at the scene other than a twelve-gauge shotgun and two hunting rifles, all registered to the victim." She paused. "But the General owns a .44 Magnum and was practicing with it at Doug Brinkley's shooting range a few hours before the murder."

Hank raised his eyebrows. "You get a statement from Doug?"

She nodded. "Yes, and I've also gotten a warrant to search the General's home and vehicle." She placed her hands on her hips. "Hank, you've seen the texts that Butch sent General Lewis a few hours before the murder."

"I have, and I agree that there's an implied threat in both of them."

She held out her palms. "Sheriff, based on the evidence we've uncovered in the last thirteen hours, General Lewis had the means, the opportunity . . ." She paused and pointed at the piece of paper on the desk. ". . . and a boatload of motive to kill Butch Renfroe."

For thirty seconds, Hank paced a circle around his small office, realizing that he had no choice. "Has she come home yet?" he finally asked.

"No. Deputy Savona has been parked at her house for the past six hours, and there's been no sign of her. She hasn't answered her cell phone or returned any of the voice and text messages sent to her." Frannie licked her lips and sucked in a quick breath. "She hasn't responded to your call and text yet, has she?"

Hank shook his head, still not believing this was actually happening. Then he gritted his teeth and spoke in a firm voice. "All right, Chief. Put an APB out on the General."

17

"I can't," Bo said, unable to meet her eye. They were inside the farmhouse now, sitting around the circular kitchen table. Lee Roy sat bolt upright by the door to the carport. He was awake now and on guard, sensing tension.

"Can't or won't?" Helen asked, the frustration in her tone palpable.

"Both. I'm sorry, General, but I haven't tried a case to a jury in over five years. You'd be better off with Lou Horn or Dick Selby. Besides, Judge Woodruff said I needed to get a job and a residence closer to my kids if I want to have any chance of regaining custody." He paused. "Taking a case in Pulaski is going in the opposite direction."

"I'll pay a retainer of fifteen thousand dollars and an hourly rate of up to four hundred dollars an hour."

"It's not about the money."

"You need a job, and I'm offering you one as my lawyer. You could still take up residence in the Huntsville city limits and commute to and from Pulaski."

"General, how can you be so sure that you're going to be arrested for your ex-husband's murder?"

"Agree to represent me and I'll tell you."

He blinked his eyes and gazed down at the table. "I'm sorry, I—"

"You're the best, Bo. People in town still ask about you."

Bo gave a weak smile. "I've been gone close to three years. I suspect the last thing anyone remembers about me is the outcome of my trial for murder." He looked at her. "Back when you charged me with murdering Andy Walton. Remember?"

"I do. I also remember dismissing all charges against you and helping you and Tom find the real killer."

"True enough," Bo said. "Even still, I suspect folks see me as a circus act. A black man whose biological father was the Imperial Wizard of the KKK." He paused and shook his head. "All those years I spent trying to bring the men that murdered Roosevelt Haynes to justice, and turns out my daddy wasn't Roosevelt but the leader of the lynch mob. How's that for irony?"

Helen sighed and stood from her chair. She walked to the door and petted Lee Roy behind the ears. "I know you've been through hell, Bo, and I can't imagine how difficult it must be to come to grips with your family history." She paused and gazed at him. "But despite all that, and regardless of your suspensions from the practice and the bogus criminal conviction that came out of you trying to prevent Jazz from being killed . . . despite all of that . . . you're still the only attorney I'd trust to handle this case."

"It's not even a case yet," Bo said.

"It will be."

For almost a minute, neither of them spoke. Finally, Bo stood and placed his hands into his pockets. "I'm sorry. I can't."

Helen gave a swift nod and grabbed the doorknob. Before exiting, she peered over her shoulder at him. "You know, Tom would be ashamed of what you've let yourself become, Bo. Whether you help me or not, your life has spiraled downhill since Tom died. You've quit and been content to sit out here on your dead friend's farm feeling sorry for yourself."

"I think it's time you leave, General." Bo felt adrenaline and anger begin to pulse through him.

"If you'd been strong and gotten your life in order, you would have never lost custody of Lila and T. J. They'd be with you now." She paused. "The truth is that you're not so sure they aren't better off with Jazz's mom and dad."

Bo ground his teeth together but said nothing.

"Whatever happened to the Bocephus Haynes who made other attorneys quake with fear any time your name showed up on a pleading? The lawyer that worked cases so hard that insurance defense lawyers were begging to settle with you. The guy that used to make even me lose sleep."

Bo turned his back on Helen and gazed into the empty kitchen. "He's gone," Bo said, feeling hate for himself return with a vengeance.

"Is he?" Helen asked, sarcasm leaking into her tone. "I don't think so. I believe that he's lurking somewhere beneath the surface, and you're just plain scared of him."

Bo tried to speak, but no words came.

"A pity," Helen said, twisting the knob and opening the door. Outside, the rain continued to fall at a steady pace. "Well, you can forget my little request. I don't want a coward like you to represent me anyway."

Bo turned his head in time to see the door slamming shut.

———

For a long time, Bo sat in the kitchen of the farmhouse and gazed out the bay window at the rain. Lee Roy had walked over to him and lay at his feet, and every so often, Bo leaned over and rubbed his hand over the bulldog's fur. "I've made a mess of things, boy," he said, thinking about what a strange day it had been. Bo let out a ragged breath.

He needed to talk with someone, and in his lifetime, there had been only one person he'd ever turned to for advice.

Bo rose to his feet and walked to the liquor cabinet, squinting at the various options before choosing a bottle of Jim Beam. Then he trudged toward the front door.

"Come on, boy," he said, and Lee Roy followed him outside and into the rain.

Bo walked past the empty carport, barely taking notice of the fact that the Sequoia was gone.

He wouldn't need a car for the journey he was about to take.

18

By the time Helen reached the Giles County line, the rain was pouring sideways, making visibility scarce. Turning her wipers on full blast, she hit her hazard lights and pulled over on the shoulder of Highway 64.

Helen waited for several minutes. A part of her hoped that the rain would subside so that she could finish this trip and face whatever awaited her; the other part prayed that the precipitation would drone on forever. That eventually, her car would be engulfed by water and carried away on a tide to some far-off place where she could start life anew. A utopia where she had never made the mistakes that had brought her to this point.

Helen grabbed her cell phone from the passenger seat, which she'd turned off during the entire time she had been at the farm. She looked at the blank screen and hesitated, noticing that the rain was only falling harder. Finally, knowing she couldn't delay the inevitable forever, she clicked it on. A few seconds later, she was greeted with the ding that indicated she had received several new text messages. Holding her breath, Helen quickly filtered through them.

The first, received at 5:07 p.m., was from Gloria. Give me a call. Need to talk. The second, also from Gloria, came in at 5:38 p.m. Where are you? Call me as soon as you get this message.

Though a bit unsettling—Gloria rarely called or texted Helen after hours—those texts didn't upset her nearly as much as the third. It was from Sheriff Springfield, received at 6:00 p.m. General, we need to talk as soon as possible. I came by your office and you weren't there, and I also drove by your house and couldn't find you. Where are you? Call me, please. It's an emergency.

Helen clicked out of the message and realized that she was still holding her breath. She exhaled and closed her eyes. She opened them when she heard another tone coming from the phone, this one indicating receipt of a voice message. It had been left at 6:03 p.m. When she clicked on it, her vehicle was filled with Hank's voice. "General, just left you a text. Where are you? Been looking all over. We need to talk. It's about the Butch Renfroe investigation. Please call me as soon as possible."

Helen sighed and replayed the message a couple more times before exiting out of voice mail. Then she went back to her texts and scrolled down to the messages that Butch had sent her the day before.

After reading them, Helen again closed her eyes and leaned her head against the steering wheel. She knew these two communications would be evidence used against her to show motive for murder. And based on the texts from Gloria and Hank as well as the sheriff's voice mail, they were closing in.

Feeling her heartbeat racing, Helen forced herself to open her eyes. The rain was showing no signs of letting up. She glanced at the time on the car stereo: 11:56 p.m.

"Screw it," she said, keeping her hazard lights on and putting the vehicle in gear. Helen Lewis had never been one to procrastinate, and she wasn't going to start now.

Praying that her instincts would be as wrong today as they'd been the night before, she pressed down on the accelerator, and the black Crown Vic flung gravel as it roared back onto the highway.

———

Helen barely made it another mile before red and blue headlights appeared in her rearview mirror. Feeling her pulse quicken, she again pulled onto the side of the road. There was a sheriff's cruiser behind her and two more pulled to a stop in front. At least three uniformed men approached the Crown Vic, and Helen noticed several other officers who stayed behind in the vehicles. She rolled down her window and tried to maintain her composure as rain droplets leaked into the interior of the vehicle.

"What's the problem, officers? I'm getting wet here."

After conferring with each other, one of the deputies stepped forward holding an umbrella over his head. Helen recognized him as a veteran member of the force named Ty Dodgen, whose wife, Cindy, taught history at Giles County High. Dodgen peered at Helen with a pained expression. "General, the sheriff needs to see you right away."

"That's good," Helen said, maintaining her prosecutorial tone. "Because I need to see him too. What the hell is going on, Ty? Do you guys need three vehicles and six officers to tell me to see Hank? And if he needs to talk with me so bad, why haven't I received anything on my dispatch radio?" Helen gestured at the system that was installed in her government-issued car, the same as it was in the deputies', and felt a cold tickle run down her arms. *Why haven't I received a dispatch?* she thought, knowing that her instincts had been dead-on this time. She decided to press the issue. "Look, it's been a long day, and I'm going to go home and change out of my court clothes. I'll call Hank on my way."

"I'm afraid I can't let you do that, ma'am," Ty said.

Helen gazed into the officer's determined blue eyes.

"The hell you can't," Helen said. "I'm the district attorney general of this county as well as the counties of Maury, Wayne, and Lawrence. I don't need your permission to go home. Now stand down, Deputy."

Helen made a motion to put the car in gear, and when she did, Dodgen drew his weapon. "General, please step out of the vehicle."

"What in the world is wrong with you, Ty?"

Ty Dodgen, who had always been one of Helen's favorite officers, stuck his chin out and stood his ground. "We have a warrant for your arrest, General."

"My *arrest*? What are you talking about? My arrest for what?"

Before Dodgen could respond, Helen saw another figure approaching the vehicle. The deputy, still holding his weapon aimed at Helen, took a step back, and Sheriff Hank Springfield took his place. The sheriff wore a rain slicker over his uniform, and water dripped off the brim of his hat.

"Hank," she managed, forcing her voice to remain steady. "What—?"

"General Lewis, you are under arrest for the murder of Frederick Alan Renfroe," Hank said, his voice low and cold as ice. "Please step out of the vehicle and place your hands behind your head."

19

As the sun began to rise over the Hazel Green farm, Bocephus Haynes awoke to hot and foul breath on his neck, face, and nose followed by the coarse feel of his dog's tongue licking all three areas. When he opened his eyes, he was inches away from the soulful gaze of Lee Roy Jordan McMurtrie. The dog nudged Bo's cheek with his cold nose and started licking again, burying his white-and-brown head into Bo's neck.

"All right, damnit. All right." Bo tried to sit up and found that the side of his face was stuck to the damp and muddy ground. Wrenching himself free, he sat up and rubbed his face, feeling the sting from his makeshift pillow of wet dirt and grass. His head felt like it had marbles in it from all the bourbon and beer he'd consumed the night before. He blinked his eyes and got his bearings. He was sitting in a clearing on the northern tip of the farm, just a few feet away from a large headstone. Bo leaned forward and crawled on his knees a couple of feet until he could reach the concrete marker. Even now, as he read the name of the man buried here, he felt a ripple of sadness envelop him.

"Thomas Jackson McMurtrie," Bo said out loud, the words sounding like they were being filtered through sandpaper. He swallowed, and his mouth tasted of bile. Had he thrown up last night? He couldn't remember, but based on how his stomach felt at the moment, a bout of nausea could very well be on the way.

"I sure have made a mess of things, Professor," Bo said, tapping his hand softly on the grave. Last night, he and Lee Roy had walked through the driving rain the mile and a half to the grave, but Bo couldn't remember anything about the walk other than collapsing at the foot of the headstone when he arrived, exhausted from the day's events. He was sure he'd cried, but he couldn't remember that either.

Bo pondered what the General had said the night before. *Tom would be ashamed of what you've let yourself become . . .*

Bo felt coarseness on his fingers and looked down to see Lee Roy licking his hand. The dog, too, was peering at the grave. Lee Roy was once Tom's dog, and one of the Professor's last requests was for Bo to take care of him.

"Lee Roy's doing really good, Professor," Bo said. "You probably wouldn't be proud of me, but you would be of him. He's kept me good company this past year."

Bo looked at his clothes. He was still wearing the shirt and suit pants that he'd worn to court the day before. They were now filthy with grass and mud stains. *Ruined,* Bo thought, just like his life.

He took in a deep breath of the fresh farm air and hung his head. "Professor, I thought living out here would be the perfect compromise. Hazel Green is almost halfway between Pulaski and Huntsville. I really thought it would work." He paused and swallowed hard. "But it hasn't. I'm stuck." He gave his head a jerk. "The General is right. I guess I'm scared of being me again. When I start being me, people get hurt. People that I love." He felt heat behind his eyes. "Now it seems like all the people I care about are either dead or gone."

Again, Bo felt his hand being licked, and he leaned down and ruffled Lee Roy's head. "I'm lost, Professor." He sighed. "And I don't have the first clue as to what to do. But one thing's for sure . . ." He straightened himself. Then he kissed his hand and gently rested it on the grave.

"I'm not going to find my way out here."

20

Helen moved her eyes around the holding cell and breathed in the stale scent of incarceration. She sat at the same metal desk where countless accused criminals had waited to be charged, tried, and sentenced. The five-foot-by-seven-foot box had three yellow cinder block walls and one glass partition, behind which Helen figured that Sheriff Hank Springfield and perhaps several of his deputies were watching her. She extended the middle finger of her right hand toward the glass wall. Then she gazed across the concrete floor of the cell until her eyes reached the sliding steel door with its small Plexiglas window. She could see the reflection of her face, but mercifully that was all she could make out. She wasn't sure she could stomach the sight of herself in the orange jumpsuit of a pretrial detainee.

A shadow appeared in the window, and Helen felt her body tense. Then she heard the swooshing sound of the door sliding open. Two men entered the cell.

Sheriff Hank Springfield had a grim look on his face. His eyes appeared red from lack of sleep, and the top two buttons of his khaki uniform shirt were unbuttoned, revealing his white undershirt. He had a day's growth of beard, and he rubbed his whiskers as he stepped to his left so that the other man could enter. Helen shot to her feet when she recognized him.

"What in the hell are you doing here?" Her eyes darted to the sheriff.

Hank held out his palms and was about to say something when the other man's voice cut him off.

"Judge Page has appointed me as acting district attorney general in light of your . . . *predicament*, Helen." Reginald "Sack" Glover's high-pitched southern drawl reverberated off the cinder block walls. Helen cringed at the sound.

"You?" Helen spat the question.

"Me," Sack said, running a hand through his thick red hair and smacking his lips, which glistened from recently applied ChapStick. He was of average height but in good shape for a man in his fifties, and his physical stature was enhanced by the custom-made clothes he typically wore. Today, he had on a light gray sports jacket, white shirt, burgundy tie, and black pants. As he approached the metal desk and took one of the plastic chairs across from Helen, she noticed a smattering of freckles on his nose. He crossed his legs and smiled at Helen. "It wouldn't be right for someone who works for you to prosecute you for murder."

"Why him?" Helen asked, looking past Sack to Hank, who had leaned his athletic frame against the cinder block wall.

"Like he said, Judge Page made the appointment, General," Hank said. "I had nothing to do with it. I'm assuming because of his prior experience as a prosecutor."

"Fifteen years," Sack chimed in, looking down at the concrete floor and gritting his teeth. "And though I know this will be hard, try to remember, Sheriff Springfield, that for purposes of this case, *I'm* the General in this room. Got it?"

Even in the dimly lit cell, Helen could see Hank's face reddening. The sheriff didn't answer the question.

"Page hates my guts," Helen rasped, wishing she had a glass of water. "Always has, the lazy bastard. The only reason he appointed you is because he knows it'll piss me off. It has nothing to do with your experience. You were a mediocre prosecutor, and that's why I fired you." She paused and glared at Sack. "I guess your placement could have something to do with all of that family money you've filtered into Page's war chest over the years."

Now it was Sack whose face blushed as red as his hair. "Well . . . whatever the reason. I'm the one who will be prosecuting you for your ex-husband's murder." He licked his lips. "I'd like to ask you a few questions."

Helen rolled her eyes and plopped down in her chair. "I've already told Hank that I won't be talking. I'll wait for my attorney."

"And who might that be?" Sack asked. "Dick Selby?" He snickered. "Old Lou Horn? I'm sure you'll probably have all the defense lawyers in town lining up to represent their old friend, General Lewis."

Helen didn't answer. Instead she peered at Hank. "How about getting this asshole out of my sight?"

Hank pushed himself off the wall. He was about to say something to Sack when the swooshing sound of the sliding door cut him off. A deputy who couldn't be much over twenty years old stepped into the cell, his eyes wide. "Sheriff, there's a man out here who says he's General Lewis's lawyer."

Helen felt her stomach tighten.

"Bring him back," Hank said, and the deputy shuffled off, leaving the door open. The sheriff looked at Helen and raised his eyebrows, but she said nothing.

"The suspense is killing me," Sack said, his tone oozing with venom. Outside the cell, Helen heard the sounds of shackled men being brought down the hall to see the jail nurse. From her own experience interviewing detainees in this very holding cell, she knew the medical office was a couple of doors down.

Seconds later, the deputy was back outside the opening to the cell. Helen couldn't see the man with him, but Hank could. She noticed that the sheriff's face had turned a shade pale. "You're the General's lawyer?" Hank asked, his voice a mixture of shock, surprise, and—*something else*, Helen thought, before it came to her.

Fear.

"Expecting someone different?"

She recognized the deep baritone even before he stepped into the cell. When he did, Sack Glover straightened his back and crossed his arms, involuntarily taking a step back to make more room for the huge man.

Bocephus Haynes wore a white button-down, faded jeans, and black combat boots. "General," he said, nodding at her. Then he peered at Sack.

"Aren't they missing you down at the store?"

Sack smiled, but there was no humor in his eyes. His family had owned Glover's Grocery for years before it was eventually bought out by Winn-Dixie. Because of the family business, Reginald Glover's high school buddies had taken to calling him "Sack," and the nickname had stuck.

Ignoring Bo's question, which was a common jab since everyone in the Giles County Bar Association knew that Sack didn't have to practice law, the red-haired prosecutor stuck out his hand. "Been a long time, Bo. Are you back in town?"

Bo shook hands with the man. "You could say that," he said. Then, turning to Hank, he shook hands with the sheriff.

"Good to see you, Bo," Hank said.

"You too," Bo said.

"I take it that your presence as Ms. Lewis's lawyer means that your suspension by the Tennessee State Bar has been lifted?" Sack asked.

"It does indeed," Bo said, turning around to face the prosecutor. "I was reinstated on March twenty-second."

"Well . . . let's hope that we don't have any more of that kind of trouble," Sack said.

"Let's hope," Bo said, his voice low as he stepped closer to the man, invading his personal space. "I'd like a few minutes with my client if you don't mind?"

Sack blinked and tried to take another step backward but was stopped by the cinder block wall. "Of course," he said. "Sheriff, let's give Ms. Lewis a chance to talk with her attorney."

"Not in here," Bo said. "I know that people can see inside this cell behind that glass wall, and y'all are probably videoing or at least tape recording everything that happens. We'll use the attorney room." He turned to Hank. "If that's OK?"

Hank nodded and gestured to the young deputy. "I'll escort Mr. Haynes to the consultation area. You bring General Lewis."

"Yes sir," the deputy said.

Bo turned to follow Hank, but Sack's voice stopped him. "After you speak with your client, let's talk."

"Oh, we'll be talking," Bo said as he exited the cell. "You can count on it."

———

Five minutes later, Helen was escorted into the attorney consultation room of the Giles County Jail. The room wasn't much bigger than a closet but had the same yellow cinder block walls. In the middle of the tiny space sat a square-shaped folding table and two aluminum chairs. Bocephus Haynes leaned forward in one of the chairs with a yellow notepad and pen in front of him.

Once in the room, Helen shuffled toward him, finding it hard to walk in the prison-issue sliders that adorned her feet.

"Sheriff said y'all could have as much time as you need," the deputy said.

"Thank you," Bo said, standing as Helen approached the table. Once the door was safely closed shut, he smiled, but Helen could tell it was forced. "I don't believe I've ever seen you in orange, General." He held out a hand but she ignored it.

"It doesn't appear that you dressed up for the occasion either."

Bo squinted at her. "I don't suit up for client meetings at the jail."

"Who says I'm your client? I thought I told you last night that I had decided not to hire you."

"You said a lot of things last night." He licked his lips. "I chose to ignore that part."

"What about all that talk about not being able to represent me? Been out of the game too long. I'd be better off with someone else. Taking my case would hurt your chance at regaining custody of your kids, yada, yada, yada. What's changed?"

He took a step closer to her. "I think it's time I start being me again."

She gave her head a jerk. "Like I said at the farm," Helen started. "You're scared of being you."

"No, that's not exactly true. I wasn't scared of being me. I was scared for everyone else." He paused. "I tend to leave a wake."

Helen felt a charge of something as she gazed into his eyes, which were as black as coal. Adrenaline maybe? Or perhaps it was hope. She closed her eyes. "And now?"

"Outside of my kids, I don't care anymore."

Unable to hold his intense gaze, Helen turned away from him and peered at the wall. She didn't have a whole lot of options. She wasn't going to hire Dick Selby or Lou Horn, and she didn't want to retain a lawyer from Nashville or Knoxville. If she did that, she'd still have to hire a local attorney to help pick the jury, and she wasn't Bill Gates. She didn't have a pot of money to throw away.

She wanted only one lawyer and needed the best.

And just as she had surmised during her wild trek to Hazel Green yesterday afternoon, Bocephus Haynes was the obvious choice. *Outside of me, there's not a finer trial lawyer in Pulaski . . .*

Finally, she wheeled and faced him. "Same terms as last night: $15K retainer and four hundred dollars an hour?"

Bo nodded. "That's fine."

"This isn't the easiest way to break back into the practice of law."

"Nothing about my life has been easy. Am I hired or not?"

A barely audible sob escaped from Helen's mouth. Then she gave her head a swift nod.

"Good," Bo said, sitting down and gesturing toward the chair in front of him. "Why don't you start by telling me what in the hell is going on?"

21

When Sack Glover entered Kathy's Tavern, he found Lou Horn sitting at a corner table in the back parlor. It was only 4:30 in the afternoon, but based on the two empty bottles of Coors Light on the table and the half-full bottle in Lou's hand, the defense lawyer had started without him. Even in the dark room, Sack could see that Lou's face was flushed a darker shade from the alcohol. "A little early to be tying a buzz on, isn't it, Lou?"

"Sack," Lou said, taking another swig from his beer bottle and gazing down at the table. He gestured at the seat across from his. "Buy you a beer?"

Sack sat down and eyed the attorney. "I better not."

Lou motioned for the barmaid, and a petite young woman with brown hair approached.

"Another round, Lou?" she asked.

"Yeah, Cassie. Bring me a cheeseburger and fries too. And whatever Sack wants as well."

"Diet Coke," Sack said. Cassie waited for more, but when Sack remained quiet, she strode away.

Lou held his bleary gaze on the barmaid's backside for a couple of seconds. Then he peered at Sack. "Did Page make the appointment?"

"A couple of hours ago."

Lou scoffed. "Well . . . congratulations, *General*." He held his beer up in mock salute and took another sip. "When can we talk deal on Zannick?"

"We need to give that some time, Lou. You know that. We can't be obvious with it. Page is in my pocket, but even Harold isn't going to flaunt a miscarriage of justice. He's too savvy for that."

"Has he said anything to you?"

"Nothing specific, but he did give me a piece of advice after the appointment that I intend to follow."

Lou smiled, his eyes a bit too unfocused for a few beers. Sack wondered if Lou had started drinking earlier or if maybe there was something else in the old lawyer's bloodstream. "And what wisdom did the Honorable Harold Page bestow upon you?" Lou asked.

"Take it slow," Sack responded, moving his hands off the table so that Cassie could set down their drinks. "Thank you, Cassie."

"Would you like something to eat, Mr. Glover?" Cassie asked. The barmaid was a trim woman in her midtwenties. She wore a sleeveless Tennessee Titans jersey, cut-off jeans, and an orange cap with a cursive *Vols* embroidered on the front.

"No, I'm good. How's your momma doing, Cassie?"

The barmaid sighed. "She's fine, I guess. The bursitis in her hip is still acting up, and she fell again in the yard last week. I tell her to take it easy, but it doesn't do any good."

"She still getting her groceries delivered like we arranged?"

A smile broke over the young woman's face. "Yes, thank you so much for that." She leaned over and hugged his neck, and the smell of wildflowers hit Sack's nostrils.

"You're welcome," he said.

"Sure you don't want something to eat?"

"I'm sure," Sack said, and she shuffled away.

"I bet if you had said *you*, she would have straddled the table and let you go to town." Lou spoke in a slurred whisper that caused Sack to lean back in his chair and reassess the man.

"You all right, Lou? You seem a little off."

"Just stating a fact. Why is it that all of the young tail in this town leave moist spots in their chair after you talk with them?"

Finally, Sack grinned, but instead of answering the question, he fired one of his own. "Can your client lay low for a few months?"

Lou drained his beer and looked toward the bar, holding the empty soldier up and pointing at it until he got Cassie's attention. Then he glared across the table at Sack. His eyes seemed to have sunken into his face, and he looked even older than his sixty-plus years. "Honestly, I don't know. Patience isn't Michael Zannick's biggest virtue."

"I understand that, but he's going to have to exercise some here. If he does, then this will work out the same way the Ennis Petrie parole hearing went." He took a sip of soda and squinted at Lou. "You and I both know that getting Ennis paroled, given his history with the Klan and the horrific crime he helped commit, was no easy task, especially with Helen arguing so hard against it. But Michael Zannick wanted Ennis out, and I made it happen. I won there, and I'll win here. The charges against Zannick will be dismissed or pled down to a hand-slap misdemeanor. He's just going to have to give it some time."

Lou peered at his beer bottle and didn't respond.

"What does he have on you, Lou?" Sack finally asked.

Lou continued to gaze into the empty bottle. "No comment."

Sack watched the other lawyer, thinking that he must be chasing the alcohol with some type of mood enhancement drug. Xanax or Klonopin maybe. "You want me to drive you home?"

Lou gave his head a jerk. "Nah, but I need to ask you a question."

"What?"

Lou motioned for Sack to lean toward him, and Sack reluctantly did so. When Lou spoke, his breath smelled like bad coffee covered by beer, and Sack's eyes began to water. "Do you really think the General killed Butch?"

Sack shifted back in his seat and exhaled the air he'd been holding in his lungs. Then he gritted his teeth. Sack had always hated everyone's persistence in calling Helen Lewis "the General," as if she were Douglas MacArthur or something. He understood that lawyers had to use the term in court. But it boggled his mind that Helen Lewis's stature had risen to the point where an experienced trial lawyer like Lou Horn would still use the title in a bar. "Do you believe Sheriff Springfield would have arrested her so quickly if he didn't think she was guilty? Hank worships Helen. Everyone in his office does."

"The case is that strong?"

Sack grinned. "As an oak tree."

Lou sighed and looked down at the table. When his right thumb began to shake, he gripped his beer bottle with both hands. "Butch was my oldest friend."

"I know," Sack said, finishing his soda and rising from the table. "And I'm going to make Helen Lewis pay for what she did." He began to walk away, but Lou's voice stopped him.

"Has the General lawyered up?"

Sack felt his stomach tighten as he nodded his head. "Guess who?"

Lou took another sip of beer. "Selby?"

Sack laughed. "Hell no."

Lou snapped his fingers. "That old professor from Alabama. McMurtrie? There were rumors that the two of them had a thing going on."

"He's dead," Sack said. "Try again."

"Perry Mason? Ben Matlock? F. Lee Bailey?" Lou snickered at his suggestions.

"We wish," Sack said, not joining in the other man's revelry.

"Who then?"

"Bocephus Haynes," Sack said.

Lou's eyes narrowed, and he took a long pull off the bottle. Then he peered up at Sack. Some of the alcohol-induced redness in the man's cheeks had evaporated. "I thought he moved away."

"He's back."

22

Bo gazed at the wooden boards that covered the front door of his law office. Almost three years ago, after the Tennessee State Bar had suspended him the first time, he had nailed the planks over the entrance. And though he owned the building, he hadn't tried to lease the space to another lawyer or vendor since barricading the place.

He wondered if part of him always figured he'd come back.

Bo ran his hand over the dusty shingle that hung to the side of the door. Despite all the time that had passed, the words on the sign were still visible.

BOCEPHUS HAYNES, ATTORNEY AT LAW.

He let his hand drop to his side and gazed up First Street. It was seven o'clock in the evening, and the sun was setting bright orange above and to the west of the ancient clock that adorned the top of the Giles County Courthouse. Bo let out a deep breath and took in the scene, which he had to admit was beautiful. Then he let his eyes wander past the majestic courthouse—where he'd tried countless cases over the past two decades— to the streets, restaurants, and stores that he knew by heart.

Was it good to be back? He wasn't sure. Bo had a lot of history in Pulaski, and much of it was bad. But he had to admit that it felt good to be working again. To be doing something, anything, besides feeling sorry for himself.

"Wide ass open," Bo said out loud, chuckling to himself. Those three words had been his mantra during his legal career, and he'd been going that speed ever since waking up this morning at the foot of the Professor's grave. After walking the mile back to the house with Lee Roy at his heels, he'd showered, shaved, and eaten a quick breakfast of cereal and coffee. Since his head had been pounding with a hangover, he'd popped three Aleve as well. Once he'd felt half-alive again, he'd hitched a ride into town with the farmer who leased the McMurtrie land. The man needed to pick up some equipment and supplies from CT Garvin's Feed and Seed, and downtown was close by. Bo sighed with relief when he saw that his Sequoia hadn't been towed but remained parked in the same lot where he'd left it the night before. After thanking the farmer and shaking his hand, Bo drove to Glenn's Flower Shop on Bob Wallace, bought an orchid, and headed to another graveyard.

Jasmine Henderson Haynes was buried at Maple Hill Cemetery, a huge expanse of land adjacent to California Drive in Huntsville. Bo placed the flower on the headstone and squatted down so that he could run his fingers over her name.

"Jazz, I don't know if what I'm about to do is right or not," he said. "Hell, I'm not sure if I know the difference between right and wrong anymore." He paused and stifled a sob. "But I've got to do something, honey." He leaned down and kissed the marker and then, after wiping his tears, walked with purpose to the Sequoia.

His next stop was the Hendersons' home in the Medical District, a neighborhood of middle-class houses a half mile from Huntsville Hospital. He hoped that Ezra would be out and that he could speak with Juanita. No such luck.

Ezra answered the door before Bo could knock. "What in the hell do you think you're doing? The kids are at school, and even if they were home, the court made it plain yesterday that you only get to see them on the weekends."

"I came here to tell you that I'm going back to Pulaski," Bo said, trying with every fiber of his being to maintain his cool. "I've been retained to represent a prominent citizen on charges of murder."

"What *prominent citizen* would even think about hiring you after what you've done with your life these past few years?"

"General Helen Lewis."

Ezra's eyes widened, but he wasn't thrown off too much. "Well . . . good luck." He started to shut the door, but Bo stuck his forearm in the opening. "One thing," Bo said, stepping into the space and making the older man retreat a step backward.

"You're in my house now, Bocephus, and I'm going to call the police if you don't leave. How'd that be? Another conviction on your record."

"I got something to say, and you're going to listen. I'm returning to work in Pulaski, but I'm not giving up my children. In six months, we'll be back in front of Judge Woodruff, and I'll be awarded custody. You understand?"

"In your dreams."

Bo leaned forward and glared at the other man, who had never thought Bo was good enough for Jazz, even when things between the couple had been stable. "In the meantime, I expect that you will make sure that they stay safe, attend school, and do what they're supposed to be doing."

"Who the hell do you think you're talking to? I asked the court for custody because I didn't think you were going to do those things. I don't need a lecture from you."

"You asked the court for custody because you're a vindictive man. A very *small* man who decided to blame me for all of his troubles instead of owning them himself."

"Get your ass off my property," Ezra said, reaching out with his hands and pressing them hard into Bo's chest.

Bo didn't budge. "I'll be seeing you, Ezra. Next weekend, I'll be here to pick my kids up."

He turned to go, but Ezra was determined to get the last word. "If General Lewis is so desperate that she asked for your help, then she must have done whatever she's charged with."

Bo didn't bother with a response. He peeled asphalt as he left his former father-in-law's house and made a beeline back to the farm, where he quickly packed his clothes and Lee Roy's food. Then he and the dog were off to Pulaski. On the way, he tried to call the Professor's son, Dr. Tommy McMurtrie, but he didn't answer. *Probably in surgery,* Bo thought. He didn't leave a message, resolving to set up a time to see Tommy in person when he visited T. J. and Lila next weekend.

After clicking off the phone, Bo spent the rest of the trek into Giles County praying that the General would relent and still let him represent her.

She did, but instead of getting the whole story in the attorney room, all Bo got was his client's cryptic promise to tell him everything in good time.

"For now, you need to find out every piece of evidence they have against me."

Realizing that the General's mind was made up and that further questions would be futile, Bo left the jail at three o'clock, after requesting a copy of all the witness statements gathered by the sheriff's office from a deputy at the front desk. The officer had smirked at him and said he'd see what he could do. If this case ran like any of the ones he'd had defending clients charged by General Lewis, Bo would be lucky to see any of the state's evidence prior to the preliminary hearing.

What goes around comes around, Bo thought, shaking his head at the irony of his client's situation.

From the jail, Bo drove out to Pecan Grove Drive and began knocking on doors, but most of Butch Renfroe's neighbors were either not home or not answering their doors. One person, an elderly woman named Bonita Spencer, opened her door for him but politely declined to discuss the case, saying she was still very upset and had told the police everything she knew. As Bo was walking away, Ms. Spencer surprised him. "I sure was sad to hear about your wife."

"Thank you, ma'am," Bo said, making a note to return in a couple of weeks to try again with Ms. Spencer.

By the time Bo left Butch's neighborhood, it was past six o'clock, and he was exhausted. But alas, there would be no rest for the weary.

Bo rolled up his sleeves and reached inside the passenger-side window of the Sequoia for his toolbox. In the back seat, Lee Roy had collapsed on his stomach, and the tip of his tongue hung out of his mouth. Bo didn't have the heart to wake him. Today had taken a lot out of Lee Roy, too, as he'd been in the truck for all of Bo's adventures since his arrival in Pulaski. Bo had kept both back windows cracked all day so that Lee Roy would have plenty of cool air, but now he rolled them all the way down. It was such a pleasant April night Bo figured that he could probably fall asleep himself on the hood of the SUV.

But sleep wasn't in the cards. He undid the latch to the tool kit and took out a pair of locking pliers and a claw hammer. Then, after scanning the four boards that crisscrossed the front door of the office and picking out the first nailhead he wanted to remove, he went to work.

He had a law firm to resurrect.

23

"I am the resurrection and the life."

Ennis Petrie whispered the words by heart, but he still gripped the pocket-size Bible tight in his right hand. They came from the eleventh chapter of John, verse 25. The story of Jesus raising Lazarus from the dead was Ennis's favorite of the Messiah's miracles, and he repeated the phrase from chapter 11 often, especially when he was anxious or scared.

When you were in prison for over four years, you learned how to control your nerves or you went crazy. Survival was the only goal. Eat. Sleep. Use the bathroom. Stay alive. Day after day after day, same routine.

It was a kind of monotonous danger. Like floating down a river in a raft with a brood of cottonmouths just under the surface of the water and gators watching on the shoreline. One false move, one wrong breath, and you could get bit. Or worse . . . Ennis had seen it happen. Men attacked in the showers, where there were no cameras. Beaten, gagged, and raped. An overzealous corrections officer taking out his frustration with a baton to the shins of an inmate who didn't know when to shut up. The man hadn't been able to walk for a week. Sometimes Ennis had hoped he'd fall in and get overwhelmed by the vipers, but a human's will to live was a tricky thing. Ennis had plenty of scares, especially since he was a former lawman, but he'd been smart and lucky, and he managed to make it out.

And now I'm surrounded by snakes again . . .

Ennis lay on a seat in the back of the abandoned bus. He could hear footsteps outside, shuffling through the gravel, but he remained still. Another thing you learned in prison was how to quiet your mind, your body, and even your breathing to remain as unmoving as a corpse.

Ennis closed his eyes and listened. The school bus garage was located on Eighth Street, just off West College, down the hill from Martin Methodist. Sometimes Ennis could hear the faint sounds of campus life. The happy screams and laughter of coeds going out for the night. The honking of horns. Even the echoes of a trumpet from band practice.

But now, though the night was still young, all Ennis heard were the footsteps growing closer. Then the squeaking hinges of the bus door opening. Seconds later, a shadow appeared above him, and then a man came into view holding a large briefcase in his left hand and a two-by-four stick of lumber in his right. "You did a good job, Sheriff. Are you ready to collect?"

Ennis sat up straight and leaned his back against the bus's window. He peered at the man standing above him. Finn Pusser had the cold, dead eyes of a contract killer. As the high sheriff of Giles County, Tennessee, and then an inmate himself, Ennis knew the varying looks of criminals. The wild and reckless eyes of an abusive husband. The puffy faces and hazy expressions of druggies. And the nervous and herky-jerky movements of dealers. Finn's demeanor impressed Ennis much more than the other types.

"Set the case on the ground."

"You're not going to count it? A hundred thousand dollars is a lot of money."

"No need. I doubt Mr. Zannick wants to cross me."

Finn smiled. "On the contrary, he wants you to stay on the payroll."

Ennis slowly shook his head. "Tell him, no thanks. I did what he asked. In return, he helped me get parole and delivered the money he promised." Ennis paused. "We're even."

Finn tossed the piece of lumber from his right hand to his left and back. Then he smiled. "Suit yourself. But remember something, Sheriff." Finn stepped forward and stuck the two-by-four an inch from Ennis's face. "It would be wise to remain a friend of Mr. Zannick."

———

Ennis took slow and deliberate breaths as he watched Finn leave the bus. Glancing out the window, he saw the gray sedan pull away, and though the windows were tinted, he knew there were other men in the car. Finn Pusser was Michael Zannick's muscle, and Ennis figured the Irishman had brought reinforcements.

Once the vehicle was out of sight, Ennis scooted forward until he could reach the briefcase. He unclicked it and gazed at the stacks of one-hundred-dollar bills. *God forgive me,* he thought, as images of what had happened forty-eight hours ago flashed through his mind. The things he'd seen. What he'd done.

Ennis closed the briefcase and set his jaw. Then he gripped the Bible in his pocket.

"I am the resurrection and the life."

24

An hour after Bo pulled out the first nail, the boards lay in a pile to the side of the door, and Bo was inserting a key into the latch. Despite the cool of the night, he was drenched with sweat from the effort and had taken off his button-down. He wiped his forehead with the front of his white tank-top undershirt and turned the key hard to the left.

Though tight from lack of use, the lock eventually gave, and the door swung open. Bo stepped inside, and a flood of memories washed over him.

Everything was as it had been the last time he'd been here. The front parlor, which Bo had used as a lobby, had a leather couch, two chairs, and a coffee table on the left side of the room. Bo smiled when he saw that the table still had the same magazines on it from three years earlier, which included a *Sports Illustrated* with Eddie Lacy in his number 42 Alabama football jersey on the cover. To the right of the sitting area was a cherrywood desk behind which, for twenty years, Ellie Michaels had managed the office.

Ellie had been Bo's paralegal, secretary, and receptionist all rolled into one highly efficient and talented human being. After Bo's first suspension in 2012, she'd retired and now lived near her oldest son in Chicago. The last time Bo had seen her was at Jazz's funeral. He wondered if Ellie might be talked into returning to Pulaski. He'd paid her well, and each time one of her five kids needed anything extra for grade school or college, Bo had managed to throw in a timely bonus. Ellie was such a good and loyal employee that any payment to her seemed small in comparison to the wonderful job she'd done.

If I begged her, she probably would come, Bo thought.

But he knew he couldn't do that. Ellie had moved on and was now a full-time grandmother. *Gonna have to hire someone,* Bo thought, pacing around the dusty lobby, which still contained some of the trophies from Bo's former life. The signed form memorializing his first million-dollar verdict, which was an SUV rollover case from 1998, was in a large frame above the couch so that every prospective client had to see it when they walked in the door. Bo peered at the framed document, signed by a jury foreperson named Kimberley Carden, who Bo could still remember. Blonde hair and fierce eyes, looking right at Bo with a twinkle in her gaze and saying loud and clear, "We the jury find for the plaintiff and award compensatory damages of one point five million dollars and punitive damages of five million dollars." Though the punitive award was later cut in half by the Tennessee Supreme Court, the rest of the verdict was upheld. Bo's client, Henrietta Stein, who was rendered a paraplegic from the accident, was able to pay for her medical care for the rest of her life and provide a future for her family.

And Bocephus Haynes became the most feared trial attorney in southern Tennessee. Despite having an explosive racialized past, juries in Pulaski, Lawrenceburg, and even as north as Nashville and east to Knoxville, took a shine to Bo. He was good in the courtroom, comfortable and confident around the jury, the judge, and his opponents. Plus, because he was a huge man with a baritone voice who'd played football for Coach Paul "Bear" Bryant, he was different. His size, his blackness, and his tortured background made him an oddity, and sometimes, in the carnival world known as trial law, a person's distinctive qualities gave them an edge. He'd learned this, his greatest lesson, from Professor Tom McMurtrie.

In courtrooms across the South, you're going to stand out. You're going to be different than your opponents. Use that. Own who you are and tell your client's story to the jury your way. If you do, you'll be successful. I know it.

Bo felt tears fill his eyes as he rubbed a thumb over the framed verdict. The Professor had believed in him. Always. Even when Bo hadn't believed, Tom McMurtrie had. He could use some of that belief now.

The sound of knocking interrupted his trip down memory lane, and he turned to see a woman standing in the doorframe.

"It was open," she said, giving him a nervous smile as she removed her knuckles from the door.

Bo wiped his damp eyes and squinted at the woman, who had to be at least six feet tall. She wore the khaki uniform of the Giles County Sheriff's Office, and the name on her lapel read "Chief Deputy Storm."

"Frannie?" Bo asked, his mouth curving into a grin. "Frannie Storm?"

"Yes, sir," she said, extending her hand. In it, she clasped a manila envelope.

Bo took the package and raised his eyebrows.

"Copies of the witness statements we've obtained so far. You asked Officer Canupp for them earlier today."

"He didn't seem too jacked up about honoring my request."

"He told Hank, and the sheriff wanted to make sure you got these tonight. My investigative report is also in there."

Bo cocked his head at her. "Why?"

"Because today was Sack Glover's first day as acting district attorney general, and Hank figures that Sack won't be offering much in the way of discovery until after the prelim." She paused and took a step closer to him. "Hank wanted you to have these now."

All Bo could think to do was repeat the question he'd just asked. "Why?"

"So you can see what you're up against. Hank thinks a lot of the General and wants to make sure she gets a fair trial." Frannie paused and licked her lips. "But the evidence is staggering, and because of the enhancers, he's afraid that Sack will seek the death penalty."

"The enhancers?"

"The victim's body was badly beaten with what looks to be a revolver. There were also items stolen from the house." She pointed at the manila envelope that Bo now gripped in his right hand. "It's all in there."

Bo glanced at the package and then back at Frannie. "Tell Hank I said thank you."

"Will do," she said, turning to leave.

"Hey."

She looked over her shoulder at him.

"Last time I saw you was at your graduation from high school. Your aunt Ellie was very proud."

"She loved working for you, Mr. Haynes."

Bo snorted and looked around the spiderweb-infested office. "I loved her, too, and I sure could use someone like her now. And call me Bo, OK? You're how old now? Twenty-six?"

She narrowed her eyes. "Twenty-nine."

He shook his head. "It can't be. Four years at David Lipscomb and then the WNBA, right?"

She nodded. "Blew my knee out on a fast break. Lost a step, and in that world, a step is all it takes."

Bo grimaced. "I know. I blew my knee out too. My junior year—"

"At Alabama," she interrupted. "First game of the season, right? You were a preseason All American, destined to follow in the footsteps of Marty Lyons, Barry Krouse, and E. J. Junior."

Bo squinted at her, and Frannie laughed. "Auntie told me everything about you, Mr. Haynes. How your football career was cut short, the beginning of your law practice, and of course when you started hitting the big verdicts." She nodded at the framed form on the wall. "Bocephus Haynes is the greatest trial lawyer in the world." Frannie mimicked the southern accent of her aunt. "She was so proud to work for you, and she'd be glad that you're back." Frannie sighed. "Even if it is in a losing cause."

"You're that confident the General did it."

Frannie nodded and again turned to leave. "I know she did." Just as she was about to turn the knob, she peered at him with eyes burning with intensity. Bo had watched Frannie Storm play ball on several occasions, and she competed with an aggressive, tough edge. She wasn't afraid to mix it up for rebounds, dive for loose balls, or do whatever else it took to win. He caught that vibe in her expression now and felt his own adrenaline begin to ramp up.

"Did she tell you about her abortion today?" Frannie asked.

"What?"

Frannie kept her poker face. Her eyes remained glued to Bo's. "The baby she aborted in 1977. Did she tell you?"

Bo shook his head and could barely find his voice. "No."

"You should ask her," Frannie said. "It was the one skeleton in the General's closet." She paused and raised her eyebrows. "My hunch is that Butch Renfroe died because he threatened to reveal her secret."

25

"October 15, 1977," Helen said, gazing at the cinder block walls of the consultation room. Then she glanced at Bo, who was studying her with his fierce obsidian eyes. He was dressed in black slacks and a blue button-down, and he'd draped his brown sports jacket over the aluminum chair. It was 8:30 a.m., and Helen had barely slept during her first full night of incarceration. Every time she closed her eyes, she saw Butch as she'd seen him last. At his house on Pecan Grove Drive, Helen tightly gripping her revolver. Everything was fuzzy after that. Helen couldn't remember when or how she'd left Butch's house or what she'd done in the hours that had passed before the beginning of the Zannick trial. The time was gone. She'd once seen a therapist who said that people sometimes completely erased their darkest moments. Like soldiers who returned from war and couldn't remember the numerous kills they were a part of and didn't want to talk or think about it. PTSD in its highest form.

Helen Evangeline Lewis knew all about posttraumatic stress disorder, and April Fools' Day 2015 at her ex-husband's house wasn't the first time she'd experienced it.

"You remember that day?" Helen asked. "October 15, 1977 . . ."

Bo blinked. "It was during football season," he said, and she could tell he was thinking hard.

"It was more than that," Helen said. "It was the third Saturday in October."

At this, Bo smiled. "My first Alabama-Tennessee game."

"At Legion Field," Helen said, her voice dripping with bitterness. "The Football Capital of the South." She sneered at him. "Or so it was written on the side of the stadium."

"You were there?"

"I was indeed," she said. "I remember pointing out to the friend I was with that I knew number forty-three out there. Bocephus Haynes from Giles County High, Pulaski, Tennessee."

"I was a freshman, so I didn't play much in the game."

"They didn't need you. Twenty-four to ten Bama was the final score as I recollect."

Bo nodded. "Good memory. Where are you going with this, General? Chief Storm said that the sheriff's department's investigation reveals that you had an abortion in 1977 and that's the motive for you killing Butch. Did you have an abortion?"

Helen returned her focus to the walls. "I'm going to tell it my way. If you don't want to hear it, then you can get the hell out. Your choice."

Bo crossed his arms and sighed. "I'm still here."

"I was dating Butch at the time of the Tennessee-Bama game, but we were fighting. It was my third year of law school, and he was angry that I had been spending too much time studying and not enough time with him. He had graduated from law school by then and was a second-year associate at a firm in Nashville. He wanted me to come there to watch the game with him, but I said no. A girlfriend said that her sister at Alabama had gotten great seats to the game, and I thought a trip away would be good for me.

"We had a great time. Even though the Vols lost the game, it was fun hanging out with some younger people who weren't perpetually stressed out. My friend's sister had brought a flask of whiskey into the game, and we had several Jack Daniel's and Cokes before the clock struck zero. By that time, we had a nice buzz, and my friend's sister's group was heading to a bar next to the stadium called the Tide & Tiger."

Helen paused and her lip began to tremble. "I was having a good time. There were some guys in the group, but so what? I hadn't done anything wrong." She folded her arms tight across her chest. "I shouldn't feel guilty about going, but even now, I still do."

"What happened?" Bo asked, his voice soft. *He's starting to see where this is going,* Helen thought.

"At first, everything was fine. We had a few drinks. The guys were nice enough, and they were buying." Again, she paused. "One of them seemed to really be into me. He kept telling me how much he liked my dark hair. How I had a striking look." She sighed and then cringed. "I had been with Butch for so long it was exciting to have someone flatter me like that. I had no interest in things going any further than some innocent flirting."

"And what about the guy?"

Helen shot Bo a glance and then returned her gaze to the wall. "After a while, I went to the restroom. When I came back, I had a full drink waiting on me. By this point, my friend was pulling on my arm, telling me it was time to go, but I wanted to stay. I was having a good time." Helen started to cry. "After drinking about half the glass, I began to feel a little woozy. I told the guy I'd been flirting with that I thought I might be sick and, a few minutes later, we left."

"Did he slip something in your drink?"

Helen nodded. "GHB."

"How did you—"

"Later. After I woke up the next morning, I checked myself into a hospital. They did a drug screen, and that's what showed up."

Bo exhaled. The room suddenly felt smaller to Helen. She cleared her throat, knowing she had to finish telling what happened. "I don't remember much after leaving the bar. Vague images, like a television screen that's losing its picture, are all I could make out. He was on top of me . . . behind me . . . inside me." She bit her lip and finally looked at Bo. Her attorney was gazing down at the concrete floor and slowly shaking his head.

"General, I'm so sorry," he managed, his voice hoarse. When he looked up at her, she could tell that he meant it.

"Me too," she said, wiping her eyes and pounding a fist on the metal table. "But it doesn't change the fact that on October 15, 1977, I was drugged . . . and raped."

———

"When did you find out you were pregnant?" Bo had waited several minutes to ask the question, and Helen was grateful for the reprieve. She was drained. The only other person she'd ever told the story to was Dr. Rose Marie Servick, a psychiatrist she'd seen for years in Nashville.

"Six weeks later, the Monday after Thanksgiving." She moved her eyes from the wall to her attorney. "Don't you want to know about the morning after?"

Bo didn't say anything. He blinked his eyes and waited.

"I woke up fully clothed on a couch in his den."

"What?" Bo asked, clearly expecting a more horrific description.

"The bastard even had the gall to ask me if I wanted breakfast."

"Like nothing had happened."

She snapped her fingers. "Nothing."

"Did you report the rape to the police?"

She guffawed. "This was 1977 in Birmingham, Alabama, and my rapist was a rich blue blood from Mountain Brook. You ever heard of that neighborhood?"

Bo had clerked a couple of summers at the Jones & Butler law firm in Birmingham, and he remembered that one of the partners had a mansion in the swanky neighborhood known as Mountain Brook. "I have."

"What was I going to say? I could barely remember anything after I was slipped the pill. They call it the date rape drug for a reason, and that was long before that type of rape became the norm on college campuses." She paused. "I would have lost. Sitting here right now, having been a prosecutor most of my life, I didn't have enough evidence to get a conviction."

"Did you ask if anyone saw him put the drug in your glass?"

"I asked my friend on our way back to Knoxville. She said she hadn't seen anything and then asked me what happened."

"Did you tell her?"

Helen grimaced at Bo. "No."

"So, you kept the rape a secret all this time?"

"Yes, I did. Are you judging me?"

He shook his head. "No, ma'am. I was just curious if you had told anyone."

She sighed. "I've seen a psychiatrist in Nashville off and on over the years, and I did tell her. Thought it might help."

"Did it?"

"No." She paused.

Bo leaned his elbows on the table. From this close, Helen could smell his aftershave and the musty scent of the man, which was pleasant and reminded Helen of the times she had visited the barbershop when her father was getting a haircut. "General, thank you for sharing this with me. If you don't mind me asking, has anything ever helped to make you feel better about what happened to you?"

She pondered the question and the man who was asking it. Bocephus Haynes had witnessed a brutal murder when he was five years old. He'd been beaten and kicked and abused by the men who had perpetuated this race crime. As an adult, he'd seen his wife gunned down by an assassin's bullet and had been covered with her blood when she was pronounced. He'd also learned truths about his own background and heritage that would make most people go insane. This man, her attorney, knew pain. He rode in the cockpit with it. He bathed in it every morning and night. She touched his hand.

"The only thing that's ever helped me is to do my job. For a while—three and a half years—I decided to be a police officer. I thought arresting the evil in this world would help me ease the pain, but I knew my real talent was in the courtroom, and only as the district attorney general could I see to it that perps like the man who raped me would be given the maximum punishment under the law."

Bo nodded, more to himself it seemed. "You're only at peace when you're working a case." He glanced up at her. "I get that."

She squeezed his hand. "I know you do."

The room was so quiet now that Helen could hear the faint sound of phones ringing, even from outside the block walls.

"General, what did you do after you learned you were pregnant?" Bo asked.

She sighed. "By that time, I'd agreed to marry Butch. When I came back to Knoxville, he was waiting on my doorstep with a ring. I was so flustered and felt so guilty—can you believe that? I felt guilty that I was raped?—that I agreed to his proposal." She hung her head. "I guess I wanted to feel normal again."

"Did you tell Butch about the pregnancy?"

She choked back a sob and stood from her chair. "Yes."

"When?"

"A week before Christmas, 1977."

"What did you tell him?"

She folded her arms so tight against her chest that it was difficult to breathe. "That I had been pregnant . . ." She trailed off, unable to finish.

"Had been?"

Helen nodded, and let out a short, choppy breath.

"Did you tell him anything else?"

She turned and looked at Bo, seeing the horror plastered to his face. "That I had aborted our child."

———

Now it was Bo who needed to stretch his legs, and he paced around the small room with his hands in his pockets. "You let him think that the baby was his?" There was a challenge in his voice that Helen didn't like.

She set her jaw and let her arms fall to her sides. "Yes, I did."

He didn't say anything, continuing to walk back and forth across the room.

She took his silence as an accusation. "I suppose you think it would have been better if I had borne all to him and told him the truth."

Bo stopped and looked at her. "It doesn't matter what I think." He paused. "And we've drifted a long way from the events of April 1, 2015. We should get back on point."

"The prosecution is going to use the abortion as the motive for murder, right? That's what you said when you stormed in here and demanded to know every detail about it."

He continued to peer at her.

"Well, are they going to try to use it or not?"

Bo nodded.

"Then you need to know the deal."

"What I really need to know, General . . ." He paused. ". . . is what happened two nights ago at your ex-husband's house?"

Helen blinked but continued to hold his eye. "Do you think it would have been better for Butch to know that I had been raped? That *our* child was actually fathered by a sociopath in Birmingham?"

"You were drugged. He would have—"

"He would have what? *Understood?* Understood how I couldn't remember being fucked all night long by some yuppie prick?"

"You were raped, General. Don't—"

"Don't you patronize me, Bocephus Haynes. You know how my rape would have looked to Butch and everyone else in 1977. I'm not even sure I could have gotten a fair trial today, much less then. All the same arguments that defense lawyers make now held more weight back in the good-old-boy '70s. They would say I shouldn't have been flirting. Shouldn't have been drinking. Shouldn't have been having any fun. That I asked for what I got."

Bo grimaced.

"Am I wrong?" She paused and turned back to the wall. "Would Butch have eventually understood?" She shrugged. "I guess it's possible. He was a good man when he was younger. Weak, too, but I didn't learn that till later. But good all the same. Butch might eventually have come to terms with what happened. But would he have had reasonable doubts?"

Bo's face was expressionless.

"You're damn right he would have," Helen continued. "And so would a jury."

"That doesn't make it right," Bo said. "Not telling him was wrong. You being drugged and raped was wrong." He sighed. "And if you didn't kill Butch, you being in this cell is wrong."

Helen collapsed back into her seat. She was exhausted.

"General?"

She looked at him.

"Tell me what happened at Butch's house on Monday night."

She bit her lip. "No. Not until we've seen everything they've got."

"That won't be until the prelim. You know that."

"I do, and don't tell me for a second that you haven't asked clients to hold off on telling you their story until you've seen the prosecution's evidence."

Bo narrowed his gaze. "I have, General, but that's usually when I think . . ." He trailed off and gazed at the table.

"Go ahead, Counselor, spit it out. You don't get your client's whole story when you think they might be guilty, right? You don't want them to burden you with information you might not need to know in order to win. Information that might put you in some kind of ethical quandary where you're helping to exonerate a guilty client. But we both know that the defendant doesn't have to take the stand or even present a case." Helen snorted. "I know well and good the burden of the district attorney general. If the prosecutor can't prove the elements of the crime beyond a reasonable doubt, then the defendant walks . . . whether he or she did the deed or not."

Bo raised his eyes. "That's really how you want to play it."

She exhaled and scratched the back of her neck.

"General, if you're innocent, and I believe that you are, the earlier I know your story, the quicker I can begin working up our defense strategy." He paused. "Give me something."

Helen leaned back in the chair and peered into her attorney's intense eyes. "OK . . . I went to Butch's house that night."

Bo let out a breath of relief. "What happened?"

"I didn't steal anything."

Bo cocked his head at her. "What?"

"According to Frannie's report, a laptop computer and Butch's wallet were stolen from his house." She paused. "I didn't take them."

"That's a hell of a place to start your story."

"I'm giving you what you need to know. The prosecution's theory doesn't fit, because I didn't steal anything."

"If you were trying to hide the fact that you had an abortion, then it would make sense that you would take his computer."

"I agree, but I didn't. I left the house without removing any of Butch's property."

"All right, what else? Why did you go to the house? And what happened when you got there?"

Helen gave a tired smile. "That's all for now, OK?" When Bo started to protest, she grabbed his hand. "Please. You're going to have to trust me. Whoever killed Butch took his computer and his wallet. Stands to reason that the real perp thought Butch had something in either his billfold or his laptop that could hurt him or her and killed him to keep that information hidden." She paused. "And one other thing. There's nothing in the witness statements you've shown me detailing an abortion. How did Frannie Storm learn about it?"

Bo crossed his arms. "I don't know, but she did. I presume because they have more evidence than what's been disclosed. Do you have any idea what that could be?"

Helen rubbed her chin and shook her head. "None."

Bo stood and put his jacket back on. "Well, I guess the prelim should be enlightening."

"So what are you going to do in the meantime?"

"I'll take another stab at meeting with the neighbors on Butch's street. Terry Grimes is who found him dead, so getting an audience with him is crucial."

"What else?"

"I'll do a thorough investigation of the victim. Butch's whereabouts in the days prior to the murder. Friends. Enemies. Colleagues. Would have done that anyway, but the theft of the laptop and wallet make it even more important. I'm also gonna need to get my law firm up and running and hire at least one assistant and a private investigator. I'll file my notice of appearance later today along with a motion for a preliminary hearing. And standard request for discovery." He snickered. "You know, the stuff that you always used to ignore, General."

Helen smirked. "There's no discovery in the state of Tennessee in a criminal case until after the grand jury issues an indictment and the defendant is arraigned. You know that as well as I do, Bo. If I were prosecuting this case, you wouldn't have any of this stuff." She waved an arm at the witness statements that Bo was now placing back into his file jacket.

"Well, I guess we should be damn thankful that you aren't the prosecutor for this case." He turned for the door. "I'll be back in a couple of days." He knocked on the door, signaling to the guard outside that he was done.

"Bo, do one more thing for me."

"What's that?"

"Find out as much as you can on Michael Zannick."

"Zannick?" He cocked his head. "If anyone knows the deal on him, it should be you, shouldn't it? Weren't you headed to trial against him on the day of Butch's murder?"

"Yes, but my knowledge was limited to the facts of the rape case. We need to know more." She paused. "If there's anyone on God's green earth who's benefitted from my arrest, it's Zannick."

Bo arched his head in understanding. "His trial was continued."

"Not only that, but guess who is the new acting district attorney's biggest financial contributor?"

"Jesus," Bo said, scratching his chin. "You think Zannick may have set you up."

The door swooshed open, and a deputy stepped inside. Since they weren't alone anymore, Helen didn't dare answer the question.

Instead, she held out her palms and shrugged.

Maybe, maybe not . . .

26

Bo drove back to his office in a haze of confusion, trying to get his arms around the story he'd heard the General tell. If Helen were anyone else, Bo was sure he'd be thinking that he was representing a guilty client.

But she's not anyone else. She's the General.

Bo had known Helen Lewis for almost thirty years. It was hard to think of her as a young law student flirting at the bar with a man. And parts of the story were still missing. How had Butch reacted after being told about the abortion? Was he upset? Did he cancel the wedding? Obviously, they were eventually married, but how did the abortion affect their relationship? And why was Helen so sure the baby she had aborted was the rapist's? Couldn't Butch have actually been the father?

Since Helen was being charged with her ex-husband's murder, the entire history was important. He banged his steering wheel, frustrated that he didn't have the full picture.

And she still hasn't told me what happened the night of the murder. Her disclosure about going to the house and not stealing anything was a start, but it provided more questions than answers. The glaring one being obvious.

Why did Helen go to Butch's house the night he was killed?

When Bo parked in front of his office, he was so distracted that he barely noticed that the front door was wide open and a long orange extension cord was running from a plug on the side of the building into the office. *What the hell is going on?* he thought, hopping out of the Sequoia and walking toward the door. Now that he was closer, he could hear the dual sounds of a vacuum cleaner and a very agitated English bulldog.

Before he reached the opening, Lee Roy ran toward him and jumped onto his chest. The dog was foaming at the mouth, and Bo caught a nice gob of slobber as he set the animal's paws back on the ground. "Easy, boy," he said as he entered the office. When he did, his forehead collided with something blunt and heavy, and Bo yelled in pain.

The sound of the vacuum cleaner evaporated, and when Bo focused his eyes, he saw a woman holding the handle of the machine with an impatient look blazed on her sweat-streaked face. "You could really use some air-conditioning in this place," she said.

"What did you just hit me with?" Bo asked, rubbing his forehead.

"Nothing. You walked straight into the back of my vacuum cleaner handle." She smirked at him. "You should watch where you're going."

He squinted at the woman, whose head was covered with a red bandana. She wore gray athletic shorts, a black tank top, and solid white tennis shoes. Then he peered over her and noticed that the cobwebs that had littered the office were gone. The stale, dusty smell had been replaced by a lemon freshener. There was a pail of water with a mop stuck in it leaning against the couch, and the rug in the lobby appeared smooth from vacuuming. "What—?"

"No offense, but your office was a pigsty. I've got the back mostly clean. You could use a new paint job in the library. I can handle that over the weekend if you'd like."

"Ma'am, who—?"

"Lona Burks," she said, extending her hand. Bo took it and felt rough calluses on her palms.

"Bocephus Haynes."

"I know. You worked a case a few years back where you interviewed some of the dancers out at the Sundowners." She paused. "You talked to me. Do you remember?"

Bo gazed down at the freshly mopped hardwood floor and back up at the woman. He remembered helping the Professor a few years ago on a trucking case, where a key witness was a stripper at the Sundowners.

"You worked with Wilma Newton?" Bo asked.

She nodded. "Do you remember me?"

Bo shook his head. "I'm sorry. Everything starts to run together when you've been doing this as long as I have. I recall that case well, but I don't recollect our meeting."

She shrugged. "I'm not surprised. I'm sure I wasn't all that helpful. Back then, I was high on meth, coke, and vodka pretty much 24-7." She sighed. "If you don't mind me asking, whatever happened with that case? If I recollect, it involved a trucking accident in Henshaw, Alabama."

Bo smiled. "That's a long story." Then he stepped closer to the woman. "Ms. Burks, while I appreciate what you've done with the place, why are you here? I had planned to call a cleaning service but hadn't got around to it yet."

She gave him a tight-lipped smile. "Well, I'm better than any cleaning crew. I work harder, and I can do more than mop and vacuum."

Bo smiled. "Are you applying for a job?"

"You might say that."

Bo leaned down and petted Lee Roy behind the ears. Since his arrival, the dog had calmed down and was sitting upright, but he didn't acknowledge Bo while he was being petted. Instead, Lee Roy peered at the woman with suspicious eyes, as if he wasn't quite sure who or what he was looking at.

As he followed the dog's line of sight back up to Lona Burks, Bo figured that he probably had the same expression in his own gaze. "Ms. Burks, why are you here?"

"Like I said. I want a job."

"Why do you want to work for me?"

"You represent General Lewis, don't you?"

Bo nodded. He had always been amazed at how fast news traveled in Pulaski. As far as he knew, there had been no press announcing his presence as counsel for the General yet, but Lona Burks acted as if it were common knowledge. *Small towns . . .*

"Well . . . ," Lona continued, ripping off the bandana and wiping her face with her forearm. Without the covering, Bo noticed that her hair was strawberry blonde and trimmed short on the sides and in the back with bangs in the front. ". . . a prick named Michael Zannick raped my little girl, and General Lewis was supposed to be prosecuting him this week." She scoffed. "Instead, she's sitting in jail for a crime she couldn't possibly have committed."

"How do you know that?" Bo asked.

"I know the General. She's tough, mean, and fair. On my second charge for possession, she said she'd get me some treatment if I pled guilty. I did, and she followed through on her end."

"You're clean."

Lona nodded. "Sober three years next month."

"Congratulations."

"I don't want or deserve your praise. I do want a job."

Bo again peered around the office. He'd been gone three hours, and Lona Burks had transformed the place from a complete dump into something a person might consider presentable. Though there was much left to do, she'd made a big dent. He looked at her. "I can hire you to keep the place clean." He paused. "Is there anything else you can do?"

She gazed down at the hardwood and leaned forward to pet Lee Roy. The dog tensed, but then Bo saw him relax when Lona's fingers began to caress his ears. "Not sure about me, are you?" she asked, and then she looked up at Bo. "I can answer the phone, and I'm sure I can learn how to file documents on the court's electronic system. I can get someone in the clerk's office to teach me that. I'm a quick learner, and I'll work my ass off."

Bo again moved his eyes around the room. "I can see that."

"How about it then?"

"Let me ask you something. Do you think this Zannick fellow might have had something to do with Butch Renfroe's murder and General Lewis's arrest?"

Lona didn't hesitate in her response. "There's not a doubt in my mind."

Bo thought back to the General's desperate plea as he was leaving the jail to find out everything he could about Michael Zannick. Helen had been ambivalent about whether Zannick had set her up, but Bo saw nothing of the sort in Lona Burks's ardent glare. "You're hired."

27

The Yellow Deli was located in the historic Heritage House on Third Street in downtown Pulaski. Founded by the Twelve Tribes, a Christian cult organization that had originated in the early '70s, the restaurant had opened its first location in Chattanooga, and since its arrival in Pulaski it had been a popular lunch-and-dinner spot for locals, tourists, and the students of Martin Methodist College. Because it remained open twenty-four hours a day from Sunday through Friday, served great coffee, and had a cozy atmosphere, the place was ideal for a college kid pulling an all-nighter to cram for a test or finish a research paper.

Michael Zannick enjoyed the food at the Yellow Deli, but even more than that, he loved the atmosphere and the diverse crowd. At noon on Wednesday, Zannick sat at his customary table upstairs and had his laptop out in front of him. He wore jeans, a black-and-gray Pearl Jam T-shirt, and a pair of red Chuck Taylor high-top Converse All Star tennis shoes with white laces. His tweed sports coat was wrapped around the back of his chair, and he was studying his computer with heightened focus. He'd already ordered his usual—the "Deli Rose," which consisted of roast beef, corned beef, pepper jack and provolone cheeses, onions, a tomato, and spicy red sauce laid out on a homemade onion roll—and was now getting about the business of sending out his second round of tweets for the day.

General Lewis arrested for murder of ex-husband.
#corruption

General Lewis, who accused me of bogus rape
charges, now on trial for murdering her ex.
#potandkettle #cleanhouse

Sack Glover, Lewis's opponent in election, named
acting DA. #justice #makeitpermanent

Zannick surveyed his three rapid-fire tweets and saw what he
had expected. Each had already been retweeted seven times in the
first fifteen seconds after he'd pressed the "Tweet" button. When you
had 1.2 million followers, that tended to happen. And though Giles
County wasn't the most social media–savvy place in the world, the
young voters—the ones who pulled all-night study sessions at the
Yellow Deli—paid attention.

"Hey, Mike," a young man said as he passed by with a couple of
books under his arm.

"What's up, Thad. How's school?"

"It's killing me, sir." The kid, who was a sophomore at Martin
Methodist College, gave Zannick a sheepish smile. "Got a history paper
due Friday and a huge calculus quiz on Monday. You'll probably see a
lot of me here the next few days."

"Good luck."

Thad frowned. "I heard your trial got continued."

Zannick nodded. "The prosecutor was charged with murder. Can
you believe it?"

"Case should've been dismissed by now anyway," Thad said. "Do
you ever read the blog Casimir's Vine?"

Though he was the one responsible for the website named in honor of the town's founder, Casimir Pulaski, Zannick furrowed his brow in feigned confusion. "Is that something put out by the college?"

"No, I'm not sure who does it, but it basically dishes on everything going on in Pulaski, Giles County, and the college. There are a bunch of articles in it denouncing General Lewis and your accuser."

"I'll have to check it out."

"Well, I hope the charges are dropped soon," Thad said, beginning to move for the stairs.

"Thank you."

Zannick turned his attention back to his computer, where his tweets had now been reposted hundreds of times. Casimir's Vine would submit a recap of General Lewis's arrest and the current status of the police investigation later tonight along with an even bigger bombshell. He ran his index finger along the scar on his upper lip and then clicked on his Facebook page. On his personal page, he had over three thousand friends. His business pages, Z Bank, Zannick Storage, and Zannick Construction, all had at least a thousand followers each. Pulling up the "Create Post" box on his personal feed, Zannick wrote: "What's on my mind? Beyond shocked that the district attorney general of Giles County, who's maliciously charged me with a crime I didn't commit, has now been charged herself with the brutal murder of my friend, attorney, and colleague Butch Renfroe. RIP Butch."

Zannick read and reread the message and then pressed "Post." Although the responses took longer to accumulate, Zannick knew that he would eventually have hundreds of "likes" and several comments. He shared his personal post on the business pages for the bank, the storage company, and his construction outfit and then logged out.

He closed his computer as his waiter was placing his food on the table. "Thank you, Henry," he said, and the man, whose beard hung well past his neck and whose hair was tied in a ponytail in back, nodded.

"Anything else, Mr. Zannick?"

"I'm fine," he said. As the waiter turned to walk down the stairs, a plump figure trudged past him going up.

Zannick faked a smile as Lou Horn approached him. Lou was supposed to meet him for lunch at noon, and the criminal defense attorney was late. "Well?" Zannick asked before Lou could even sit down.

"Your trial has been rescheduled for June first," Lou said, plopping down hard in the seat. Even from a couple of feet away, Zannick could smell the alcohol on the man's breath. Lou coughed and leaned his elbows on the table. "Sack should still be the district attorney general then, and once some time has gone by, I'll approach him again about settlement. I mentioned it to him last night, and he said it was too early to talk deal."

"A deal?" Zannick asked, throwing in some exasperation in his tone. "How about an outright dismissal?"

Lou grimaced. "Let's be patient for now and see what happens."

"Patient?" Zannick raised his voice, causing the defense lawyer to cower. "Listen to me, Lou. I want it gone. Over. Done. Dismissed. I've got a multimillion-dollar investment with Hoshima riding on this. Do you understand?"

Lou looked behind him and then did a sweep of the upstairs to make sure he was out of earshot. Then he leaned over the table. "Mike, with all due respect, you had sex with a fifteen-year-old girl. Even if she begged you to screw her, it would still be statutory rape under the laws of the State of Tennessee."

"I won't testify, and a jury will be left with whether they believe the word of a sixteen-year-old tramp whose mother is a known road whore."

Lou lowered his voice to a whisper. "Lona Burks has been straight and sober for three years, and Mandy's extracurricular activities in the boys' locker room, which were only confirmed by one witness, are likely to be excluded under the rape shield rule." Lou again did a sweep of the room. "I don't know a damn thing about Mandy Burks other than

General Lewis was prepared to stuff that girl's story straight up our ass on Tuesday if we hadn't been saved by the bell."

Now it was Zannick who edged forward, his nose only a couple of inches from Lou's. "That *bell* that was rung was my corporate lawyer and the president of my bank. Let's show a little respect for the dead."

Lou gazed openmouthed at Zannick. "Respect for the dead? You were blackmailing Butch. Same as with me and Terry. Do you expect me to believe that you're *sad* that he's gone? Besides, everything that's happened since his murder has been solid gold for you."

"For *us*, you mean."

Lou leaned back in his chair and grabbed a roll of silverware. He unrolled the napkin and wiped sweat from his forehead. "For us," he finally said. "Look, Mike, Butch Renfroe was my friend for thirty years, and I . . . I'm having a hard time with it."

"Is that why you smell like a bar?"

Lou wrinkled up his face. "I'm battling a bad cough and a sore throat, and a pinch of Jack Daniel's helps the pain."

"Finn says you've been nursing the pain every night at Kathy's Tavern for several hours for the past month."

Lou's cheeks turned red. "I've been ending my workdays at Kathy's for almost two decades. Long before you bought your first piece of property in this town."

"Maybe so, but I'd be careful if I were you. I have a lot on the line here, and I'm not counting my chickens until the rape charge is dismissed." He paused. "And if I go down, I'm still taking you and Terry with me. Your little sex worker ring will be public knowledge, and you'll spend the rest of your life in prison. Got me?"

Lou gazed down at Zannick's uneaten sandwich. "I understand that, Mike." He paused. "Do the Hoshima folks know about Butch's death?"

"Yes, and they're concerned, but I think they're also beginning to believe my pleas that General Lewis had a vendetta against me. With

Sack as acting district attorney, and with the bomb that's gonna drop tonight, Helen Lewis will never be the head prosecutor again."

"What bomb?"

"You haven't heard yet?"

Lou slowly shook his head.

"You will."

———

Lou left two minutes later, saying that he was late to another appointment. The old lawyer apologized profusely, but in all honesty, Zannick was grateful that he was gone. The man was a dinosaur. A puzzle piece easily manipulated. The key to this crazy world, Zannick knew, was always having something on someone. When you had the power to cripple someone's life if you shared clandestine information, well, then that person would do almost anything you asked.

Zannick ate his sandwich alone. As he was finishing the last bite, his cell phone buzzed on the table. Seeing the familiar number, he wiped his mouth and clicked the "Answer" button.

"Hello, Finn."

"Good news and bad news."

"Let's start with the good."

"A source in the sheriff's office has confirmed that they found a press release in Butch Renfroe's safe during their search of the home."

Zannick rubbed his index finger over his scar. "And does it mention the bombshell?"

"Indeed, it does."

"Good. So the Vine can go with the story?"

"Yes."

"What's the bad news?"

A pause on the other end of the line followed by a frustrated sigh.

"Finn?"

"It seems our friend, the recently evicted Mr. Rowe, is continuing to squat on our property. Want me to call the sheriff's office again?"

For at least fifteen seconds, silence filled the line. Michael Zannick took a sip of tea and winked at a petite woman who was walking up the stairs with a backpack strapped to her shoulder. "No," Zannick finally said to Finn, pausing for emphasis. "The sheriff's deputies haven't communicated the message clearly enough. I'd like you to handle the situation."

There was another half beat of silence and then Finn's voice, firm and cold. "Ten-four."

28

The lights in the house were off when Bo pulled up the gravel driveway to what was once his cousin's farm off Highway 64. Bo had sent several texts and tried to call Booker T. numerous times since arriving back in Pulaski yesterday afternoon, and finally, about thirty minutes earlier, Bo had received a cryptic text to meet here. Bo had texted back, asking whether Booker T. had permission to be on the land in light of the recent foreclosure, but Booker T. hadn't responded.

He's mad at me, Bo thought, figuring that his cousin had every right to be pissed off. *I disappeared for over a year without one word.*

As with Ellie Michaels, the last time Bo had seen Booker T. was at Jazz's funeral. They had shared a hug, and Booker T., like every other person at the ceremony, had told Bo how sorry he was.

Since then, which was over sixteen months ago, they hadn't seen or talked with each other. Booker T. had reached out several times with calls that Bo had let ring without answering and texts that were also ignored. At some point, he'd quit trying.

Bo parked in front of the dark barn and gazed at the one-story rancher that, until the foreclosure, had been his cousin's home for the past four years. The house and farm had been the crowning achievement of his cousin's farming career, and Bo felt a pang of sadness and guilt as he examined the property now, remembering how Booker T.'s enormous son, Jarvis, who was already collecting football scholarship offers in the ninth grade, had played basketball with T. J. on the goal attached to the barn. Squinting in that direction, Bo saw that the goal was now without a net and was bent down as if someone had hung on it too long after dunking.

Bo glanced at the clock on the dash of the Sequoia: 9:30 p.m. His first full day back practicing law had been long, exhausting, and fairly productive. With the help of Lona, he'd gotten the phones, the power, and the water all turned on that afternoon. Plus she knew an IT guy who had come out and had looked at the computers. "They're old as Methuselah but should still work well enough for word processing and internet searches." Bo had spent the rest of the day reviewing the witness statements provided by Frannie Storm the night before, surfing the internet for any information on Michael Zannick, and dictating his notice of appearance, request for discovery, and motion for an expedited preliminary hearing. Lona had typed up the pleadings that afternoon on the lobby computer; she wasn't nearly as fast as Ellie had been, but she worked her ass off and had the one thing that the defense of General Helen Lewis desperately needed.

Passion.

At 6:30 p.m., she left the office, saying she needed to get home and make Mandy dinner. Bo had almost said that he wanted to meet Mandy, but that could wait until later. If Michael Zannick was somehow involved in a frame-up of the General, then Bo needed to know everything he could about the prosecution's rape case against Zannick. That would include talking with the victim. As she was walking out the door, Lona said she would go to the courthouse tomorrow and get a tutorial from one of the clerks on how to file documents and then would have everything filed by lunch.

Assuming that got done, the preliminary hearing would be set in approximately thirty days. Then, when the judge found probable cause for the arrest, the case would be bound over to the grand jury. After that, the grand jury would issue an indictment, and the court would set an arraignment date. At the arraignment, General Helen Lewis would plead not guilty and then . . .

. . . *trial.*

He sighed as the enormity of the case began to set in. The General had been charged with first-degree murder. Sack Glover hadn't provided notice yet of whether he would seek the death penalty, but with the enhancers mentioned by Chief Storm last night . . .

. . . *he will.*

Bo rolled down his window and let the cool night breeze filter into the interior of the car. The only noises he could hear were the chirping of crickets and the distant whine of a cow. The air smelled like honeysuckle with a faint whiff of manure. He reached for a beer from the six-pack he'd picked up on the way and popped the top. As he took his first sip, the sound of a shotgun blast caused him to spill half the drink down his neck and chest.

"Sonofa . . ."

He lunged for the glove compartment, where he kept his Glock, but before he could unclick the box, he was blindsided with a punch that busted his mouth wide open. Before he could gather himself, he felt huge hands grabbing him by the shirt and pulling him out the window of the car. Then he was lifted high into the air as if he was being pressed like a barbell.

Only one person on earth was capable of manhandling him like this. "Put me down, dog."

"As you wish, cuz."

Suddenly Bo was flying in the air, landing hard on his shoulder but rolling to his feet just as he'd been taught as a linebacker in football. He glared at the enormous man standing in front of him.

Booker Taliaferro Washington Rowe Jr. was a mountain of a human being at six feet six inches tall and well over three hundred pounds. He was built in the box shape of a refrigerator, which had made him a ferocious offensive lineman for Giles County High and, later, Alabama A&M.

"What in God's name are you doing?" Bo asked, spitting blood onto the ground.

"Whipping your ass . . . *dog*." Booker T. strode forward, and Bo could tell that his cousin's eyes were glazed. The strong scent of alcohol and body odor filled the air.

"You can try," Bo said, taking a fighter's stance with his left foot in front of the other.

Booker T. smiled and swung his fist in a wild arch toward Bo's face.

Bo ducked, hearing the wind swoosh above him from the force of the missed punch, and fired a left jab that connected with his cousin's jaw and then a right cross that found the base of Booker's T's nose.

The big man dropped to his knees from the force of the blows, and Bo backed away from him. "Came out here to talk, not fight."

Booker T. rose to his feet and glared at him. "Don't feel like talking. Would have liked that a year ago. Hell, even six months. But now." He scoffed and moved forward, his hands up now to cover his busted nose but no less motivated. "Think you can breeze back into town like nothing's happened. Like you didn't ignore me, the land you own, and every damn part of your childhood and past for the past year and a half."

"My wife was murdered."

Booker T. took another step toward him. "I know that. I was at the funeral, remember? Your *hero* died too. Old Professor McMurtrie finally kicked the bucket." Booker T. spat at him, and the saliva landed a couple of inches from Bo's feet. "You cared more about that white man than you did your own flesh and blood. Rented his farmhouse. Hell, I heard you even took his dog off him."

"You need to shut your mouth, fat boy," Bo said. He found himself moving closer, squeezing his fists together.

"Why don't you close it for me? What about your kin, *dog*? What about your blood?" He spat again. "While you was looking after that old professor, my life has been dying on the vine. Lost my farm. Thelma walked out on me and took the kids. My boy, Jarvis, won't even speak to me no more. And I'm a gnat's ass from filing bankruptcy."

"Why didn't you ask for help?"

Booker T. stepped forward and swung another wild punch with his right hand, missing again, but this time he leaned back and avoided Bo's oncoming jab. As Bo stumbled off balance, he felt his right kneecap explode in pain as Booker T. kicked him.

Bo fell to his knees and saw his cousin's boot coming at him again, this time connecting with his solar plexus. The air went out of his stomach, and he struggled for breath. Then he was getting picked up and thrown again, this time over Booker T.'s shoulder. The big man hauled him a few steps and, without warning, slung him into a trash bin adjacent to the barn.

"That where you belong."

Bo gasped for air inside the almost empty receptacle. The strong aroma of spoiled meat hit his nostrils, and he gagged, making it even harder to catch his wind. He heard a thud, and the side of the can was dented from another kick from Booker T.

"Ignoring me for over a year. Leaving me when I needed you most and taking care of some white man's stuff." Another thud and Bo heard the sound of plastic crunching, as the trash bin began to cave in. Then he was moving as the can was tilted over on its side. The air went out of him again.

Booker T. was now kicking the can over and over again, causing it to roll like a barrel. The world was spinning as Bo bounced against the sides of the bin, the dented-in portion wedging into his rib cage and causing him to howl in pain.

"How does that feel, Bocephus? You enjoying this ass beating? If anyone ever deserved—?"

And then his voice drowned out like someone had turned off the TV.

For several seconds, Bo blinked his eyes and tried to steady himself. He started to say something, but then he heard his cousin's voice again. "Keep your mouth shut, Bo. Don't talk. Don't move."

Bo thought he heard the sound of wheels on gravel and then the thud of car doors opening and closing. He crawled to the edge of the trash bin, but the can was facing the barn, and he couldn't see what was going on. He heard the crunching of feet on gravel. Multiple feet and likely different shoe types. And finally, a voice.

"You alone, Rowe?" The accent was either Irish or Boston or perhaps a mixture of both.

"Yeah."

"Where's the wife and kids?"

"Gone," Booker T. said.

"Gone on vacation or gone for good?"

A pause. "That's none of your damn business," Booker T. said.

"Tsk, tsk, tsk. I hope your money troubles aren't impacting your family life."

There was no response, and Bo felt his heartbeat begin to pick up. The dizziness had subsided, and he listened hard.

"You're trespassing again," the other man finally added when Booker T. hadn't said anything.

"I need some more time."

"Time's up, Rowe. Time's been up. Bank has foreclosed. Sent you an eviction notice. I hung it on your door and gave you a month to get out, and that was forty-five days ago. We've looked the other way several times and called the sheriff twice."

"Did you call him tonight?"

"Not yet. Tonight, I figured I'd deliver my own message."

Bo heard the unmistakable sound of a pistol cocking.

"Please, Finn. This is my land."

"No, sir. This property belongs to Z Bank. So . . . let's see here. I'm thinking that I came out here to check on things since I'm the head of security for the bank. Saw you out here. You're clearly drunk and out of control. You fired your shotgun at me and then, in a courageous act of self-defense, I had to shoot you in the—"

"Stop!" Bo yelled. He had crawled out of the trash bin when he'd heard the click of the handgun, and now he was standing to the side of the receptacle. His heart pounded in his chest as he took in the long-haired man pointing what looked to be a 9-millimeter semiautomatic pistol at Booker T.'s knees. Behind the man, Bo saw two other figures dressed in dark clothes. He couldn't tell if they were men or women, but they were both carrying guns that were now aimed at Bo.

"Well, I don't believe we've been formally introduced," the long-haired man said, gazing at Bo while still holding his weapon on Booker T. "You would be Mr. Haynes, right?"

"Bocephus Haynes."

"I heard some news today about you, Mr. Haynes. Didn't you recently take on a new case?"

"Who are you?" Bo asked.

"Oh, I'm sorry. My name is Finn Pusser. Head of security for Z Bank." He kept the gun pointed at Booker T. "You and Mr. Rowe are trespassing on land owned by the bank."

"And I was just telling my cousin that we needed to be leaving," Bo said.

Finn snickered. "From the looks of your face, Mr. Haynes, it appears that Mr. Rowe wasn't heeding your advice. Same as he hasn't been following the directives of the sheriff's office to stay off this property. It's time a message was sent that he can understand." He paused. "Seems to me that I still need to exercise some self-defense. You *boys* . . . got all riled up out here, tied one on, and decided to meet my pleas to leave peacefully with gunfire."

Bo felt his cheeks and neck flush with an anger that he hadn't felt since he was a teenager playing football for Giles County High and an opposing coach of an all-white team had referred to him as *boy*. "What did you call us?" he asked, his tone low.

Finn held the gun steady on Bo's chest. "In all this excitement, I can't remember."

"You done poked the bear," Booker T. said, his voice hoarse and dry.

Bocephus Haynes took a step toward Finn, ignoring the weapon. Adrenaline radiated down his body from his face to his toes. "I called the police," he grunted.

"No, you didn't," Finn said. "Your phone is in the car. You didn't call anyone. You have no video of this. No tape recording. You're up shit creek without a paddle."

Bo took another step closer to Finn. He and Booker T. were now standing side by side, and he could hear the rapid patter of his cousin's breathing. "You're not going to kill us, Mr. Pusser. Wouldn't it be a public relations disaster for a brand-new lending institution like Z Bank if its head of security gunned down two local citizens in the middle of the night? Especially with both of the victims being longtime fixtures of Pulaski and former All County football players on the Giles County Bobcats? You may not realize it being from out of town and all, but folks have a long memory in these parts when it comes to high school football. And with my racially charged past, this little killing would make the front page of every newspaper and media outlet in the southeast if not the whole country." Bo steadied his breathing and kept his voice low and calm. "You can't use force to carry out an eviction. It's illegal. So if you decide to wound us in lieu of killing, I'm going to report you to the sheriff's office tonight. Then, first thing tomorrow morning, I'll file a lawsuit against you and Z Bank and set up an interview with the local newspaper to discuss the racist comments I endured from the head of security of the new bank in town." He paused. "Or you can let us go and avoid all of that hassle."

Finn squinted at Bo. "You're an incredible talker, Mr. Haynes. I'm sure you're an excellent lawyer." Then he aimed his gun at Booker T.'s left shin. "This is going to sting a little, Mr. Rowe."

"No!" Bo screamed, lunging in front of his cousin and flinching in expectation of the shot.

But when the sound of gunfire erupted, it didn't come from a handgun or either of the semiautomatic weapons being held by the two people behind Finn.

Instead, the blasts of a twelve-gauge shotgun crackled through the air. One shot . . . two . . . three. The front windshield of Finn's black Cadillac Escalade shattered, as did the back glass. The figures behind the longhaired man ducked to the ground.

Finn also crouched but kept his gun pointed at Bo. "You've stuck your nose in the wrong person's business."

Another crackle lit up the air, and Finn dropped his weapon, screaming in pain. Seeing an opening, Bo crawled on his hands and knees toward Finn's gun, but his cousin beat him to the punch.

Booker T. grabbed the pistol and aimed it at Finn, who was writhing in pain on the ground as his crew continued to peer around the dark farm for where the shotgun blasts were coming from.

"I ought to put an end to you," Booker T. growled. "You and your bank ruined my life. I got *nothing* 'cause of you people."

"Don't," Bo said, trying to speak in a calm tone but out of breath from the excitement and rush of the last few seconds. "He's not worth it."

After several tense seconds, Booker T. took a step backward, keeping the gun on Finn. "Get out of here."

Finn was on his knees, still cradling his right hand, which was covered in blood. "You bastards are going to jail," he gasped. Then he climbed to his feet and walked toward the Escalade. After one of his crew swept the glass off the seat, he climbed inside the passenger seat. Thirty seconds later, the car was gone, the only remaining sign of it being the dust from the gravel that had spewed upon the SUV's departure.

For a long while, the only sound was Bo's and Booker T.'s shallow breaths. Even the crickets seemed to have been driven away by the gunfire.

"Glad you brought reinforcements," Booker T. finally said, turning to the woodlands behind and to the east of the barn. "Why don't you call whoever it is out?"

Bo was silent. "I didn't bring anyone with me, cousin."

They looked at each other. "Then who was that out there that just saved our asses?"

Bo gazed in the direction of the woods. "I have no idea." Then, after wiping a sheen of sweat from his forehead and spitting a strand of blood on the gravel, Bo peered hard at his cousin. "Booker T., what in the hell have you gotten into?"

29

Bo awoke the next morning to the pleasant aroma of coffee. His body ached all over from the butt whipping he'd received from his cousin, his upper lip fat and swollen and his midsection bruised from being kicked.

When he opened his tired eyes, he was gazing out at Walton Farm. A thousand acres, a third of which was used for livestock and the rest for corn, were now illuminated by the rising sun, which glowed a stark orangish red. Bo was slumped in a rocking chair on the porch with a shotgun lying across his chest. As he leaned forward and placed the gun against a wooden coffee table, he couldn't help but admire the stunning view. His biological father had placed the "Big House," as Andy Walton had called it, at the highest point on the land, and it seemed that Bo could see for miles in every direction.

"You ain't much of a guard dog," Booker T. grumbled, walking out on the porch with two steaming mugs in his hand.

"Where'd you find the coffee?" Bo groaned, rubbing his bruised ribs.

"There's a Keurig in the kitchen," Booker T. said, handing Bo's cup to him and then taking a sip from the other. He looked better than he had the night before. Sober and clear eyed. "I keep it and a box of K-Cups here so I can have a pick-me-up when I'm working the fields." He nodded over the railing, and his expression softened. "Bo, I'm sorry I got you into my mess."

Bo took a sip of the coffee, and the heat scalded his throat and burned his swollen lip. Still, he needed the caffeine. He glanced down at the wooden porch and saw that all six bottles of Yuengling that he'd brought with him last night had been drunk, and there was also a bottle of Bombay gin perched on the floor that looked a quarter full. "Did we tie one on last night?" Bo asked, the details of the night foggy after the confrontation with Finn Pusser. Once Pusser and his two minions had left, Bo had said he had a crazy idea for where they could bunk down for the night. Then Booker T. had followed him a quarter of a mile down Highway 64 to the property Bo had inherited by virtue of his being the only "surviving issue" of Andrew Davis Walton.

Booker T. chuckled. "I'd already drunk enough gin to float the *Queen Mary* before you arrived. But you pounded those beers you brought. You were pretty shaky after everything that happened, and you drank that six-pack in about thirty minutes while I told you my sad tale."

Bo sipped the mug and rubbed his sore chest. "Correct me if I get the details wrong. You took out a two-hundred-thousand-dollar loan from Z Bank to finish paying for the irrigation system on your farm and some of the other properties you lease, including this one." Bo pointed to the vast expanse of land out over the porch railing. "Then, when last year's corn crop went in the tank, you went under."

Booker T. shook his head. "Tried to get another loan from FNB, but I was in the hole too far. When I couldn't pay my employees, they all left. Lost all the farms I was leasing except this one here and would have lost it, too, but the owner wasn't paying attention." He glared at Bo and spoke in a soft and bitter voice. "Even tried to call the owner, who happens to be my rich cousin, but . . . he was having his own problems."

"I'm sorry," Bo said, hanging his head. "I really am." He sighed. "But Booker T., you can't be trespassing anymore. Finn Pusser wasn't messing around last night."

Booker T. leaned his ample girth over the railing and gazed out at the vast expanse of land. "OK, then what am I supposed to do, Bo? I've got no job, no money, and no place to live."

Bo took another sip of coffee and touched his swollen lip. "What time is it?"

"It's 6:32 a.m."

Bo closed his eyes. "I need to get to the office."

"Where are you staying?"

"The office."

"Why don't you stay here? I mean, hell, it's yours."

Bo peered up at him. "You know I can't."

Booker T. blinked and gazed down at the porch. "Yeah . . . I guess not. I'm sorry I even suggested it."

Bo waved him off and stood from the chair. He set his coffee mug on the table and stretched his tired limbs. "Booker T., where are you living now?"

"In my truck." He let out a sigh fueled with regret. "How did everything get so complicated, Bo? All I ever wanted was some land of my own. Live off the fruit of my labor." He shook his head. "That was the American dream for me."

"Life's not ever as simple as it sounds," Bo said. "If you need an example, look at my crazy life." Bo leaned over the railing, being careful not to press too hard on his aching rib cage. "Booker T., why don't *you* live out here?"

Booker T. turned to him and raised his eyebrows. "Here? At the 'Big House'? Naw, cuz, I can't do that. I'm not as spooked by this place as you, but I still couldn't live in the home of Andy Walton."

"Just for a while," Bo pressed. "You can stay rent-free until you get your feet back on the ground. And in addition to farming the land, I'd like to hire you to do something else."

"And what might that be?"

"I need to do something with this property, and I don't have a clue as to what. I want to hire you as a consultant to help me figure things out."

Booker T. guffawed. "Bo, I'm a farmer, not a developer. I think you're already doing what you should do with this land. Besides, working your farm is the only job I have left, and I don't want to lose it too."

Bo ran a finger over his lips and then stuck his hands in his pockets. "Do you think the employees you lost would come back to work for you if you were able to pay them?"

"In a heartbeat," Booker T. said. "They all hated to leave in the first place."

"What about the farms you were leasing? Would the owners take you back and let you start farming their land again?"

Booker T. bit down on the fingernail of his thumb. "I think a few would."

"Got any equipment left?"

Booker T. pointed out a hundred yards to the south. "A combine and two tractors that I've been keeping in your barn."

Bo gripped his cousin's arm. "Look, I wasn't there to help you when everything went crazy, and I can't help you get your farm back." He paused and squeezed Booker T.'s arm. "But I want to help now. How much do you need to get operational?"

Booker T. blinked his eyes. "Bo, I can't take your charity."

"Not charity, cuz. I'm going to *loan* you some money. But the terms are going to be family friendly." He smiled. "No interest, and you can pay me back when you can. Now, how much?"

Booker T. gazed down at the wooden floor and rubbed his chin. "Fifty thousand dollars?"

"That's not near enough, and you know it."

Booker T. bit on his thumbnail again. "A hundred fifty?"

"Done," Bo said. "I'll transfer the money tomorrow."

Booker T.'s eyes had moistened. "Thank you, cousin."

"You're welcome," Bo said. "I'm also going to pay you a fifty-thousand-dollar consultant's fee for helping me with Walton Farm." Bo gestured over the railing.

"You still call it that? Even though it's yours now."

Bo gripped the wooden railing and gazed out over the rows of corn. "Until we can do something else with it, that's all this property will ever be to me."

———

A few minutes later, they stood by their respective vehicles. As Booker T. was opening the door to his pickup truck, he peered at Bo. "Thank you for coming last night, Bo. I . . . needed a wake-up call."

"You almost got more than that. If it hadn't been for . . ." Bo trailed off and looked past his Sequoia to the north and in the direction of Booker T.'s old farm.

"Any ideas on who our guardian angel is?" Booker T. asked.

"No. You?"

Booker T. gave his head a jerk. "None, but whoever he or she is, my shins will be forever grateful." He paused. "Bo, I promise I'm going to make good on what you're doing for me. I'll pay back the loan and . . ." He paused and swept his eyes around the property. ". . . we'll figure out something to do with this place."

"I know," Bo said, patting his cousin's back and stepping up into his vehicle. He turned the key and rolled down the window, gazing at his cousin, who had placed his enormous hands on the window seal.

"You going to be around?" Booker T. asked. "I mean, I never even asked you why you're back in town."

"I never had a chance to tell you. I was too busy getting my ass kicked and then trying not to get killed."

"Tell me what?"

"I'm representing General Lewis."

"The General?" Booker T. wrinkled up his face. "She in some kind of trouble?"

Bo frowned at him. "Haven't been paying much attention to the news lately, have you?"

"Been out of sorts . . . as you saw last night."

Bo coughed and rubbed his lip. "She's been charged with the murder of her ex-husband, Butch Renfroe. Did you know him?"

Booker T. blinked his eyes and peered down at the gravel driveway. "I did."

"With all your dealings with Z Bank, did you have much contact with Butch?"

Booker T. nodded, his eyes still lowered. "Yep."

"How?"

"He gave me my loan." Booker T. raised his eyes to Bo's. "And he wouldn't give me an extension despite how many times I asked. I didn't figure Michael Zannick would grant me any mercy, but I'd known Butch for a lot of years. I thought he'd help me, but he wouldn't budge."

"When was the last time you saw him?" Bo asked. He'd forgotten about the soreness in his ribs and lip.

"Monday."

"This past Monday. April 1?"

"April Fools' Day," Booker T. said, gazing past Bo to his truck.

"He was killed that night. Did you know that?"

"He was very much alive the last time I saw him."

"And where was that?"

Booker T. kept his eyes on his truck. "Sounds like you might be suspicious of me."

"Should I be?"

Booker T. arched his neck and started to walk away. "Thanks for your help, Bo."

"Booker T., we aren't finished here!"

He looked over his shoulder at Bo. "We are for now."

30

When Bo parked in front of the office, he saw Sack Glover standing outside his door holding a manila envelope in his hand. Bo glanced at the dash: 7:35 a.m. He climbed out of the Sequoia and peered at the acting district attorney general. "Awful early, dog."

"Bo," Sack said, extending his hand, which Bo grasped with a firm grip before letting go. "You look like hell. I hope you haven't gotten into any trouble already."

Bo rubbed his fat lip and glanced at his shirt and slacks, both of which had dirt and grass stains on them, not to mention streaks of caked blood. For a couple of seconds, he pondered whether he should share his near-death experience the night before with the prosecutor. What Finn Pusser had done constituted attempted assault and probably several other crimes. But as he gazed up at Sack Glover and took in Sack's custom-tailored navy suit and perfectly coifed hair, Bo remembered that the new DA was in Michael Zannick's pocket. If Bo had any intention of reporting the incident at Booker T.'s farm, it wouldn't be to this man. "What can I do for you, Sack?"

The prosecutor glanced through the window of the office and then back at Bo. "Is that Lona Burks in there?"

Bo followed his gaze and saw Lona sitting behind Ellie's old desk. She was typing furiously on the computer with an intense expression on her face. Bo wondered if Lona ever relaxed and then remembered what she'd said about her prior addiction to drugs and alcohol when she was a dancer at the Sundowners. *Always on guard,* he thought.

"It is," Bo said. "Do you know Lona?"

"Not really," Sack said, but Bo could tell he was lying.

"Well then, like I said, what can I do for you?" Bo approached him and pointed at the envelope. "You got a steak in there for me?"

Sack smiled. "It's a copy of the arrest warrant along with the letter mentioned in last night's Casimir's Vine blog." He handed the envelope to Bo.

"Casimir's what?"

"Vine. It's a blog written by an anonymous local group." He paused. "You haven't seen last night's entry?"

Bo shook his head, feeling a nervous twinge in his stomach. "Enlighten me."

"Somehow the Vine got word that our investigation had uncovered a letter written by the victim. Ordinarily, I wouldn't provide discovery this soon, and I'm pissed off that Frannie Storm gave you copies of those witness statements and her report." He shrugged. "But since we obviously have a mole in the sheriff's department, I thought it only fair to give you a copy of the letter."

"Big of you," Bo said.

"Read it and let's talk." Sack walked past him toward his car, which was a silver Porsche 911 sedan. Not the vehicle of your average public servant.

"Hold on."

Sack opened the door to his car but waited to get in. "What?"

"Are you seeking the death penalty?"

Sack narrowed his gaze. "I have no choice. The evidence is clear that she executed the victim, badly beat either the man or the corpse—Melvin Ragland is still trying to come to a conclusion on that—and stole property from his house, including but not limited to his computer and his wallet."

Bo grunted. "You really think Helen Lewis is capable of such a gruesome crime?"

Sack smiled, showing off bleached white teeth. "I don't think, Bo. I know. The evidence is overwhelming and conclusive." He paused. "You'll see at the preliminary hearing. The best thing for the General, the town of Pulaski, and Giles County is for your client to plead guilty."

"You got an offer?"

"Life without parole."

Bo scoffed. "Get out of here, Sack. And don't get too comfortable in my client's seat. She'll be back in it real soon."

"You think so?" Sack asked, a huge grin plastered to his face. "Read the letter in that envelope." He paused. "Then tell me what you think."

———

A few seconds later, Bo entered the office.

"Jesus, what happened to you?"

Bo ignored the question. "I ran into Sack Glover on the sidewalk."

"What did that asshole want?"

"Wants us to plead the General to life without parole."

"In his wildest wet dream."

Bo couldn't help but laugh.

"I hope you told him no," Lona pressed.

"I didn't tell him anything. I have a duty to report plea offers to clients, but I know the General will refuse that one."

"If that's his settlement offer, then he must be seeking the death penalty."

Bo nodded. "He mentioned a blog entry on something called Cashmere's Vine."

"Casimir's Vine. Like Count Casimir Pulaski." Lona snatched a piece of paper off the desk and handed it to him. "Already printed it out for you."

Bo took the page and only had to see the title before the nervousness he'd felt in his stomach was back with a vengeance. "Jesus

H. Christ," he whispered. Then he read out loud. "Victim Allegedly Murdered Because of Threats to Reveal General Lewis's Abortion." Bo looked up from the page at Lona.

"Is it true? Did the General have an abortion?"

Bo set the page down on the desk and squeezed his hands into fists. "How many people read this thing?"

Lona frowned. "The website says it has over twelve thousand followers."

Almost half the county, Bo thought, closing his eyes and gritting his teeth. *All poisoned now* . . . "This is not good."

31

"This is fantastic," Sack said, pushing a copy of the blog entry across the desk.

Gloria Sanchez looked down at the paper but didn't touch the page. She'd already read the article, and it had made her sick to her stomach. "How did this information get in the hands of the Vine?"

Sack held out his palms. "Beats me. But let's not look a gift horse in the mouth. You know how this county feels about abortion."

Gloria folded her arms across her chest. "Did you leak it?"

Before Sack could answer the question, the door to the district attorney general's office swung open. Chief Deputy Sheriff Frannie Storm strode through with a look of contempt on her face. "Are you the mole?" Frannie asked, pushing past Gloria and walking around the desk to stand in front of Sack.

"I don't know what—?"

"Answer me!" Frannie said, grabbing Sack around the collar and pulling the man to his feet. "Did you give the Vine information about the press release we found at Butch's house?"

"No," Sack said, his voice struggling to remain calm. "Now take your hands off me, Chief, or I will file an assault charge against you."

"Go for it," Frannie said, releasing her grip and taking a step back. She whirled toward Gloria. "Do you know anything about this?"

"No," Gloria said, feeling heat on her neck and face. "I'm as mad about it as you."

Frannie made a fist with her right hand and punched the palm of her left so hard that the popping sound caused Gloria to jump. "I'm going to find out who the mole is, and when I do, I'm going to cut his balls off, put them in a jar, and throw it in the Elk River."

"That's kind of a sexist thing to say, isn't it?" Sack asked, faking a smile.

"Fuck you," Frannie said, turning to leave. "Got a minute, Sanchez?"

———

Out in the hallway, Frannie spoke through clenched teeth. "He's loving it, isn't he?"

"Like a pig in mud," Gloria said.

"Do you have any ideas about who leaked the letter?"

Gloria glanced at the door and then back to Frannie. "The jackass in there is the one who benefits the most."

Frannie started to move for the door again, but Gloria blocked her. "Don't, OK? It won't help." Gloria paused.

The chief squinted down at her. "Are you going to be second chair on this trial?"

Gloria bit her lip. "We haven't discussed assignments yet, but . . ." She trailed off.

"But what?"

Gloria opened her mouth but closed it before saying anything. Her face had grown pale.

"What's wrong, Sanchez?"

Gloria averted her eyes, gazing upward at the top of the rotunda. "It's just that I, um, doubt I'm going to have a job here much longer. The rumor is that Sack is going to clean house as soon as the interim tag is removed." She sighed. "Ironic, isn't it? If we're successful in convicting General Lewis, then I'm out of a job."

Frannie shook her head. "It is what it is." She turned to leave but then peered over her shoulder at Gloria. "You sure that's what's bothering you? You look like you're about to throw up."

Gloria again bit her lower lip. She did feel nauseous and had since learning of Butch Renfroe's murder. "I'm sure."

32

April 1, 2015

FOR IMMEDIATE RELEASE

To Whom It May Concern:

In December 1977, Helen Lewis, my fiancée at the time, had an abortion. Helen was in her third year of law school and felt that a baby would stunt her career before it even began. She did not tell me, the father of the child, until after she had gone through with the procedure.

For thirty-eight years, through our engagement, marriage, and eventual divorce, I have kept this information secret at her request.

The people of this county deserve to know the truth.

Frederick A. Renfroe

Frederick A. Renfroe

After Bo had read the letter, he slid the piece of paper across the table to Helen. "Is that Butch's signature above his typewritten name?"

Helen glanced down at the page, reading the press release again to herself. Then she nodded.

"Did you know he was going to do this?" Bo asked, the challenge in his voice palpable.

Helen peered at him without blinking. "This proves nothing."

"That's not an answer to my question."

"It's the only answer you're going to get."

"All right, then let's look at the blog, which was published last night and goes a little further." Bo removed a couple of stapled pages from his file jacket and read in a deliberate tone. "'Victim Allegedly Murdered Because of Threats to Reveal General Lewis's Abortion. A source in the Giles County Sheriff's Office has revealed that Frederick Alan "Butch" Renfroe, who was brutally murdered in his home on Monday evening, was killed because of a secret he had threatened to reveal about his ex-wife and the accused, General Helen Lewis. Our source indicates that in 1977 Helen Lewis had an abortion and that Butch Renfroe, the father of the aborted fetus, had threatened to disclose this secret to the press and to General Lewis's opponent in November's election, Reginald "Sack" Glover. Our source further indicates that the victim left behind a letter confirming General Lewis's abortion. If true, this would be a powerful motive for murder, as this revelation could potentially cost General Lewis her job. Now it appears that the loss of her position is a foregone conclusion. The bigger question is . . . did General Lewis murder her ex-husband? Stay tuned for more coverage of this controversial case from the Vine.'"

Bo slammed the sheets of paper down on the metal table and looked at his client. "Where did this information come from, General?"

Helen found it hard to breathe, and she gripped the table with both hands. When she was able to exhale, she forced herself to remain calm. "The letter signed by Butch is hearsay. So is the blog. None of this is evidence, but they've now poisoned the jury venire." She shook her head. "So which funeral service do you think I should use? How about Carr and Erwin? My momma and daddy were buried by them, and they do a hell of a—"

"General, that's not helping."

"Well, what *is* going to help? Half of Giles County now knows I had an abortion, regardless of whether Sack Glover is able to introduce any evidence of it at trial. And do you need a reminder about which way this county votes?"

Bo looked at the cinder block wall.

"Well, let me give it to you anyway," Helen continued. "In the 2012 presidential election, which Barack Obama won in a landslide, the state of Tennessee was overwhelming in its support of Mitt Romney, and Giles County voted about 70 percent Republican." She let out a ragged breath. "Regardless of your politics, the reality is that this county doesn't favor abortion and would never support someone who had one, regardless of the circumstances. I can kiss my job goodbye, and the trial is a formality at this point. Just get the needle ready."

"We could ask for a change of venue."

Helen laughed. "To where? California? The whole state of Tennessee is bad for us on this, Bo. Hell, the entire southeast. We're screwed six ways from Sunday, and you know it."

Bo slapped his knees and stood. "Chin up, General," he said, walking to the door. "We haven't seen all their evidence yet, and you're right. The press release and the blog entry are hearsay. They don't come in, and leaking that information to the press was the epitome of bush league." He paused. "Let's not panic until we get through the prelim." He stopped. "OK?"

Helen nodded, but her eyes were filled with concern. "Bo, you came in here so wired that I didn't have a chance to ask you about your face."

"What about it?"

"You look like you were on the wrong side of a brawl."

Bo smirked. Since his return from Walton Farm that morning, he'd showered, shaved, and changed into khaki pants, a blue button-down, and a navy-blue blazer with no tie. His lip was still swollen, but there was nothing he could do about that. "Don't you worry about me." He banged three times on the door.

"Where are you going now?"

Bo's eyes radiated anger. "To raise some hell."

33

Bo didn't knock before barging into Sheriff Hank Springfield's office. Hank and Frannie were standing and discussing something, and both of their eyes went wide when they saw him.

"Look, Bo," Hank started. "I know why you're mad, and you have every right—"

"Don't tell me what you know, and don't tell me about my rights." Bo walked slowly into the room. "My client deserves a fair trial, and your office's leak has made that damn near impossible." He glared at the sheriff and then gave the same look to his young chief deputy.

"I'd file a motion for change of venue, but my client reminded me that it wouldn't do one damn bit of good in this state. Regardless of how you feel about abortion, the issue is a magnet for outrage. People . . . jurors who don't believe in abortion will be prejudiced against her."

"That's why you have jury selection, isn't it, Bo?" Hank asked, his tone defensive.

"That all you got?" He shot a glance at Frannie. "How about you, Chief? Do you understand the magnitude of this disclosure?"

Frannie bit her lip and met his eyes. "It was going to come out in the trial anyway."

Bo scoffed. "That's where you're wrong, rookie. Everything you've leaked so far is rank hearsay. Unless you have a witness with knowledge of the abortion and Butch's threat to reveal it, it doesn't come into evidence. But now, every person in Giles County already knows about the abortion. This office poisoned the well." He turned back to Hank. "What kind of ship are you running here, Hank? I thought things were corrupt when Ennis was sheriff." He turned for the door.

"Mr. Haynes." Frannie's voice was firm. "I'm truly sorry for what happened. When I find out who the mole is, I'm going to personally see to it that he never works another day in this office."

Bo smirked. "That's good, Chief. I'm sure that'll make my client happy." He slammed the door before he had to listen to their response.

34

When he reached the parking lot of the jail, Bo felt his phone vibrating in his pocket. He was so pissed off that he answered without even looking at the number. "Bocephus Haynes."

"We need to talk about what happened last night." The Irish accent stopped him cold.

"How did you get this number?"

"That's not important," Finn said. "What is important is that Mr. Zannick would like to see you today. Actually, he'd like to see you right now."

"I'm busy," Bo snapped. "I've had an emergency arise in my new case."

"I see. Well, if you don't meet me and Mr. Zannick at the Sundowners Club off Highway 64 at twelve noon, you're going to have another emergency." He paused. "How would a trespass charge affect your child-custody situation?"

Bo's stomach tightened. Though his custody dispute with the Hendersons was of public record, he was stunned that Finn Pusser was aware of the case. Bo looked at the time displayed on the top of his phone: 11:30 a.m. He was supposed to meet his banker at noon to go over the terms of the loan he was about to make Booker T., but that would have to wait. Though he wanted to tell Finn to go to hell, he squelched his anger. "I'll be there," he finally said, and the mobile clicked dead in his hand.

Bo took a deep breath and exhaled, sticking the phone back in his pocket. He turned back toward the faded brick façade of the sheriff's department building, which housed the jail and Hank's office. He again thought of reporting Finn Pusser to the authorities. *He could've killed us last night,* Bo thought. *And now he's blackmailing me.*

But as quickly as the idea popped into his mind, he dismissed it. Blackmail or no, Bo and Booker T. had trespassed on private property last night, and it sounded like Booker T. had been trespassing a lot lately. Bo didn't want to make any more trouble for his cousin. Also, after the events of this morning, he wasn't sure he could trust the sheriff's office.

And he relished the opportunity to have an audience with Michael Zannick.

Bo walked briskly toward his car, thinking of the mysterious stranger who had saved his and Booker T.'s lives the night before. He hadn't had much time to contemplate their rescuer, but like his cousin, he was grateful. He was also curious. Had someone been following him yesterday? Or perhaps tailing Booker T.? Or maybe the hero was trying to get back at Finn?

He flung the car door open. All he had were questions, and the answers would have to wait. For now, Bo had other fish to fry.

Seconds later, he was on the road headed toward Highway 64.

35

At 11:55 a.m., Bo pulled into the gravel lot of the Sundowners Club. At this time of day, there were only two other cars in the area, both of them pickup trucks. Bo undid the glove compartment and snatched his Glock out, then stuffed the weapon down the front of his pants.

As he walked across the gravel toward the front door, Bo could almost feel his skin crawl. He had a lot of history with this particular place, almost all of it bad and none of it involving strippers. On August 18, 2011, Andy Walton was murdered as he was leaving the Sundowners. Forty-five years to the day earlier, Bo had witnessed Andy and nine of his Klan brethren lynch Roosevelt Haynes at the clearing on Walton Farm. As almost everyone in Pulaski had known that Bo had spent his life trying to bring the men who had killed Roosevelt to justice, when Andy had been brutally murdered, Bo had been the obvious choice as the perpetrator.

Bo had been charged with the crime, but luckily, with the help of Tom McMurtrie and Rick Drake, he had been exonerated. Now, as he looked at the concrete walls of the Sundowners and its neon beer signs, which appeared dull in the middle of the day but which would shine brightly once the sun went down, Bo felt hate in his heart. Hate for this world, which had taken Jazz and Roosevelt and his mother too soon. A world where he'd believed for four and a half decades that the face of evil was Andy Walton only to learn that face was his father.

A world where the sheriff's department would leak news of an abortion to prejudice the jury panel against one of its most prominent and best citizens.

And a world where a rich prick came to a small town, opened a bank, and gave a bunch of good people short-term loans that they couldn't pay off, and then foreclosed on their properties, taking everything those people had worked for their whole lives. And if the prick could rape a fifteen-year-old girl and get away with it, he did that too. Why?

Because that's the world we live in.

Bo spat on the gravel, touched the handle of his gun, and pushed through the heavy front door.

———

Not counting the bartender, there were three men in the Sundowners Club when Bocephus Haynes walked through the front door. Bo saw Finn Pusser at a table in the back of the place. He appeared to be dressed all in black. Next to him was a slight-looking man whom Bo didn't recognize. Bo assumed the stranger must be Michael Zannick. Bo made eye contact with Finn, and the longhaired head of security for Z Bank gestured for him to approach. As Bo zigzagged his way through the tables of the club, he noticed the lone dancer on the big stage in the middle. She was a heavyset, buxom woman who was leaning over the stage and rubbing her breasts in the face of the Sundowners' one spectator. As Bo walked past the stage, he couldn't help but chuckle as he recognized the patron. "Clete, that you?"

Clete Sartain pulled back from the dancer and squinted up at Bo with eyes glazed over from what appeared to be, based on the bottle on his table, one of several Natural Lights he'd consumed since his arrival. He rubbed his snow-white beard, which, taken with his thick similarly colored hair, had made him the obvious choice to play Santa

Claus during the Christmas festival held every December in downtown Pulaski for as long as Bo could remember. As Bo peered down at him, he figured that Clete must be pushing eighty years old now, though he didn't seem quite as heavy as he used to be.

"Bocephus Haynes," Clete said, smiling and standing up. "I will be damned."

Bo shook the man's hand. "You will be if you spend much more time in here," Bo joked, and Clete let out a hearty cackle.

"You got that right."

"You still working at Johnson's Foodtown?"

Clete had been a fixture at the grocery store for years as a salesclerk. "Nah, retired last November. My back couldn't take the sweeping anymore." He rubbed his beard. "I thought I'd be able to spend a few years traveling with my wife, but she had a brain aneurysm in January." He jerked his head. "Dead before she hit the ground."

"I'm sorry," Bo said. "I know what that's like."

"I know you do." Clete squeezed Bo's shoulder, and his grip was feeble. "I'm sorry about Jasmine. She was always nice to me at the store."

Bo nodded and smiled toward the stage. "If you don't mind me asking, Clete, what are you doing in here?"

He frowned. "I got nobody in town no more. My son's family is here, but they don't pay me any mind. With Edna gone, there's no one for me to talk to." He glanced at the stage. "Jess is good company."

"It didn't look like y'all were doing much talking."

"We do," Clete said, scratching his beard again. "All that gyrating she's doing is just for show." He cocked his head toward the back. "Boss man gets mad at her if she doesn't rub her boobies in my face every once in a while." He shook his head. "Don't do no good. I haven't felt the slightest tingle of a boner since George W. was president." He leaned in closer and lowered his voice. Bo could smell the beer on his breath. "You got business with the two guys in the back?"

"You might say that."

"Well, watch yourself. Everyone in this town sings the praises of that boy, but I think he's trouble." Clete was now whispering. "And I'd bet a case of Natty Light that he did rape that Burks girl."

Bo patted Clete's shoulder. "Thanks for the advice." He started to walk away but then thought of something else. "Clete, how often do you come here?"

He looked up at the ceiling as if he were trying to do advanced math. Then he peered back at Bo with a twinkle in his gray eyes. "Every day. I mean, except for Sunday. They ain't open on the Sabbath."

"Gotcha," Bo said. "I'll be seeing you, OK?"

Bo continued his trek toward the back. While he walked, he noticed that the song playing on the speakers was "Baby Got Back" by Sir Mix-a-Lot. He looked over his shoulder and saw the stripper, "Jess," shaking her backside in front of eighty-year-old Clete Sartain.

When he reached the table, Bo stopped and gazed down at the two men, feeling adrenaline rage through his veins as he remembered what Finn Pusser had done and said last night as well as the threats he'd made on the phone half an hour ago.

Neither Finn nor the other man had risen. Both were seated with their legs crossed, looking at ease. Their relaxed nature put Bo further on edge.

"Glad you could make it," Finn said. There was a cast on his right hand, and he was picking at it with his left. He glanced at the Glock, which was clearly visible in the front of Bo's pants, but the sight of the weapon didn't seem to bother him. "Sit down for a minute, Mr. Haynes. Mr. Zannick would like to have a few words."

Bo hesitated but then sat in the chair closest to Finn. From this vantage point, he was looking directly across the table at the other man. "So you're Michael Zannick?" Bo asked. "I've heard a lot about you."

"And me you, Mr. Haynes." Zannick made no move to shake hands. Instead, he looked at Bo as if he might be a biologist sizing up an exotic plant.

"So, you got me here," Bo said, choosing his words carefully. "What do you want?"

Zannick opened his hands palms out as if he had nothing to hide. There was a scar on the man's upper lip that appeared to be the surgical remains of a cleft lip repair. Bo had sued a physician once for botching a cleft palate surgery, and during that case, he had studied thousands of pictures of the typical and expected scarring left after the procedure. Zannick's mark fit the mold. The businessman wore a gray Pink Floyd T-shirt under a brown blazer. The clothes made him appear to be in his twenties, but the lines on Zannick's forehead gave him away as older. "I would like to discuss what happened on my property on Highway 64 last evening."

Bo crossed his right leg over his left. "Not much to discuss. That land used to be my cousin's, and I met him out there thinking he still owned it. When I realized my mistake, we tried to leave, but your hired gun here attempted to kill us." Bo paused. "He also called me a *boy*, which is offensive and racist in this part of the world." Bo glared at Finn. "And if he hadn't been armed and had two sidekicks with him that were also packing, I would have unscrewed his head and pissed down it."

Zannick tapped his fingertips on the table. "Finn tells me that you and Mr. Rowe had someone armed who was helping you."

Bo peered at Zannick, unable to read anything in his blank gaze. Though Bo didn't have the first clue who had come to his and his cousin's aid last night, he wasn't about to confess that here. "A good thing we did."

"Well . . ." Zannick pressed back from the table. He smiled but his eyes remained lifeless and seemed to hold no feelings. Bo couldn't tell whether he was mad, irritated, or happy. "I think what we're describing is a rather large miscommunication." He paused. "Though I certainly would have every right to take this matter to the police, given your cousin Mr. Rowe's repeated trespassing on my property, I've decided to refrain from doing so provided that you'll also refrain from getting the authorities involved because of Finn's . . . *aggressive* behavior and that you won't say anything to the newspapers or media about the incident."

Bo glanced at Finn, noticing that the longhaired brute's neck had turned bright red. He obviously wasn't in agreement with his boss's compromise.

"You've got a deal," Bo said, focusing on Zannick. He didn't like it, but he damn sure didn't want another bogus criminal charge on his record.

"Excellent," Zannick said. "Now, let's talk about the property you own on Highway 64. I understand it's about a thousand acres."

Bo shook his head, impressed by the younger man's 180-degree change in direction. "Before we do, mind telling me why you wanted to meet here?" Bo turned his index finger in a circle.

"I own the Sundowners now," Zannick said, moving his eyes around the nearly empty space. "And Finn manages it for me."

"Man of many hats," Bo said, looking at Finn. "Well, I should be heading on," Bo said, rising from his chair.

"How much for the land you own on Highway 64?"

Bo squinted at the small man. "It's not for sale."

"Everything is for sale," Zannick said.

Bo placed his hands on the table and leaned toward him. "You think you sound cool saying that?"

Zannick ran a finger over his scar. If he was bothered by the slight, he didn't show it. "I understand you're representing the woman who murdered my bank president."

"That's right," Bo said. "And I understand that Butch Renfroe was also your corporate lawyer."

"Man of many hats," Zannick mimicked.

"I'd like to see Butch's office at the bank and maybe take a tour of the place. Could be important in my case."

Zannick frowned. "I'm sorry, Mr. Haynes. I'm afraid I can't allow that. While we'll be glad to cooperate with the sheriff's office's investigation, we won't be cutting General Lewis's lawyer any favors. You might say I'm not her biggest fan." He stood from his chair. "Let me know if you change your mind about selling your property."

Next to Zannick, Finn had risen from his seat as well, and for a few seconds, none of the men spoke.

Bo started to walk away but stopped after a few steps and peered back at them. "Mr. Zannick, where were you on the night Butch Renfroe was murdered?"

"Ahh, the criminal defense lawyer wants to know if I have an alibi." He rubbed his hands together. "Just like *Law and Order*."

"Where were you?" Bo asked again.

"I don't have to answer your questions," Zannick said, stepping around the table, "but I will in this case." He took another step closer to Bo. Now that he was out in the open, Bo saw that Zannick was about five foot nine inches tall, couldn't weigh much over 150 pounds, and was wearing jeans and Chuck Taylor Converse All Stars. "I was here at my club until around nine o'clock, and then I met a young lady for a drink at my house on Highway 31."

"Who?"

"A woman named Cassie Dugan."

Bo blinked his eyes. The name sounded familiar, but he couldn't quite place it.

"Oh, you have to know Cassie," Zannick said. "Let me give you a hint." He paused, clearly enjoying himself. "Kathy's Tavern."

Bo peered down at the floor for a half second, and then it clicked. Cassie Dugan was the longtime bartender at Kathy's. Attractive, nice . . .

. . . and known and liked by almost everyone in town. Zannick couldn't have a better alibi.

"Any other questions?" Zannick asked, his mouth curving into a wide grin.

As he sized up the man who had managed to buy up half of Pulaski in sixteen months, Bo could feel the hate begin to burn inside him again. "Not right now."

———

Michael Zannick remained standing as Bo left the Sundowners. Eventually, Finn approached and stood beside him.

"What do you make of him?" Finn asked.

"A fly in the ointment," Zannick said. "He shouldn't upset our plans." He paused. "Still, best to watch him from here on out. I doubt he's done poking around."

"Will do," Finn said, holding up his bandaged hand. "I owe him one too."

"And you'll get retribution. But for now, just track him."

36

A little more than half a mile from the Sundowners Club, Bo pulled into the gated drive that led to Walton Farm. A gold-plated *W* was still emblazoned on the front of the black gate.

Bo would never sell this land to Michael Zannick. Not after what he'd done to Booker T. But Bo knew he needed to do something with it, and hopefully his cousin would figure out the best use of the property.

Bo took a deep breath and exhaled. In the last three days, he'd reopened his law office and had been retained to handle what would likely be the most important case in his career. If he was successful in his defense of the General, then he'd have the boost of all that positive publicity. His firm would be reborn, and more importantly, he would exonerate a woman he admired. Bo didn't have a lot of friends in this world, but Helen Lewis was one of them.

But was victory even possible?

Bo put the car in gear, remembering the smug look on Michael Zannick's face. *I need some help,* Bo thought. Lona Burks was doing a great job so far, but he needed someone to help him investigate Zannick and any other potential suspects.

Having been out of the game for five years, Bo couldn't think of any private investigators from his heyday who hadn't either retired or died. For a case of this magnitude, he would have loved to use his old friend, Rel Jennings, but Rel had been killed a year and a half ago.

"Damnit," Bo said out loud as he turned back onto Highway 64. But then, just as he was about to reach the intersection with Highway

31, he remembered something. Pulling his wallet from his back pocket, he saw the card stuck between a wad of bills. He took it and noticed that the words had faded from being stuck in his billfold for a couple of days, but he could still make out the name and the number.

Bo turned onto Highway 31 and pulled over to the shoulder of the road. He dialed the number and tapped his fingers on the dash.

The man answered on the fourth ring. "Hooper."

Bo smiled. "You said you'd tell me your first name if I hired you."

37

Helen had done everything she could do to repress the memory of being raped.

It wasn't human nature to punish yourself. As a police officer and prosecutor, she'd observed this phenomenon with children who'd been molested by loved ones and who, despite being the victims of such despicable and defenseless crimes, maintained relationships with their molesters. Some of these children were even loyal and loving toward the monsters who had taken their innocence.

Therapists talked about closure, and perhaps a few folks actually obtained it. For Helen Lewis and many other victims of hideous atrocities, survival depended more on denial. On manipulating the mind into thinking of the tragedy as if it had happened to someone else. Or that it hadn't happened at all.

Was that healthy? Helen didn't know and didn't care. It was easy to have an opinion about sex crimes and abortion.

That is, it was until you or someone close to you was a victim.

Had Tom McMurtrie lived, would she have ever told him about what had happened to her in the fall of 1977? She liked to think so. She had loved Tom. He was the kindest and strongest man she'd ever met.

And he loved me too . . .

———

Helen lay on her cot and stared up at the ceiling. Her cheeks were damp with tears, but she made no move to wipe them.

How fast, she thought, *a person's life can change.*

On a dime. In an instant. In literally a second. She'd seen this play out in over twenty-five years as a prosecutor, and she'd witnessed it in her own life. One decision. One wrong turn. One chest x-ray.

Snap. The world flipped on its axis.

Helen fixed her jaw and thought about the press release she had been shown that morning by Bo. *It was supposed to be our secret. Butch had promised to never tell . . .*

They had broken up when Helen told him that she'd aborted the child. Butch said that he could never look at Helen the same way again and couldn't believe that she had had the abortion without at least telling him. He was angry and questioned whether the child was even his since he had used protection during all of their sexual encounters. He specifically asked about her trip to Birmingham and whether she had met someone.

Helen wanted to tell him the truth. And though the night of her assault was a haze, she knew the rapist had not used a condom.

But she couldn't bring herself to do it.

She left school in January of 1978 with one semester left, though she had plenty of credits accumulated to graduate, which she did despite not attending the ceremony. Her diploma was shipped to her home.

For several months, she traveled. She had some money saved up from summer clerkships, so she got in her Volkswagen Beetle and drove the Bug to New York City. She spent a week in Manhattan. Watched *Death of a Salesman* on Broadway. Took in a Yankees game and saw Reggie Jackson hit two home runs. She went to her first and only disco and danced with some graduate students from NYU.

On the way back to her hotel from the club, she was accosted by two men on the sidewalk. One pulled a knife, and the other made a move for her purse. After the rape, Helen had never gone anywhere without a handgun, and she pulled the weapon on the men. Seeing the two thugs back down and cower at the sight of her sidearm gave her the first sense of empowerment that she felt since Birmingham.

From New York, she went to Las Vegas. She gambled enough to know she had no talent or passion for it and then drove on to California, where she remained for a month. She enjoyed the climate and energy of Los Angeles and relished the state's more liberal stance on women in the workforce. There were times when she thought about looking for an apartment, but she didn't.

Instead, she drove cross-country from LA all the way to Key West, Florida. Along the way, she practiced target shooting in towns that had ranges and watched the first season of *Dallas* on televisions in hotel rooms from Phoenix to Miami.

Tired from her travels and out of money, Helen returned home to Pulaski in November of 1978. Hungering for the power she had felt after holding off the two muggers in New York and hoping to follow in her father's footsteps, she took a job with the Giles County Sheriff's Office. For three and a half years, she worked her way up from deputy to corporal to sergeant. Because of her expertise with a handgun and quick instincts, she was a good cop and liked the work despite feeling slighted and disrespected at times because she was a woman. Regardless, she never regretted wearing the badge. It made her appreciate the officers when she later became a prosecutor. But she saw too many of her arrests pled down or dismissed and became frustrated with the bureaucracy of the department. Real power would come from being the one who made the decision whether to go to trial or not.

Only the district attorney general could ensure that justice was done.

Helen went back to Knoxville in 1982 and took and passed the Tennessee State Bar Exam. A few months later, she accepted a job as an assistant prosecutor with the district attorney general's office for the Twenty-Second Judicial Circuit.

She ran into Butch when he moved to Pulaski in 1983. After a couple of chance encounters, he confessed that he hadn't been able to get over her. Helen hadn't been with a man since the rape, and she loved Butch for his devotion. If she was honest with herself, she was also afraid of what it might be like with another man.

They married in 1984, but she knew by the time of the ceremony that it wasn't going to work.

Butch was loyal but feebleminded and easy to manipulate.

They never discussed the abortion during their marriage, only hinting at it a few times when they were having difficulty conceiving a child. Despite Butch's weakness, Helen knew the divorce was as much her fault as his. She craved the power she had obtained as the head prosecutor, but her need to dominate in the courtroom had eventually transferred over to their marriage. After a while, Butch couldn't take the constant battle for alpha supremacy. First he had started drinking too much, and eventually he had been unfaithful.

Helen sighed, tired of torturing herself with this lonesome train of memories. She sat up in the cot and gazed at her reflection in the Plexiglas window across from her.

When she tried to think about the moments when she was in Butch's house the night of April 1, 2015, the images came in and out in the same way that memories of her rape did. She could see Butch sitting drunk and helpless on his couch. She could feel the anger and bitterness in her veins. She could sense the cold metal of the gun she held in her hand.

The revolver, she thought, remembering that the weapon hadn't been in her glove compartment the day after the murder. *I left it at his house,* she thought. *And when that comes out at the prelim . . .*

. . . I might as well accept life in prison.

She gazed around the holding cell, and depression began to set in. She thought of the choice she had made in 1977. The lies she had told. The lives she had hurt. And then she lay down on her side and closed her eyes.

I'm exactly where I should be.

38

At 4:55 p.m. on Friday, April 5, 2015, five minutes before the close of business, Gloria Sanchez walked into the Giles County Sheriff's Office. She'd given the General four full days to come clean on what she had done, during almost all of which her hero and mentor had been incarcerated.

She'd expected that by now Helen Lewis would have given up any hope of a successful defense. That her attorney, Bocephus Haynes—widely regarded as the best lawyer in town—would have convinced her of the futility of pressing forward.

But instead of a confession, the only things that had come from the defendant were motions for discovery and a preliminary hearing. For all intents and purposes, it appeared that the General was going to fight.

Gloria strode down the narrow hallway past the booking desk, nodding at the deputies, sergeants, and lieutenants she'd come to know over her past thirty-six months as General Lewis's top assistant prosecutor. She'd learned so much from Helen Lewis. How to size up a case. Its strengths. Weaknesses. And most importantly, its theme. What was the case all about? With many crimes, the theme ran parallel to the motive for the act. Revenge. Greed. Hate. Love.

Gloria had also learned the work ethic required of a prosecutor. The hours it took to memorize the facts of the case and what every witness and document brought to the table. It wasn't enough to know the material. To do the job the way it must be done, a prosecutor had to sufficiently prepare so that nothing fell through the cracks.

Finally, Helen Lewis had taught Gloria the importance of making a decision. To plea a case or try it. To give in to a discovery request or stand your ground. To cross-examine a difficult witness or to pass. *You must prepare. You must work your ass off. And then, inevitably, each case requires you to choose. To decide on a course of action. You can't run from it. You can't hide. At the end of the day, it's your responsibility to choose.*

Gloria could hear the General's harsh voice in her mind as she made her way down the hall to the chief's office. When she reached the door, she didn't hesitate, nor did she knock.

When she turned the knob and entered the office, Frannie Storm met her eye with a scowl. The chief deputy sheriff was on the phone. She clasped a hand over the receiver. "What do you want, Sanchez?"

"I'm the mole," Gloria said, her voice unwavering.

"What?" Frannie said, hanging up the phone without saying goodbye.

Gloria could feel her heartbeat thundering in her chest as she took a step closer to the chief's desk. "I'm the mole," she repeated. "I leaked the press release to the Vine."

PART THREE

39

"ALL RISE!" Ricardo Cassidy said, his voice scratchy from what sounded like a bad cold.

Bo and Helen stood from their seats at the defense table and watched as the Honorable Susan Connelly strode to her place behind the bench. Her Honor was a petite woman in her late forties with dark brown hair. Before taking the bench, she'd been a spitfire criminal defense attorney who'd gone to battle with Helen a few times. Helen had always admired Susan's work ethic and her street smarts. Breathing a soft sigh of relief, she knew that Susan was by far the better draw for her case than Harold Page. With only two judges in the district, it was a coin flip as to whether you'd have a competent, fair judge or a lazy, dimwitted oaf. Helen was happy to have won the toss.

After taking the bench, Judge Connelly grabbed a blue file folder, glanced at the top of it, and then spoke in a firm voice. "State of Tennessee v. Helen Evangeline Lewis." She looked up from the bench. "Are the parties here?"

"Yes, Your Honor," Sack Glover said, his high-pitched drawl causing Helen to involuntarily grit her teeth. She peered at the prosecution table and saw that Sheriff Hank Springfield and Chief Deputy Frannie Storm made out the rest of the prosecution team. Helen was surprised to see no sign of Gloria Sanchez, who'd always been her top assistant and easily the best assistant prosecutor on the roster.

Sack probably thinks her loyalty to me will get in the way of her job, Helen thought.

"Yes, Your Honor," Bo said, his baritone voice projecting loud and clear as he stood and buttoned his jacket.

"Very well," the judge said, standing and looking past the parties to the gallery. "I see that there are quite a few members of the press and also some spectators here this morning." Helen followed Her Honor's gaze and noticed that almost every space was occupied on the lower level of the courtroom and that there were a few folks up in the balcony. "Please be reminded," Connelly continued, "that there are to be no pictures taken during this preliminary hearing. And if I hear a phone ring, buzz, vibrate, or make any noise whatsoever, I'm going to have Sundance confiscate it and throw the owner in jail for contempt of court." She paused. "I hope I've made myself clear."

After allowing several seconds of silence as she continued to glare around the room, Judge Connelly looked at the prosecution table. "General Glover, please proceed."

———

For the next seven hours, Sack Glover rolled out the state's evidence against Helen Lewis. As Bo watched and took notes, he couldn't help but be reminded of Sack's warning on the sidewalk outside his office that the evidence against the General was "overwhelming."

It was.

Based on the shell casings found on the floor of the home and the bullet fragments lodged in the victim's chest cavity, County Coroner Melvin Ragland opined that the cause of Butch Renfroe's death was two gunshots from a .44 Magnum revolver, one in the head and one in the sternum. Ragland further testified that, based on the temperature of the body and the degree of rigor mortis, the approximate time of the victim's death was between 9:00 p.m. on April 1, 2015, and midnight on April 2. Ragland also testified that Butch Renfroe's face, shoulders, and chest had numerous red-and-purple bruises, which Ragland opined had come from the revolver. Ragland said he couldn't give an opinion whether the wounds were made before or after the victim was shot.

Sheriff Springfield then testified that, based on his department's search of the defendant's home, vehicle, and office as well as his own personal knowledge, General Lewis owned a .44 Magnum revolver but that said weapon hadn't been located. Moreover, no revolver of any kind was found at the victim's home. The only guns owned by Butch Renfroe were a shotgun and a couple of rifles.

Next up was Doug Brinkley, owner of a local shooting range that Bo himself had used on occasion, who testified that the General had come to shoot on the night of the murder and that he'd opened the range after hours for her, as he had done on many occasions. When asked whether the General had a .44 Magnum revolver, Brinkley answered with a tight smile. "A Smith & Wesson .44. Like Dirty Harry, except with a snub-nose barrel."

There were no laughs from the gallery. Having watched all of Clint Eastwood's movies, Bo was familiar with the reference, but he kept his expression neutral. *Never let them see you sweat,* the Professor had always advised. Brinkley testified that he'd watched the General shoot on several occasions and that she was insanely accurate with the revolver.

"Did she shoot the .44 on the night of April 1, 2015?"

Brinkley cleared his throat and glanced with wide eyes over at the defense table. "Yes. I went back and looked at the targets she'd shot at the next morning, and it appeared that the only gun she fired was the .44."

The next witness was Bonita Spencer, who testified to seeing a black Crown Victoria parked outside Butch Renfroe's home sometime after 9:00 p.m. but before 10:00 and seeing General Lewis step out of the car and walk around the side of the house. Spencer testified that, about thirty minutes later, she looked out the window and the car was gone.

On cross-examination, Bo asked Ms. Spencer if she saw any other vehicles or people on the street near Mr. Renfroe's home after 9:00 p.m.

"Well, I went to bed right after the news at 10:30. The only other thing I remember seeing is a Ford truck driving kind of slow by Butch's house."

"When would that have been?" Bo asked, feeling a tingle of hope in his chest.

"Maybe 10:15 or so? It was when I pulled the curtains to go to bed, so somewhere around 10:15 or 10:30."

"Could you see the driver of the truck?"

"No. It had tinted windows."

"What about the color of the vehicle?"

She took a long time with her answer, gazing up at the ceiling. "I'd say it was either blue or black. Probably black. It was a dark truck."

"Is there anything else you remember about the vehicle?"

"Yes," she said. "The back windshield had a Confederate flag emblem on it."

"A Confederate flag?" Bo asked, envisioning the symbol in his mind. "You mean there was a blue X with a red background?"

She crinkled up her face. "I think so. I can see cars and people pretty good out my window, but that car decal was small. I'm not sure if the background was red. Seemed like it was darker, but there was an X and I thought it was the Confederate flag."

"Anything else you remember about it?"

She cocked her head. "No. Only that the truck was going really slow when it passed Butch's house."

———

After a short break for lunch, the afternoon started with the finger-print and DNA evidence, which was also bad for the home team. Chief Frannie Storm testified that print analysis of the victim's house showed matches for the defendant on the knob of the side door of the victim's home and on the victim's shirtsleeves. The only prints found in the house belonged to the victim, the defendant, and the victim's neighbor, Terry

Grimes, who was the person who found the victim after Butch had failed to show for their morning workout. Frannie then testified that particles of blood, hair, and skin were uncovered in the den where the body was discovered and that microscopic fragments of blood were located in the defendant's car and on the defendant's clothing. Frannie said that all the DNA evidence had been sent off to the crime lab in Nashville.

Frannie then summarized the sheriff department's search of the victim's home, car, and clothing, concluding that Butch Renfroe's laptop computer and wallet were missing.

Finally, Frannie testified to the discovery of the press release in the safe of Butch Renfroe's home. Over Bo's hearsay objections—the rules of evidence were more liberal at a preliminary hearing as opposed to trial—Frannie read the letter.

When Sack said he had no further questions for Frannie, Bo expected the state to say it was through. They clearly had more than enough evidence to show probable cause, which was the threshold for the judge to bind the case over to the grand jury.

"Anything further, General Glover?" Judge Connelly asked.

"We have one additional witness, Your Honor. The state calls Ms. Gloria Sanchez to the stand."

———

As she watched her top assistant—her right hand—these past three years walk through the double doors and take the witness stand, Helen felt as if the air had been kicked out of her. She glanced at her lawyer, and Bo raised his eyebrows as if to ask, *What could this be?*

Helen shrugged and turned her attention back to the action.

After Gloria was sworn in, Sack quickly covered her background as an assistant district attorney employed by the defendant. Then he cut right to the chase.

"Ms. Sanchez, did you witness a conversation on April 1, 2015, between the victim and the defendant?"

"Yes," Gloria said, and Helen felt the hair on her arms begin to prickle. *She lied to me,* Helen thought.

"When and where did this conversation occur?"

"In this courtroom at approximately two o'clock in the afternoon."

Sack paused, clearly relishing the moment. "Please describe to the court what you saw and heard."

Bo started to stand, presumably to make a hearsay objection, but Helen placed her hand over his. *"No,"* she whispered. *"I want to hear."*

"I had just come out of Judge Page's chambers," Gloria began. "I had dropped off the jury instructions for the Michael Zannick rape trial. I decided to exit his chambers through the courthouse because I knew the General liked to do her final trial prep in here. When I entered the courtroom, I heard shouting."

"Who did you hear?"

"General Lewis was standing in the jury area." Gloria pointed straight ahead to the twelve built-in chairs that made up the jury box. "She was yelling into the gallery at a man."

"What did she say?"

Gloria licked her lips and glanced at Helen. When she did, Helen could see the angst in her assistant's eyes. "Well, I didn't catch everything, but the man had just asked her how she thought her supporters at the First Baptist Church would feel about what she did in December of '77."

Jesus H. Christ, Helen thought, turning around and gazing at the burgundy curtains that covered the windows of the courtroom. There were times when she felt the thick, flowing drapes were the perfect decoration, as they made it seem as if you were in a theater or an opera house instead of a courtroom. They certainly jibed with the drama that was unfolding right now. *She witnessed the whole thing . . .*

Helen gritted her teeth as Gloria described Butch's promise to keep his lips sealed if Helen dismissed the charges against Zannick, and Helen's retort that she was being blackmailed.

"What happened next?" Sack asked.

"The man whispered something I couldn't hear." Gloria paused. "Then he made his threat."

"What did he say?"

"He said if she hadn't dismissed the charges against Zannick by the time opening statements began in the trial, then he was going to tell Sack . . . you . . . everything." She licked her lips. "He also said that he'd drafted a press release for the *Pulaski Citizen* and all the local radio and TV stations, which he would distribute the second she began her opening. Then he asked her whether prosecuting Zannick was worth losing her whole career."

Sack waited a full two seconds before asking his next question. "Then what happened?"

"The General got mad and yelled, 'Frederick Alan Renfroe.'" Gloria sucked in a quick breath. "And Mr. Renfroe said he was sorry but that he had no choice."

"Then what?"

"The General said he was bluffing. That he didn't have the balls to blackmail her." Gloria paused. "And Mr. Renfroe said he wished he was bluffing."

"What happened next, Ms. Sanchez?" Sack asked, his scratchy drawl ringing out over the courtroom.

"General Lewis screamed at him."

Sack approached the stand and spoke in a lower voice. "What did the defendant scream?"

Gloria turned and looked directly at Helen. "That she was going to kill him."

"What were her exact words, Ms. Sanchez? Do you remember them?"

Gloria nodded and turned back to the judge. "She said, 'I swear to God, Butch, as Jesus Christ is my witness, I will kill you dead.'"

40

Judge Connelly didn't bother to order a recess when Sack Glover announced that he had no further witnesses and Bo confirmed that the defense wouldn't be presenting any evidence. Instead, she cleared her throat and said that she was ready to rule.

"After considering the evidence presented by the prosecution today, it is the finding of this court that there is probable cause to believe that on April 1, 2015, the defendant, Helen Evangeline Lewis, committed the crime of first-degree murder in wrongfully causing the death of Frederick Alan Renfroe." She paused and peered down at the parties. "This case will now be bound over to the grand jury."

———

An hour later, in the consultation room of the jail, Bo was reminded of the feeling in a locker room after a blowout loss. He and Helen both gazed down at the concrete floor.

"Maybe we should do this in the morning," Bo suggested. "After we've had a moment to process everything."

Helen smiled, still looking down at the floor. "Juries don't get to sleep on evidence. We shouldn't either." Finally, she raised her eyes. "Look at me."

Bo did as he was told.

"What do you think?" Helen asked.

"Based on what I just heard, I believe that a jury would convict you and sentence you to the needle." He paused. "How about you, General?"

"Same," she said.

Bo stood. "General, you've got to tell me your version of what happened. We've seen their case now, and it is staggering. We knew the revelation of your abortion was their motive, but our assumption was that all they had was hearsay evidence. Instead, they actually have direct eyewitness testimony from a close confidante of yours, Ms. Sanchez, who witnessed you threaten to kill Butch because he was blackmailing you with the abortion. So . . ." He slapped his hands together. "You already admitted that you went to Butch's house the night of the murder, and Bonita Spencer puts you there between 9:00 and 10:00 p.m." He began to pace. "What happened?"

Helen bit her lip but remained quiet.

"What's the deal?" Bo said, his voice rising, unable to control his agitation anymore. "You killed him, didn't you?" He walked over to the table and put his hands on it. "You went to Brinkley's range, did a couple of hours of target practice with your .44, and then went over to Butch's house, parked on the curb, walked around back where you knew from being married to him for so many years that he'd probably leave the side door unlocked, and then put three slugs in him and pistol-whipped his sorry ass." Bo smirked. "Or did you beat him with the revolver first and then shoot him? Melvin wasn't sure. Can you clarify?"

"What do you think, Counselor?"

"I just told you. Based on what I heard today, we are completely, 100 percent screwed."

"Sounds like I need to hire another attorney. Maybe you're not up for the challenge. Being out of the game for so long has made you soft and weak."

Bo ground his teeth together. "No attorney, not F. Lee Bailey, not Johnnie Cochran." He paused. "Not Tom McMurtrie. None could help you if they didn't know your side of the story."

"I'll tell you," Helen said. "But not now. I'm too tired, OK? Come back in the morning."

Bo stared hard at her. "I'll come and I'll listen, but there's something you need to start thinking about."

"What?"

"Sack's offer of life without parole is looking pretty good right now. If the forensic analysis of the hair fibers confirms that you were in the house, and if the blood in your car matches Butch's . . ." He trailed off.

Helen returned Bo's hard look and pressed off the table with her hands. Once she'd risen to her feet, she folded her arms across her chest. "I'll never take that deal, Bo, and you know it. It's all or nothing."

Bo nodded. "If that's the case, then you get some rest and be ready to tell me everything first thing in the morning." He walked to the door and rapped his knuckles on it three times for the guard. "If you don't, I'm gonna walk. I didn't sign up for this gig so that you could sabotage any chance of us winning."

"Don't you threaten me."

"Tomorrow," Bo said as the guard opened the door.

41

Bo was still fuming when he arrived back at the office. It was almost 6:00 p.m., but Lona was still at her desk and working on the computer. She stopped typing when he stepped inside the lobby.

"I heard," she said. "I'm sorry."

"It was to be expected."

"I know . . . but I heard the evidence was pretty bad. I've become friends with Sue Barnes, one of the clerks over at the courthouse. Sue taught me how to do electronic filing, and she has a brother in addiction recovery. She's been good to me. One of the few people in this town . . . besides you . . . that's given me a chance. Anyway, Sue said the rumors floating around the courthouse are that General Lewis almost had to have killed him based on what Sack Glover presented today."

"That's not an exaggeration," Bo said, hearing the defeat in his tone. "If the General would tell me what the hell happened, maybe we could get somewhere. Maybe there's an angle."

"Maybe she did it." Lona's voice was quiet, and she was looking down at her desk.

"Maybe," Bo said. He looked at the computer. "You get the complaint drafted in that new wheels case?"

Her face broke into a smile. "Yes. I was glad to have something else to work on. Sounds like a winner."

"We'll see," Bo said, but he was also happy to start building a case list again. Last week, Jess Reynolds, the dancer at the Sundowners that he'd seen with Clete Sartain a month ago, came in complaining that she'd been rear-ended on College Street at the intersection on Ninth Street. She had busted her mouth and had sprained her neck in the accident, and her fifteen-year-old son, who had been riding shotgun, had broken his arm. The case wouldn't set the world on fire, but a clear liability car wreck with medicals that would likely be $25,000 to $50,000 each would likely result in a settlement of around $300,000 if Bo's instincts were still true. Not a bad case at all and certainly worth taking old Clete to dinner to repay him. He would do that as soon as he got back from his trip. He still needed to talk with Clete about Michael Zannick and Finn Pusser.

"You headed out tomorrow for the beach?" Lona asked.

"Right after lunch, I'm driving to Huntsville to pick up Lila and T. J., and then we're off to Destin for Memorial Day weekend."

"And you're going to meet with that potential witness I mentioned?"

Bo nodded. "Seeing Darla Sunday afternoon. I hope she's of help."

"No one would know more about the secrets of Pulaski than Darla. She's one of the smartest people I've ever met."

"Sounds good. Listen, it's late. You should probably be getting home."

"Right after I finish this complaint."

Bo smiled and shook his head. "You're a machine."

———

A minute later, he was in the library of the office, which he'd converted into his bedroom. He pulled a cold Yuengling out of the minifridge in the corner and plopped down on the sofa, which converted to a bed at night. He pressed the cold bottle to his forehead and closed his eyes, wondering if the General was going to make him walk in the morning.

If she won't tell me the deal, then I'm gone.

"Bo?"

He looked up to see Lona standing in the doorway, wringing her hands together. "Can I ask you a small favor?"

"Anything."

"Next Thursday afternoon, there's a settlement docket for Michael Zannick's rape charge. I haven't heard a peep from Sack Glover or anyone else in the DA's office about it, and I'm worried that Zannick is going to buy his way out of it. He and Glover are thick as thieves."

"The case normally wouldn't be pled out or dismissed unless the victim agrees. Who's the judge?"

Her face fell. "Page."

"Damn."

"Yeah. I don't trust him, and I think he wants to settle this case. Sometimes I think the whole town wants it to go away. Especially with Hoshima delaying signing that plant deal until the charge is addressed."

Bo took a sip of the beer, which tasted crisp and cold. "What's the favor?"

"Will you come to the settlement docket? I was also thinking of suing Zannick for money damages. Would you be Mandy's attorney?"

Bo took another drink from the bottle and exhaled. "I'll definitely attend the docket." After drinking another sip of beer, he nodded at her. "And I'll represent her too. But let's see how the criminal case plays out first. We wouldn't want to file a civil lawsuit against Zannick until after the criminal trial. If we file suit before then, Zannick's defense attorney will argue that all Mandy is after is money. I've seen that happen, and it can be devastating to the chances of a conviction."

"OK, that makes sense." She leaned in and hugged his neck, and he could smell her perfume, which reminded Bo of fresh strawberries. "Thank you."

"You're welcome."

Lona turned to go but paused again in the doorway. "The Reynolds complaint is in your chair."

Bo gave her a salute, and she ambled down the hall. A minute later, he heard the front door open and close, and she was gone.

Taking his beer with him, Bo stood and walked down the hallway to his private office and picked up the complaint that was lying in his chair. After reviewing the document for several minutes, he realized there was only one word to describe it. "Perfect," he whispered, and he could smell the faint scent of Lona on the page and in his office.

He wrote the word *file* on top of the document and trudged down the hall toward the lobby, which was now dark. Lona had turned off the lights when she left. Bo placed the complaint in the spiral outbox on Lona's desk and took another sip of beer.

He didn't notice the man sitting in the waiting area until the visitor spoke.

"You should probably lock your door at night."

Bo wheeled so fast that his beer fizzed over and began to spill out of the bottle. "Who are you?"

In the unlit room, all Bo could make out was the shadow of a man. But the voice sounded familiar. "You don't recognize me, do you?"

"I can't see you."

The man stood and stepped into the light. He had a crew cut of light red hair and was clean shaven. Nothing about his appearance resembled the lawman he'd once been. Only the voice . . . and perhaps the eyes, all of which were cool and calm. Bo had always thought that Ennis Petrie could have stepped on a rattlesnake and talked the reptile out of biting him.

"Ennis?"

The man nodded.

"You've got a lot of nerve." Bo gazed past the visitor to the couch, where Lee Roy lay chewing on a massive bone. "Thanks for the warning, boy."

"He's a fine dog, Bo. I've been working on him for several weeks."

"What?"

204

"Around this time each night, after your assistant leaves for the day but while you're still in the back, I've been peeking my head in the door and giving him a few treats. Usually he barks a couple times and then settles down. Something I doubt you'd even pay attention to or remember. Tonight, I gave him a rawhide bone, too, and he didn't make a sound."

"He should be barking like there's no tomorrow," Bo said, shaking his head at Lee Roy, who continued to chomp away, oblivious to his master's irritation.

Ennis's mouth curved into a tiny grin. "You know, dogs . . . especially bulldogs . . . have fantastic instincts. Your boy here knows that I mean you and him no harm." He paused. "We need to talk, Bo."

"I've got nothing to say to you."

"Then I'll talk and you listen."

Bo opened his mouth, but the words wouldn't come. He couldn't believe that Ennis Petrie, the former sheriff who had been convicted of conspiracy to commit the murder of Roosevelt Haynes in 1966, was actually standing in his office. "Then talk," he said.

"Are you aware you're being followed?"

Bo snorted. "Yeah. Very aware. Gray sedan and a burgundy pickup." He paused. "They've been keeping their distance, and with good reason." Bo tapped the pocket of his trousers, where he kept his Glock. "I don't bring knives to gunfights." Bo stepped toward the former sheriff, keeping his hand on his pocket with the pistol. "Now, why are you here?"

Ennis rubbed his chin and held out his hand in a stop gesture. "I'll tell you in a second, but first let me ask you a question. You know who visited me the most when I was in prison?"

"I wouldn't have thought you had any visitors. A scum like you."

"I had one. A repeat customer." He scratched his neck. "Finnegan Pusser."

Bo felt his stomach clench. "That so?"

Ennis nodded. "It is. Michael Zannick's right-hand man. I think they might be half brothers or something."

Bo gritted his teeth. He was past due to hear something back from his private eye about Zannick, and it irritated him to be learning this information from Ennis Petrie. "What did Zannick and Finn want with you?"

"In return for pushing Sack Glover to expedite my parole, I gave them information."

"What kind of . . . *information*?"

"Dirt," he said, and his face curved into a sheepish grin. "Dirt on a few men in Giles County."

"And you delivered?"

"I was the sheriff for over twenty years. You learn a lot of things about a lot of people."

"Who were the men you had dirt on?"

Ennis took a step closer to Bo. The former sheriff's biceps bulged out of his tight-fitting gray T-shirt. The old Ennis Petrie had been potbellied and pear shaped. This version looked cut from the pages of a bodybuilding magazine. "There were three. Lou Horn. Terry Grimes." He paused and took another step toward Bo. They were now a foot away from each other. "And Butch Renfroe."

Bo took a slow sip of beer, squinting at the lawman while still holding his hand close to his pocket. "I'm listening."

"In the 1990s and 2000s, when Larry Tucker ran the Sundowners Club, there were rumors of a prostitution ring that was quartered at the strip club. A few of the dancers participated, and a lot of powerful men. The trucking tycoon from Tuscaloosa, Jack Willistone. You remember him, don't you?" Ennis smiled.

Bo nodded.

"He was a part of it. Your daddy was too. Andy . . ."

Bo squeezed the bottle tight in his hand but otherwise kept his expression and demeanor neutral. "You gonna get to the point?"

"My sources told me that the leaders of this sex-for-pay operation were Butch, Terry, and Lou." He licked his lips. "Lou helped line up the talent, Terry worked his political and business connections to drum up clients . . . and Butch handled the money and the paperwork."

Bo felt his heart rate begin to pick up steam as he thought of the laptop computer stolen from Butch Renfroe's house the night of the murder. "Did you ever press charges against any of them?"

"Never had enough evidence. A lot of smoke but no fire."

Bo grunted and shook his head. "Did you ever tell the General about your suspicions or what your sources had told you?"

He snorted. "The General had no tolerance for pie-in-the-sky cases. I didn't want to bring anything to her that I couldn't prove. Especially not a scandal that could implicate a lot of the town brass."

Bo rubbed the back of his neck. "Why are you telling me this?"

"Because I'd bet a gold nickel that Finn Pusser and Michael Zannick used the information I gave them to put pressure on Butch, Terry, and Lou. With Zannick charged with rape and that Japanese auto plant hanging in the balance, I think Zannick must have threatened to roll on the three stooges unless they got him out of this jam."

Bo drained the rest of his beer and set it on his desk. "Ennis, if you didn't have enough to charge Butch, Terry, and Lou, then how could you have given Zannick enough heat to put any pressure on them?"

Ennis smiled. "Zannick is a savvy bastard. I bet he's got at least one of them on tape or video saying something incriminating after being challenged with the dirt I shared."

For several seconds, Bo thought through what the former sheriff had just disclosed. Then he peered hard at Ennis. "Why are you telling me this? Sounds like you owe Zannick and Finn."

"I don't owe them nothing. I delivered what they wanted, and they helped me get parole. We're even as far as I'm concerned."

Bo shook his head and started to turn the lobby lights back on.

"Stop," Ennis said. "I don't think anyone is watching you right this minute—I didn't see either of the vehicles you mentioned when I walked in—but, if I'm wrong, I don't want them to see me in here."

Bo removed his finger from the light switch. "So answer me this, Ennis. Why are you here? You think you owe me something?"

"Yes, I do."

Bo scoffed. "Well, I don't want your help." He approached and leaned in so close that they were almost nose to nose. "I wouldn't trust you as far as I could throw you. Now get the hell out of my office."

Ennis nodded, but instead of walking toward the front door, he pushed past Bo and down the hall.

"Now where are you going?"

"You've got a back door to this place, don't you?"

"Yeah. So what?" Bo asked, hustling behind his unwanted visitor. "If memory serves, you arrested me at the back door four years ago for the murder of Andy Walton."

When Ennis reached the end of the hall, he stopped. It was even darker in this part of the building, and all Bo could make out was the other man's eyes.

"I'm sorry, Bo. I really am. For what happened in the Walton trial. For being a part of the lynch mob that hanged Roosevelt. For everything. Is there any way you can forgive me?"

"No," Bo said, his voice so cold that it gave him a shiver.

Ennis again nodded. "I don't blame you." He grabbed the door handle and then looked at Bo with a concerned gaze. "I was at the courthouse today, Bo. I saw how bad it was."

"You? How—?"

"No one hardly recognizes me anymore with my hair cut short and without my mustache. I had a beard at the parole hearing, and now that's gone too." He paused. "Besides, I sat in the balcony."

"So, you were there. So what?" Bo tried to make his voice sound bored, but it didn't take. He had to admit that he was curious as to why the former lawman had shown up.

"It's hard for me to believe that General Lewis would be capable of such a brutal killing."

"Coming from a man who participated in the lynching of a black man in front of a five-year-old boy, that doesn't mean a whole lot."

Ennis cleared his throat. "I guess not, but I want you to think about something. Remember Gloria Sanchez's testimony at the end of the hearing. She said she heard Butch tell the General to dismiss the rape charges against Michael Zannick or he would reveal her secret, right?"

Bo shrugged. "Yes."

"So Butch Renfroe, a corporate attorney and president of a bank, was resorting to blackmailing his ex-wife with—if it was an abortion— the most personal and explosive of secrets. All for what?"

Bo blinked. "To get Zannick off."

"*Exactly*," Ennis said. "Butch knew with the trial about to start that he was running out of time."

"And he pulled out all the stops," Bo added, gazing down at the floor and then back at the former lawman.

Ennis winked and started to turn the knob. Then he stopped and cracked the blinds, peeking outside.

"See anyone?"

Ennis shook his head but continued to gaze out the window. "One last thing, Bo. Finn Pusser almost killed you the other night at your cousin's farm. Whether he's keeping his distance now or not, I'm not sure I'd want him following me if I were you."

Bo felt a cold chill run down his arm. "How do you know about that?"

"A little birdie told me."

"Did that bird own a shotgun?"

Ennis turned and smiled at Bo. "Maybe."

Then he grabbed the doorknob and left the office.

42

At 8:00 a.m. the next morning, Bo trudged into the consultation room with bloodshot eyes.

"You look like hell," Helen said. "Anything the matter?"

"Didn't sleep much." He held out his palms. "Well?"

Helen leaned forward and placed her elbows on the desk. She made a tent with her hands and peered at her attorney. "I went to Butch's house that night."

Bo smirked. "Tell me something I don't know."

"I didn't steal anything from his house."

Bo cocked his head at her. "Again, this is old news."

"The prosecution's story doesn't fit, because I didn't take anything." She paused. "I also didn't dispose of my revolver."

Bo felt his whole body tense as he took the seat across from his client. "You admit to being in Butch's house with a .44 Magnum revolver?"

She nodded.

"But I didn't take it with me when I left."

"Why?"

"Because Butch took it away from me. We fought. I wanted to shoot him, but I couldn't do it. I hit him several times with the gun, but he finally wrestled it away from me."

Bo's eyes widened and, for the first time since he'd agreed to take the case, he felt the winds of hope in the air. *That fits,* he thought. *All of the prosecution's evidence would fit that story . . . as long as someone else came along and finished Butch off.*

"Thank you, General," Bo said.

"I'm sorry to keep this from you for so long," Helen said. "I've been a prosecutor for a long time, and I worked with Sack Glover for years. I wanted you to have the full benefit of his story before I told you mine."

"Do you remember what time it was when you left Butch's house?"

"I got there around nine thirty, and it was a little after ten when I left."

"Which, based on Melvin Ragland's time-of-death range, would still leave two hours for the true killer to do the deed." Bo paused. "Any ideas?"

"Zannick," Helen said. "His trial was about to start, and we had the goods. Mandy Burks was going to testify that he forcibly raped her. Even if the jury didn't find for us on that charge, there was still the statutory offense, which I think we definitely would have won on. Zannick does jail time, and he loses the Hoshima contract."

Bo stood and began to pace. He thought best when moving. "OK, I hear you on Zannick, but I asked him what he was doing the night of the murder, and he said point-blank that he was with Cassie Dugan."

"The bartender at Kathy's Tavern?" Helen asked.

"Correct."

"Have you confirmed—?"

"The next day I went in and had a beer at Kathy's and asked Cassie if she was with Zannick, and she said she was with him all night and the next morning."

"So, she's his girlfriend?"

"She was that night," Bo said.

"Well, a prick like Zannick probably has someone to do his dirty work."

Bo nodded. "There's a longhaired Irish-speaking man named Finn Pusser who manages the Sundowners Club. I'm pretty sure that he's Zannick's heavy."

"Where was he the night of the murder?"

"Don't know."

Helen smiled. "That's where I would focus my energy. Everything in my gut tells me that Zannick set me up to avoid prison time and to keep his precious Hoshima project." She paused and wrinkled her nose.

"What?"

"You might also look at Lou Horn."

Bo tensed as he recalled his interaction with Ennis Petrie the night before and the prostitution ring that Ennis said Lou was involved in. "What could Lou have gained by killing Butch and framing you for it?"

"I have no idea," Helen said. "But Lou was nervous as a long-tailed dog in a room full of rocking chairs the morning of trial. He also said he was sick on Monday afternoon and bought a recess until Tuesday."

"And Butch was killed Monday night," Bo added, thinking it through with her.

"Right." She snapped her fingers.

For a long time, the room was silent, and then Bo gazed at Helen. "All of these theories involve a frame-up, and obviously Zannick and perhaps Lou would both benefit from you being in here." He took a step closer to her. "But how would they benefit from Butch's death aside from you?"

She shrugged. "Butch was Zannick's corporate lawyer and was also running Z Bank for him. Maybe he found out some things he didn't need to know." She stopped. "They could kill two birds with one stone." She snapped her fingers again. "You know something else I've been thinking about?"

"What?"

"Ennis Petrie got parole the Friday before Butch's death. He was out of jail at the time of the murder."

Bo felt a tickle in his stomach as he again remembered his strange interaction with the former sheriff the night before. "What would Ennis have against Butch? And why would he want to kill someone a few nights after he was released?"

"He might not have wanted to. He might have had to." Helen set her jaw. "Sack Glover all but begged that hearing board to grant Ennis parole, and Sack is in Zannick's pocket big time."

"You think maybe Ennis agreed to kill Butch in return for Zannick arranging his release?"

"It's not the craziest idea in the world. Ennis is no stranger to brutal killings—you know that firsthand—and he probably wouldn't have had any qualms about throwing me under the bus since I put him in jail to begin with."

And that might explain why he's been trying to help since Butch's murder, Bo thought. *He did the deed and feels guilty about it.*

"Ennis came to see me last night," Bo said, watching Helen for her reaction.

She crossed her arms and squinted at him. "Well . . . what did he want?"

"To tell me that he'd investigated Butch Renfroe, Lou Horn, and Terry Grimes for being involved in a prostitution ring in the '90s and 2000s. He could never prove it, so he didn't involve you." He paused. "But he did mention the ring to Finn Pusser when Finn visited him in prison."

Helen gazed up at the ceiling and wrapped her hands around the back of her head. "That could explain why Butch was so desperate to have me dismiss the charges against Zannick." She lowered her eyes to Bo. "Zannick could have been blackmailing him with the prostitution ring and threatening to disclose if he were convicted of Mandy Burks's rape."

"Which would also account for why Lou was so nervous at the trial docket."

"Him getting sick never seemed right either," Helen said. "It always felt like a stall tactic."

Bo finally sighed. "All of this sounds good, but the only thing we have now is speculation and theories. Whether it's Michael Zannick,

Finn Pusser, Lou Horn, or Ennis Petrie, we need some evidence." He paused. "And if this is a frame-up, why would the framer take your gun with him? Seems like it would be more beneficial to shoot Butch with your gun and leave it at the scene to be found. The true killer would likely be wearing gloves, so the only prints on the weapon would presumably be yours."

Helen met Bo's eye and didn't blink. "I've thought of that, too, and you're right. It doesn't fit a frame-up theory, but you and I both know that criminals make mistakes. Perhaps the killer forgot to wear gloves before using my gun and didn't want to risk his prints being found on the handle. Or maybe he intended to leave the revolver but got distracted by his efforts to steal the laptop. There are dozens of possibilities."

Bo nodded his agreement before sighing again. "We need evidence, General."

"My testimony that I didn't steal anything, didn't shoot Butch, and had my revolver taken away from me before I left his house is evidence."

Bo peered at her. "That would require you to take the stand."

"I have to take the stand, Bo."

"Are you sure? Given all the evidence and the admissions you'll have to concede . . . and the questions you'll get about the abortion."

She stood from her chair and put her hands on her hips. "I've been the district attorney general of this county for over twenty years. That jury has to hear from me." She paused. "This town has to hear from me."

Bo tended to agree with her, but he didn't say so. "We'll talk trial strategy when we get closer to time." He turned to leave.

"Bo?"

"Yeah."

"Do you know if Zannick's rape trial has been reset?"

Bo remembered what Lona had told him the night before. "There's a settlement docket next Thursday."

"Trial is normally the Monday after the settlement docket," Helen said, sighing. "Promise me something."

"What?"

"Don't let that bastard cut a deal."

Bo stifled a sigh. *There's only so much I can do.* But then he fixed her with a hard gaze. "I'll try."

43

Ennis Petrie liked to walk the streets of Pulaski at night. When the sun went down, he couldn't feel their eyes on him, nor could he taste the shame of having once been someone in this town. He knew, of course, that after four years in lockup, many people had forgotten about him, and those who hadn't probably wouldn't recognize him after the weight loss, the crew cut, and the shaved face.

Regardless, during the daylight he could feel their eyes burning into him.

He'd had an identity for over two decades as a lawman. A strong and faithful public servant. The high sheriff, by God.

And then an awful mistake he'd made as a young man came back to strip everything he'd ever worked for away. Now, all anyone would ever think about when they heard the name Ennis Aaron Petrie was . . .

Racist.

Killer.

White supremacist.

Bigot.

That was his new identity. All because he'd joined the Ku Klux Klan back when many prominent citizens were members and because he'd made the horrible choice to tag along when his friend Samuel Baeder had asked if he wanted to be part of something "big."

Should he have put a stop to what was happening once he realized what was going down? Yes, he damn well should have. He had assumed that they were only going to scare Roosevelt, not actually kill him, but he eventually should have stopped them.

But he didn't. He'd been the youngest one there, and any action on his part against the mob would have ended his career in law enforcement before it had even begun.

He'd been scared of the consequences, and a good and decent man had been murdered.

Does one act of cowardice define a whole life?

These were the things he thought about as he walked up Jefferson Street, where an out-of-town car was normally parked outside Ms. Butler's Bed & Breakfast. Ennis would gaze at the license plates of the cars sometimes, recognizing neighboring Tennessee counties as well as some from over the state line and into Alabama. Mostly these cars belonged to couples who came to celebrate an anniversary or a birthday.

Ennis envied these folks who would breeze into town, enjoy some good food and the companionship of their lovers, and walk around the historic downtown square or maybe head over to the Amish country of Ethridge. They came to Giles County with fresh eyes.

He wondered about these people sometimes. Their backstories. Whether any of them had made a terrible mistake in their life. Whether they had asked Jesus for forgiveness.

Ennis had sat on the third pew of First United Methodist Church for thirty-two years. He stood when it was time to sing hymns, and he always put something green in the collection plate. He attended Christmas Eve night service and was an usher once a month. His wife, Sheila, was on the finance committee, and his daughter, Ellen, was married in the church. His granddaughters were baptized by the Reverend Shep Griffith when they were six months old, and Ennis put his hands on their tiny shoulders while Shep sprinkled holy water on them.

Ennis stood and said the Lord's Prayer with a hundred other members every Sunday for three decades. He sang, he prayed, and he tithed. He did what Christians were supposed to do.

But he hadn't known Jesus until he was sent to prison.

He hadn't really prayed until he was incarcerated next to men who were doing hard time for murder, rape, arson, and any number of other felonies. Forty bunks in a pod. Grown men putting up sheets around their cot so they could have sex. Going to sleep with one eye open, hearing the moans of those having relations, and feeling the adrenaline of knowing there would be a fight at some point during the night. There was an altercation daily in prison, and every inmate had a weapon of some kind. The pointy end of a pin top. A clothes hanger bent into a long, sharp wire. Shoelaces used as a choking device. To survive, Ennis spent every waking hour either in the weight room pumping iron, the library reading and writing letters for other inmates, or the commissary, where, because of his education and history as an officer, he had landed a job passing out goods to other inmates. He made himself valuable, stayed as quiet and still as possible, and never made eye contact with any inmate he didn't know. Because of its implied challenge, eye contact almost always led to a fight. A battle for territory and space. When he did sleep, it was never restful. Ennis hadn't seen combat, but he figured army officers who were engaged in a lengthy battle probably slept in the same manner. Shoulders tense. Stomach tight. Ready to move in an instant.

During those sleepless nights, Ennis prayed. He begged the Lord to help him and bargained with Jesus that, if he ever got out, he'd make amends.

Sheila filed for divorce six months after his sentencing. Ellen took her two kids and moved with her husband, David, to Portland, Oregon. She wanted to be as far away from her father as she could possibly get. Ennis did not see his ex-wife, his daughter, or his two granddaughters, Belle and Mae, at all during his imprisonment.

The only contact he received was a cryptic phone call from his daughter on Christmas Eve. *"Mae has cancer. A rare form of leukemia, and they aren't sure how to treat it. Her medical expenses are already through the roof. I guess we all have to pay for your sins. Merry Christmas, Dad."*

She hung up the phone before Ennis could even say hello. He prayed harder that night than he ever had before, repeating over and over again his favorite verse. *I am the resurrection and the life. Please, God . . . please heal my granddaughter. Please make a path for me to help.*

After spending his first three years of imprisonment at the West Tennessee State Penitentiary in Henning, Tennessee, Ennis was given the opportunity to serve out the remainder of his sentence at the Giles County Jail in Pulaski. Despite the danger of being incarcerated next to inmates who he might've had a role in arresting, he jumped at the chance to be closer to home. With his family gone, Pulaski was all he had. The town. The people. *His* people.

Then Finnegan Pusser began visiting him in the jail. The hope of an early release and a large sum of money began to become a reality. His prayers had been answered.

He never thought he was doing anything wrong. He didn't lie to Finn. He simply shared information about a few of the townspeople who were bad apples anyway. If Finn used the information to hurt them, then so be it. He should have known there would eventually be a catch for him to receive that much money, but at the time, he didn't think about it. *Beggars can't be choosers . . .*

Ennis took the $100,000 he received from Finn Pusser, rented a car, and drove to Portland. After finding his daughter's house, he waited until he knew she was home. Then he put the briefcase full of cash on his daughter's doorstep, rang the doorbell, and waited a block away. He saw her open it and cried when she cried. The only thing he'd put in the case other than the money was a faded picture of Mae and Belle sitting on Santa Claus's lap when they were both toddlers. He'd kept the picture with him at all times during his incarceration.

He drove home, praying that the money would serve some helpful purpose. He had known he didn't deserve to be in his daughter's or his grandchildren's lives, but he had hoped to one day give restitution for the sins of his past.

Did Jesus approve of his actions?

Ennis wasn't sure. The ambiguities and different interpretations of the Bible confounded him. After reading the whole book during his four years on the inside, he found that the only parts he could stomach to read again were the gospels. *Stick to Jesus,* he thought. When he thought of the other characters in the good book, it was hard not to see the hypocrisy. King David, having Bathsheba's husband murdered so that he could sleep with her. Solomon and his horde of women. Jacob, who tricked his brother, Esau. The ridiculous rules and laws of Exodus and Numbers. It was so easy for a person to use a section or passage of the Bible for his or her own agenda.

Ennis thought of his encounter with Bocephus Haynes the night before. *He'll never forgive me, and if I were him, I wouldn't either.*

Then he closed his eyes and thought back to the Friday before April Fools' Day, a few hours after he'd been granted parole. Of meeting his true benefactor, Michael Zannick, for the first time and receiving the young man's congratulations and thanks.

And a final request.

Ennis had agreed and complied. To get the money he had needed for Mae, he had had no choice. Now he cringed at the consequences of his actions. *I prayed for forgiveness . . . I prayed for a fresh start . . .*

. . . and all I've managed to do is make another awful mess.

Ennis turned west and walked up the hill and past the college. He saw a few students leaving the fine arts center with books under their arms and stressed-out expressions on their faces. Then he paced past the school-bus garage and hung a right on Eighth Street, finishing his trek at Exchange Park, where he used to umpire Little League baseball games at night. By now, the lights were out, and the only remains at the park were empty popcorn cartons and a few half-drunk Gatorade bottles. He went to the storage unit where he kept his blanket, bag of clothes, and shaving kit hidden in an old equipment sack. He cleaned up in the sink of the boys' bathroom, and a few minutes later, Ennis stepped through the gate to the field and lay down on the hard bench inside the covered dugout. He'd prefer to sleep on the outfield grass, but he didn't want to take a chance on being spotted.

Though he was still homeless, he'd finally landed a job working as a janitor and gofer for a Mexican food truck on Industrial Boulevard that had popped up between the Sun Drop Bottling Company and Magneti Marelli Suspensions. The pay was minimum wage, but the money would keep him fed and clothed until he could figure something else out.

He lay on the hard surface of the bench with his eyes open for a long time. He thought of Roosevelt Haynes. The look of fear and anguish in the man's eyes as the noose closed around his neck. He also imagined his granddaughter Mae, her hair taken by chemotherapy and clinging to life. He prayed that the money he'd left on his daughter's porch would help in some way. And that it would be worth the sacrifice he'd made to get it.

Before sleep finally came, Ennis saw the image of another face. One he knew would haunt him too.

The face of Butch Renfroe.

God forgive me, Ennis prayed.

44

The town of Destin was a slice of heaven on the panhandle of Florida's Gulf Coast. Originally a small fishing village, the area's white beaches and emerald-green waters made it one of the most popular vacation spots in the United States, attracting families and tourists from all over.

Bocephus Haynes sipped on a bottle of 30A Beach Blonde Ale, a local brew, and gazed out at Destin Harbor, where a yacht was making its ascent toward the narrow channel that would take it out into the gulf. From his perch on a picnic table at Darla's Oyster Bar, he could see past the harbor to the condominiums on the other side and beyond that to the Gulf of Mexico.

"Nice spot you have here," he said, taking a long pull on the bottle and leaning forward to make sure he could still see his kids. T. J. and Lila were about fifty yards down the Harbor Walk and were sizing up the many boats that were tied to the dock. T. J. had Lee Roy on a leash, and the dog, who had never been to the beach or, for that matter, around much water at all, was wagging his stub of a tail and keeping his head low to the ground and sniffing everything in sight.

"Thank you. I'm pretty proud of it," the woman sitting with him said.

Bo had met Darla Ford during his own trial for the murder of Andy Walton four years earlier. Darla had been a key witness for the defense, as she'd been a dancer at the Sundowners Club at the time of Walton's killing and the last person to see the old man alive. Darla had been the most popular dancer at the Sundowners for years and had saved and invested her money well, always planning to eventually chase her dream of opening an oyster bar on the Gulf Coast. And now here she was, running one of the busiest restaurants in Destin.

"You should be," Bo said, looking around and noticing that, even at 4:30 in the afternoon on a Sunday, the place was full of couples and families both inside the bar and out on the patio where Bo and Darla were now. "I trust business is good."

She snorted. "We aren't at the level of Boshamps or Harbor Docks yet, but we're getting there. The locals seem to enjoy the relaxed vibe, and the new breweries popping up everywhere appreciate that we're trying out their beers. You like that one?"

Bo nodded. "Very much."

"We're still making inroads with the tourists. It's hard to compete with places like the Crab Trap and the Back Porch, which have been around forever, but we're surviving."

Bo pointed at the tables that were occupied behind and in front of them. "Looks as if you're doing better than that."

She didn't answer, and the smile faded from her face. "Mr. Haynes, I'm sorry to cut to the chase, but Sundays get busy around here. How can I help you?"

Bo took another sip of beer and set the bottle down on the table. "Did you hear about the murder in Pulaski in April?"

She grimaced. "Butch Renfroe. I danced for him many a time back in my heyday at the Sundowners." She spoke as a matter of fact with no shame or embarrassment. Darla was a businesswoman then just as she was now. Looking at her tanned olive skin and toned, petite body, it wasn't difficult to imagine Darla in her prior life. She was a very attractive woman.

"I represent General Helen Lewis, who has been charged with Butch's murder."

Darla folded her arms across her chest. "Never liked the General much, but I respected her. She was a mean bitch, but she didn't bullshit you. I got into a few scrapes with the law—it was almost impossible not to as a stripper—and she was fair with me." She hesitated. "Butch and General Lewis were married and divorced, right?"

Bo nodded.

"Well, what do you want from me?"

"Lona Burks said I should talk with you."

Her face darkened. "Really? Lona and I were never close. She did cocaine and meth, and that wasn't my style. I nursed a drink for show when I danced, and I normally threw away the beverages that were bought for me by patrons."

"Lona's been sober for three years and is now working as my legal assistant."

"I'm glad to hear that. She was always smart. Just made bad decisions. Glad to hear she's making better ones."

Bo took another sip from the bottle and collected his thoughts. "You said Butch would come into the Sundowners."

"All the time."

"Who would he come with?"

"Mostly other lawyers. Lou Horn was a frequent flier with Butch. So was Ray Ray Pickalew."

Bo grimaced. Ray Ray Pickalew had been his local counsel during his trial four years ago. He'd been killed in the aftermath of the case, taking several bullets that were meant for Bo.

"Were Horn and Butch tight?"

She shrugged. "Seemed like it."

"Anyone else you can think of?"

"Sometimes Terry Grimes would come in with Butch. Grimes was a county commissioner, and he always seemed nervous and out of place. Probably afraid voters might think differently of him if they found out he enjoyed looking at strippers."

Bo scratched his chin. Grimes was the one who had discovered Butch's body. He was a neighbor, a friend, and according to Ennis Petrie, a coconspirator with Butch in a decades-long prostitution ring. Bo had tried several times to arrange a meeting with the man, who was still a commissioner, but Grimes had thus far been coy and unresponsive.

"I guess you never had any contact with a man named Michael Zannick. Or Finnegan Pusser?"

She shook her head. "I've heard of Zannick, though. He's the boy wonder who's taken the town by storm, right? I have a good friend who's been out with him a few times."

"That wouldn't happen to be Cassie Dugan, would it?"

She smiled and nodded. "Sweet Cassie. I tried for years to convince her to be a dancer at the Sundowners. She could have tripled her income. But Cassie wasn't having it. Her momma taught at the high school and would have been mortified if she learned that her baby was dancing the pole." She paused. "I had hoped that Cassie might have found her meal ticket with Zannick, but based on my last conversation with her, he was teasing her."

"Is that so?"

Darla nodded and glanced at her watch. "Anything else?"

Bo drank down the rest of his beer and sighed. Then he asked the questions he came to ask. "Darla, you lived in Pulaski for a long time and obviously had contact with a lot of people, good and bad, in your line of work back then. Can you think of anyone who might have had a grudge against Butch Renfroe?"

She looked up at the clear sky and frowned. "I really can't. Butch was a softie. I never even saw him get in an argument with anyone." She paused and lowered her eyes to the table. "But all of those guys would have things they wanted kept hidden."

"What things and what guys?"

Darla continued to look down. "Butch, Horn . . . Grimes."

Bo felt gooseflesh on the back of his neck. "What would they want to hide?"

She looked up at him with a blank poker face. "I'm sorry, Mr. Haynes, but I would rather not say. I gave that life up a long time ago and am doing good here in my new one. I don't want to be implicated in anything that's going to drag me back down."

Bo thought about her answer for a half second and decided to plunge in. "Were you aware of a prostitution ring organized by Butch Renfroe, Lou Horn, and Terry Grimes that they operated out of the Sundowners?"

Darla's face flushed red. For the first time, anger seemed to be seeping into her demeanor. "Aware?" She paused. "Yes."

"Did you participate in it?"

"No comment," she said, shooting off her chair. "This conversation is over."

Bo also stood and reached out for her hand. "Darla, please. The General's life is at stake here. If you know of anything that might be helpful—"

"I'm sorry, Mr. Haynes. I really am. But this world is a mean place, and I've learned that you've got to take care of number one."

"But the General—"

"Fuck the General. I don't owe her anything, and as I recall, I've already done you a big favor in your life. I'm not doing any more. Now let go of my hand."

Bo did as she asked and watched her stride toward the door leading inside. Before reaching it, she wheeled around to face him. "If you want to know the ins and outs of that ring, the person you'd be wise to talk with is your new assistant."

Bo opened his mouth and then closed it.

"Don't come back, Mr. Haynes," Darla said. "Ever."

As he turned his eyes back to the Harbor Walk, where his children and dog were still milling about, he felt frustrated and confused.

But not deterred. If anything, he was invigorated.

And whatever the secrets were that Butch Renfroe, Lou Horn, and Terry Grimes had in their closets . . .

. . . *they might be worth killing to keep hidden.*

45

On Thursday, May 28, 2015, at 3:55 p.m., Bo walked through the double doors of the circuit courtroom in the Giles County Courthouse. He felt a combination of butterflies in his stomach and adrenaline as he approached the bench, where Judge Harold Page was already flipping through some documents. Below His Honor, Lou Horn and Michael Zannick huddled together at the defense table, while Sack Glover was sitting on the prosecution side with his legs crossed and jotting some notes down on a yellow pad.

When the doors jarred closed, all the men turned to look at Bo. As a six-foot four-inch man practicing law in a predominantly white county where he was the only black trial attorney, Bo was used to other lawyers staring at him when he entered a courtroom, but those looks were normally more of curiosity. The predominant vibe he felt emanating in this room was irritation.

"What are you doing here?" Sack asked as Bo made his way toward the front.

While he approached them, Bo noticed that the gallery, which had been full for Helen Lewis's preliminary hearing, was empty and that there were no other attorneys in the courtroom.

Bo ignored the prosecutor and focused on the judge. "Your Honor, I understood that there was a settlement docket this afternoon." He glanced to his left and right. "I'm here for the Michael Zannick matter. Are there not any other cases set?"

Page grunted. "I called the other cases this morning. I don't remember your name being listed as an additional attorney for Mr. Zannick."

"I represent the victim, Your Honor. Ms. Amanda Burks."

Page raised his eyebrows and moved his gaze to Sack Glover. Bo did the same. Sack's face had turned as red as his hair. "Judge, we've reached a settlement of this case," Sack said, slamming his pen on the pad and standing up. "We've been trying to communicate with Ms. Burks, but she hasn't been responding to calls. I—"

"That's a lie, Sack, and you know it."

"Don't come in here and make accusations you can't back up. Who do you think you are?"

Bo glared at him. "I'm Bocephus Haynes, lawyer for the minor victim, Amanda Burks, and Mandy's mother has asked that you communicate with me."

Sack looked up at the bench for help. Judge Page had taken off his glasses and was chewing on one of the stems. "Well, General Glover, I'd suggest you tell Mr. Haynes the terms of the settlement agreement."

Sack's mouth formed a tight grin. "Of course, Your Honor. After reviewing the facts and having discussions with defense counsel, I've agreed to dismiss the charges against Mr. Zannick upon the payment of court costs and the completion of one hundred hours of community service."

Bo shook his head and looked at Lou Horn. The crusty old attorney, who was rounder than Bo had remembered, had a pasty red tint to him. If Bo didn't know any better, he'd swear the man had probably already had a few alcoholic beverages. "Well, that's quite a sweetheart deal, Lou. Mr. Zannick must be paying you well."

"I felt it was a fair deal given the he-said-she-said nature of the allegations and the credibility of the victim compared to the defendant."

As Bo was about to speak, he heard the squeak of the double doors opening and then the thud of them closing. He turned, but he already knew who would be there. Aldos Stanley, the gray-bearded editor-in-chief of the *Pulaski Citizen*, stepped into the courtroom, nodded at Bo, and took a seat in the front row of the gallery. He had a spiral notebook with him, opening it and pressing his pen to paper.

"Who invited him?" Sack asked.

"I did." Bo said. "I wanted him here to see the acting district attorney general try to dismiss charges against one of his biggest campaign contributors on a rape case without talking to the victim." Bo paused. "On apparently a special setting for a settlement hearing after all the other cases were heard this morning."

"Bo, I don't like the use of the press in this fashion," Judge Page said. "I'm tempted to hold you in contempt."

Bo frowned. "For reminding the press of the docket? There's nothing privileged or confidential about a settlement docket, is there, Judge?"

Page scowled but didn't say anything. "I take it that you, as the victim's attorney, do not approve of the deal reached between Mr. Glover and Mr. Horn."

"I do not approve," Bo said. "I will never approve of a settlement of this case, and I think it is unethical and immoral for Sack Glover to be the prosecutor for this case. General Helen Lewis should be the prosecutor."

Page held his scowl. "General Lewis has been stripped of her duties, Bo, as you well know, being her attorney too." He exhaled and looked first at Sack and then Lou. "Gentlemen, under the circumstances and based on the issues raised by the victim's attorney, I do not feel I can approve the settlement you've reached. Also, until we can get some resolution on whether it is appropriate for General Glover to prosecute this case, I'm going to have no choice but to issue another continuance." He stood from the bench. "This hearing is adjourned."

46

An hour later, at a table in the back of Kathy's Tavern, Bo and Lona clinked glasses. Bo was drinking a cold Yuengling from a frosty mug, while Lona had a Diet Coke. After informing his assistant of Judge Page's decision, she had insisted that they celebrate their victory.

"How can I ever repay you?" Lona asked. "Those turds were about to throw my baby's case out the window."

"I was glad to do it," Bo said. "I just wish I could do more."

"You can sue the prick."

Bo drank another sip of beer. "Not yet. There's a one-year statute of limitations, and we still have a few months before it expires. I don't want to sue Zannick until the criminal charges are resolved."

She nodded her agreement.

"But in the meantime, let's get Mandy into the office so I can speak to her, and then I'll work on getting something drafted. As soon as there is a conviction or, worst case, a dismissal under the terms set out today, we can file suit."

Lona brought her glass up for another toast. "Sounds good."

This time, Bo didn't join in the toast.

"Is something wrong?" Lona asked.

"I was thinking that there *is* something you can do for me."

"Anything," she said.

"Good." He drained the rest of his beer in one long gulp. "I need you to tell me everything you know about the prostitution ring that was run out of the Sundowners Club by Butch Renfroe, Lou Horn, and Terry Grimes."

47

On the second floor of the Yellow Deli, Michael Zannick stirred Splenda into his glass of unsweet tea. It had been a long time since Zannick had been angry. Up until this afternoon, almost everything about his sixteen months in Pulaski had gone exactly as he had planned it. But Bocephus Haynes had thrown a wrench into his plans when he showed up as Mandy Burks's lawyer and blew up the settlement.

Zannick peered across the table at his phone. He'd already been forced to break the news to Ichiro Hoshima, the president and great-grandson of the founder of the Japanese auto manufacturer.

Mr. Hoshima had been polite but had reiterated the company line since the rape charge had been filed. "We want to do this deal with you, Michael, but we can't take the risk of signing the contract and then have you be convicted of a sex crime." He had paused. "And we aren't willing to announce a deal until you are exonerated. Otherwise, we risk having a public relations nightmare."

Zannick had said he understood and had told Ichiro that he would keep him apprised of the status.

Now, Zannick glared at his phone as if it were a traitor. Finally, he snatched the device and made the call.

Finn answered on the first ring.

"I think it's time I heed your advice as it concerns Mr. Haynes," Zannick said, pausing and sipping his tea.

"You want me to send him a message?"

"Yes, I do, but I don't want any screwups in the delivery like you had with Mr. Rowe."

"Don't worry, brother," Finn said, his tone grim. "The message will be delivered."

48

Lona wrung her hands and gazed at her half-drunk Diet Coke. Next to it, the cheeseburger she'd ordered was untouched. "I'm sorry. Those days are hazy. I was messed up on coke and meth so much that everything kind of runs together."

Bo reached out and touched her hand. "Thank you for telling me. If you don't mind me asking, who was looking after Mandy on the nights you worked at the Sundowners?"

"My aunt Kathy watched her for me. She's dead now. Passed about three years ago."

Bo nodded. "Around the time you quit drugs and went to rehab. Was her death what cleaned you up?"

Lona finally looked at him. Her eyes had glistened over with tears. "Not really. Kathy was good to me, but she never told me the deal. It was the General who helped me get clean. When I finally got busted for possession, she was hard on me but fair. She placed me in a good rehab program, and it took." She wiped her eyes. "I owe her."

Bo took a sip of water. Once Lona had started telling her knowledge of the ring, he'd stopped drinking beer, thinking it wasn't appropriate given the circumstances. "I hate to recap, but I'm a lawyer, and that's what I do. You've told me that the dancers you are aware of who were in the ring were Darla Ford, yourself, Tammie Gentry, Candy Peterson, and Richelle Cooper."

She nodded and bit her lip.

"None of who still live in Pulaski, correct?"

"Correct. Darla is obviously in Destin, and I don't know where the others are."

Bo sighed and ate a bite of a french fry. Unlike his assistant, he had wolfed down his cheeseburger, which was the house specialty. "Even if we were to find the others, I suspect their attitude will be the same as Darla's."

"They aren't going to incriminate themselves."

Bo pointed the fry at her. "You remember Terry Grimes being one of your customers?"

She again averted her eyes, peering at the framed photographs of the country music singers who'd played at the club. "Terry was a regular."

"Were all of your . . . times with him at the Sundowners?"

"Mostly, we were up in one of the two VIP rooms, but not always. Terry liked to use the Sands Motor Hotel out by Highway 64."

"The one by the interstate?"

She nodded. "I'd meet him there on Sunday afternoons after church. He said he told his wife he had to do paperwork at the dealership and that was the only time he could do it." She paused and shook her head. "We'd swim in the pool and have a couple of vodka and tonics. Then, when he was good and loose, we'd go up to a room, do a couple of lines of coke on the pocket mirror I kept in my purse, and then . . ." She trailed off.

"What about Butch Renfroe or Lou Horn? Did you ever meet either of them as part of the ring?"

She gave her head a jerk. "No. I had other suitors, but Terry was who always requested me."

"Was it Terry who paid you?"

"No. I got my money from Larry Tucker. He owned the Sundowners and took a percentage off the top of the ring because most of the trysts happened at his club."

"I see," Bo said, picking up another fry but then setting it down without eating it. "So Terry might say that he was just having an affair."

She held out her palms. "I guess he could, but Larry paid me for each trick I turned."

"Larry's dead, and I assume all the payments were made in cash."

She nodded and then placed her hands over her face. "I haven't been much help, have I?"

Bo again squeezed her hand. "On the contrary, this information is very helpful. It gives me an angle to work with Terry Grimes. He's been avoiding my calls and attempts to see him. This prostitution ring is a possible alternative theory to Butch's murder."

"You think Butch was planning to confess the ring and implicate Terry and Lou and he got killed for it?"

Bo leaned back in his chair and sighed. "I don't know, OK? But Terry Grimes is who found him, and the only prints in the house other than Butch's and the General's belonged to Terry." Bo popped his knuckles on the table. "He's our best option as an alternative killer, and I don't think the sheriff's office has done near enough to investigate him." Bo stood from the table. "You ready?"

"I'm sorry I ruined our celebration."

"You did exactly what I asked you to do. Thank you, Lona."

She stood and leaned toward him, grabbing him tight by the forearm. "If you need me to testify to what I did with Terry, I'll do it. The General saved my life."

Bo shook his head. "I can't let you do that, Lona. You have a daughter to think about."

"And you have a case to try and win. If I'm your best evidence of the ring, you have to call me." She paused and squinted at him. "Unless you think that my testimony is not credible because, in addition to being a coke and meth addict and a stripper with a criminal record, I was also a road whore."

Bo didn't say anything.

"That's it, isn't it? My testimony is worthless because I'm worthless."

"That's not true."

Lona turned and walked toward the exit.

"Lona, wait." As Bo began to follow after her, he observed two men rise from a table in the corner.

Bo ran to catch up with her and grabbed her by the hand. In his peripheral vision, he saw the men approaching and then passing them. One had on a plaid flannel shirt, and the other a camouflage T-shirt and matching pants. They looked like two good old boys who had gone hunting and were drinking a few beers afterward.

But Bo knew better. One of the men drove a burgundy pickup truck and the other a gray sedan. He'd seen them parked outside his office. At the courthouse. Even down from Davis & Eslick Grocery when he'd dropped in for some milk. He'd last seen them on Saturday evening when he was coming out of the Hickory House after meeting Booker T. for a steak.

"Please let me go, Bo. I'm sorry. I know you're probably right, but I—"

"I need you to sit at the bar for a second," Bo said, noticing that the two men were now walking out the front door. Bo had never seen them together, and his instincts were on high alert. He'd thwarted the settlement of the rape charge against Michael Zannick a couple of hours earlier, and he sensed that tonight's assignment for the two followers was more involved.

Bo looked past Lona to the bar, where Cassie Dugan, dressed in a number 16 Peyton Manning Tennessee Volunteer jersey, cutoff jeans, and a brown-and-gold Giles County Bobcats mesh cap, was pouring whiskey into a glass over ice. "Cassie, can you bring Lona here another Diet Coke?" His tone was harsh and direct. The bartender raised her eyebrows.

"Yes, sir," Cassie said.

"I need you to do something else for me."

"What's that?"

"Call the police."

Her face went pale. "Why?"

Bo felt adrenaline surge through his veins. "Just do it."

49

Bo sensed movement the second he opened the door. Ready for it, he crouched and saw a piece of lumber barely miss the top of his head. Bo saw Finn Pusser's eyes go wide with shock as his beating stick split open when it hit the front door to Kathy's Tavern. Bo flung a left jab that connected with the man's nose and a right uppercut that landed so hard he heard bone crack. Finn's head shot back, and he groaned in pain. He fell to the sidewalk and rolled, reaching underneath his shirt for what was sure to be a handgun of some kind.

Before Finn could bring the weapon forward, Bo kicked him in the ribs. Finn's hand dropped to his side, and Bo kicked him again. Then again and again. He reached into his pocket and pulled out his Glock, putting his size-eleven loafer on Finn Pusser's neck. "You listen, and you listen like you never have before. You've had your way in this town for a long time, but you're dealing with something different now. Something you can't control." He eased his foot off the man's neck.

"You think you're some kind of badass, don't you?" Finn spat blood out of his mouth. "You weren't the target tonight, Haynes." He laughed and spat another stream of blood out of his mouth. "You really should've changed the locks on your office."

Bo stepped away from Finn, darting his eyes down First Street toward his law firm. He blinked, and then he saw the burgundy truck pulling away.

"What did you do?" Bo asked, screaming down at Finn, who was now rising to his feet.

"I'd run if I were you. You might at least be able to save your dog."

"What?" Bo asked, feeling a wave of panic wash over him. He took another step backward and heard the first police siren. Then, turning toward his office, he started to run but only made it a few feet before the world turned blood orange.

And his eardrums filled with the sound of the explosion.

50

Bo felt like he was reliving a nightmare.

In his recurring dream, which he'd lived out second by painful second a year and a half ago, he ran toward Jazz, reaching her just as the bullets entered her body and killed her. He couldn't stop her from being murdered, and now he wouldn't be able to stop this. His white Sequoia had exploded. So had Lona Burks's Mustang coupe. The fire from the two vehicles had spread, and by the time Bo was within twenty yards of his building, the flames had consumed the entire front of his office.

Where Lee Roy likes to sleep.

"No!" he screamed, running around to the rear of the building. "Lee Roy!"

When he reached the back door, he saw smoke but no flames. Bo took off his suit jacket and wrapped it around his neck. "Lee Roy!" he screamed, praying that his dog had run to safety, but there was no sign of him.

Bo sucked in a deep breath and stepped toward the door. He was about to barrel through it when a figure came out of it covered in a blanket and collapsed on the ground. Before Bo could fling the quilt off the person, something wiggled out from underneath.

Lee Roy's white-and-brown coat of hair was charred dark black, but otherwise the dog seemed unscathed by the explosion. Bo dropped to his knees and let out a howl, wrapping his arms around the animal, who licked his face.

Then, blinking his eyes and getting his bearings, he looked behind the dog to the figure who was taking off the blanket.

Ennis Petrie coughed and struggled for breath as the wail of fire truck sirens permeated the night air. Ennis crouched in front of Lee Roy and petted him behind the ears. Then he looked at Bo. "Don't tell anyone I was here."

Bo couldn't think of anything to say. He was in shock.

Ennis patted his back and brushed past him.

Cradling his dog in his arms, Bo turned and watched the former lawman until he disappeared from view.

51

At the sheriff's department thirty minutes later, Bo gave a statement to Chief Deputy Frannie Storm about what had happened, telling her everything except the part about Ennis Petrie saving his dog. Frannie had driven Bo and Lona to her office in her patrol car, and Bo was now sitting in a chair in the large conference room and sipping a cup of coffee. Behind him, Lona Burks paced and fretted. "Have you sent anyone to Zannick's place yet?"

"We need to make sure we understand what happened first, Ms. Burks," Frannie said, her voice calm and deliberate.

Lona came to an abrupt stop and put her hands on her hips. "Well, I can tell you exactly what happened. Bo showed up at Michael Zannick's rape charge settlement docket today. Bo represented my daughter's interests and made sure the judge didn't approve the sweetheart deal that Sack Glover had proposed that would have dismissed the charges against Zannick. Then Bo gets attacked a couple of hours later, our cars get blown up, and his office nearly burns to the ground." She glared at Frannie. "I'd say it's pretty obvious who's behind this. Same prick who raped my daughter."

Frannie wrote in longhand on a notepad and then looked at Bo. "Bo, we've detained a man named Finnegan Pusser. Is he the man who . . . attacked you?"

"Why the hesitation, Chief?" Bo asked.

Frannie's mouth formed a tiny smile. "Because we can't question him until he gets out of the hospital. According to the ER doctor, he has a broken nose, cracked chin, and four broken ribs."

"Did you see the shattered piece of lumber at the front door of Kathy's Tavern?"

Frannie nodded. "What happened?"

"I stepped out of the door, and Pusser swung and missed." Bo paused and glared at the chief. "I didn't miss."

"What is Pusser's beef with you?"

Bo cocked his head at Lona, who still had her hands on her hips. "What she said. We got the best of Michael Zannick at the settlement docket today, and this was retaliation."

"You're confident of that?"

Bo stood from the chair. "Listen, rookie, I don't have time for this mess. I need to go check on my office, or what's left of it." He headed for the door with Lona in tow.

"Mr. Haynes?" Frannie called after him.

Bo didn't stop or even acknowledge her.

"I'm sorry," Frannie said.

"You been saying that a lot lately," Bo said, pausing at the door with his back to the chief deputy. "And you're going to be saying it a lot more when a jury finds Helen Lewis not guilty of her ex-husband's murder."

52

Bo entered the jail the next morning with a renewed sense of purpose. The adrenaline rush that he'd experienced the previous night when he'd fended off Finn Pusser and then witnessed the dual explosions of his and Lona's cars hadn't dissipated.

All his senses were engaged. When he stepped into the consultation room, he didn't bother with pleasantries. "I went to Michael Zannick's rape charge hearing yesterday and blew up the settlement agreement that he'd reached with Sack Glover."

Helen let out a sigh of relief. "What was the deal?"

"Dismissal of the rape charges on payment of court costs and one hundred hours of community service."

Helen flew off the chair like she'd been shot out of a rocket. "That sorry, lazy sack of shit."

"Relax, General," Bo said, holding up his hands. "As attorney for the victim, Amanda Burks, I objected to the proposal and obtained a continuance of the settlement docket and trial until such time as the Honorable Harold Page can figure out whether there is an ethical dilemma with Sack Glover prosecuting his chief campaign contributor."

Helen smiled. "How'd you manage it?"

"I set out my position . . . and I invited Aldos Stanley to the proceedings."

Helen clapped her hands together. "Smart move. Page has never been one to invite publicity."

Bo started to agree and then heard several loud knocks on the door. He got up as Frannie Storm entered the small room. She glanced at Bo and then at Helen. "The grand jury has issued an indictment against you, General. Your arraignment has been set for June 5 at 9:00 a.m., which is a week from today." She turned to Bo. "I wanted you to hear the news as soon as possible."

"Big of you," Bo said. The chief deputy wouldn't be getting any thank-yous from him. Once Chief Storm had left the room, there was a period of silence as Bo and Helen processed what they had been told. At the arraignment, Helen would plead not guilty. Then Judge Connelly would set the case for trial.

Helen cleared her throat. "Have you learned anything more about that prostitution ring?"

"I've confirmed its existence with Darla Ford . . . and Lona Burks."

"Lona?" Helen asked.

Bo gave a solemn nod.

"Will either of them agree to testify?"

"Darla won't. She wouldn't even admit to the ring, but her reaction to my mentioning it gave her away. Lona will, but . . ." His voice trailed off.

"But she's not a credible witness."

"No, she's not. But even if she was, we still don't have any evidence linking the ring to Butch's murder."

"But we're closer," Helen said.

Bo grinned. "Yes, we are."

"And you should have more information this afternoon, right?"

Bo nodded and leaned his back against the wall. He pulled his phone out and checked the time. It was already past ten, and he was due in Decatur at one.

And I have a stop to make along the way . . .

"I've got to go, General." Bo returned the cell to his pocket and headed for the door.

"Bo?"

He looked over his shoulder.

"Keep at it." She smiled at him, and it was the first time he'd seen even a tinge of happiness in her face since she'd shown up at the Hazel Green farm the night after Butch Renfroe's murder.

"Wide ass open," Bo said, winking at her as he left the jail.

53

Terry Grimes Ford/Buick was located on West College Street a half mile past the Legends Steakhouse. Bo took a cab to the dealership and walked into the all-glass display area in no mood to be accosted by car salesmen. "I need to see Terry Grimes," Bo told the twenty-something blonde who greeted him with an energetic "What can we do for you, sir?"

"I'm sorry, Mr. . . ."

"Haynes. Bocephus Haynes. I need to see Mr. Grimes right away."

"Well, Mr. Grimes is showing a car to someone. Could you—"

"Wait? No, I can't wait. If Mr. Grimes isn't standing in front of me in two minutes, I'm going to start ranting and raving about how racist this place is and how a black man can't even get an audience with the manager." Bo took out his phone. "Pulling up my Facebook page now. Smile for the camera, Goldilocks."

The saleswoman hustled away, saying she'd be right back with Mr. Grimes, and Bo took in the display room's dimensions. There were three sets of entrance doors, and Bo noticed surveillance cameras above each of them. *This place has cameras all over,* he figured.

Seconds later, Terry Grimes came striding forward with a fake smile plastered on his face. "Well, hello, Bo. Come to check out our new line of Explorers?"

"Maybe," Bo said. "But first I want to talk about that prostitution ring that you, Butch Renfroe, and Lou Horn have been running out of the Sundowners Club for the past twenty years." Bo turned to the blonde saleslady, whose mouth hung open in shock. "Might want to give us some privacy, ma'am."

"Yeah, Tyra, let me have a moment alone with Mr. Haynes."

Once she was gone, Terry started to speak, but Bo beat him to it. "In your office," Bo said. "Now."

Terry again smiled. "Right this way."

———

As Bo curled through the display room and into the bowels of the dealership, he noticed cameras in the corners of each hallway. Once they were inside Terry's office with the door closed, Bo sized up the six-term county commissioner. Like Sack Glover, Terry wore a custom-fit suit, and his salt-and-pepper hair didn't have a follicle out of place. The ever-present smile was still there, but the man's eyes were hard and unblinking.

"First things first," Bo began. "I need to rent an Explorer for the time being. A black one. Leather seats. Plush, with one of those back-up cameras. I like those."

Terry folded his arms across his chest. "OK. Fine. When do you need—?"

"Now," Bo said. "Have Goldilocks or one of your other goons bring it around front. Fill out the paperwork for me, and I'll be back this evening to complete it."

"How long a lease?"

"The minimum. Just need something temporary."

"Fine, we'll set you up with a twelve-month program. We're open until 11:00 p.m., so swing by any time and you can sign everything." He paused. "Mind telling me why you need a car in such a rush?"

"Mine blew up last night. You might have heard about it."

Terry wrinkled his face up in confusion.

"No?" Bo asked, cocking his head. "Terry, come on now, you mean to tell me that a politically connected gossipmonger like yourself didn't know that two vehicles exploded on First Street last night and almost burned down the law office of Bocephus Haynes?"

"I heard about a fire but didn't know you were involved," Terry said, smiling again.

"Tell me something, Terry. When your wife asks if you've been stepping out on her, do you smile that same smile when you lie to her? Or how about when your doctor asks about the rash you keep getting on your balls or the purple tint to your lips? Herpes is a bitch, ain't it?"

Terry made a tent with his hands and placed them on his stomach. "Are we done here, Bo? I have other cars to sell."

"No, we're not done. I know about the prostitution ring. I know *all* about it. Some of those old strippers at the Sundowners Club have loose lips, and one of them just so happens to work for me now. Clandestine Sunday afternoons at the old Sands Motor Court. A little swimming. A few cocktails. A line of coke. And finishing things off with a nice pickle tickle or two. Sound familiar?"

Terry's smile had faded into a toothless grimace, as if he was trying to pass gas and hadn't succeeded yet. "I'd like you to leave. And I think I'm going to forgo leasing you that car."

"Oh, really. Well, the first thing I'm going to do when I get back in the display area is tell everyone there that you told me that you wouldn't sell a car to a nigger. Then I'm going to go live on Facebook. Ever heard of going live? My son and daughter do it all the time. It drives me crazy. But yeah, Terry, I'm going to go live and tell all of my friends what a racist organization this is. Might even set up an exclusive with Aldos Stanley of the *Pulaski Citizen*. How'd that be?" Bo rose from his seat and walked to the door. As he grasped the knob, he spoke without looking at Terry. "I think you're dirty, Terry. You ran whores in this county for two decades while maintaining your squeaky-clean image, and I'm planning on telling this county exactly who Terrence Robert Grimes really is."

"I'll sue you for every dime you own."

Bo finally turned and looked over his shoulder at the car salesman. "Truth is an absolute defense to slander." He smiled. "I know this because I'm a lawyer. At the trial of Helen Lewis, Pulaski is finally going to know all about your sins."

"Even if you could prove what you're talking about, how in the world would any of that be relevant to Butch's murder?"

Bo grinned. "I don't know, Terry. You were the one who found him dead, weren't you? You're the one who called the police. You're the one whose fingerprints are found all over his house."

"I was his neighbor, and he was my friend."

"Yeah, dog. I look forward to hearing your explanations." He paused. "I'm sure the jury will too."

———

A minute later, Bo brushed past the blonde-haired saleswoman, asking her as he passed, "Is my ride ready?"

"Right out front, Mr. Haynes. The keys are in the ignition."

Bo blew her a kiss as he exited the building.

———

Back in his office, Terry Grimes sucked on an inhaler and tried to remain calm. *Who in the hell does he think he is talking to me like that?* After catching his breath, he grabbed his phone and clicked the number for Lou Horn.

"Yeah," Lou answered on the first ring.

"We got a problem," Terry said.

"Zannick?"

"No," Terry said, wiping sweat off his forehead. "Worse. Bocephus Haynes came to see me this afternoon."

"And?"

"And he knows about the ring."

For a long ten seconds, the only sound on the other end of the line was Lou's ragged breathing. Then, after coughing and clearing his throat, he summed up the situation with succinct perfection. "Shit."

54

Decatur, Alabama, is a midsize town that sits on the banks of Wheeler Lake along the Tennessee River. Bo had spent very little time in the town during his legal career and had to use the GPS on his phone to direct him to his private investigator's riverfront office. Though his new car had been a means to an end—he had wanted to rile up Terry Grimes—he had to admit that the Explorer drove pretty smoothly. Regardless, he'd be returning it tonight without signing the lease.

When he exited the elevator, he saw a nondescript door with the following legend stenciled across the top: HOOPER, PI.

Bo knocked on the door, and when there was no answer, he turned the knob.

When he walked inside, he stepped into a large conference room with a huge window overlooking the water. Hooper was seated at the table wearing the same crimson Alabama cap he'd had on when he had driven Bo home the night of the custody hearing along with an oxford button-down, khaki shorts, and sandals. No one would confuse the man with Columbo. He had earbuds in his ears and a half-eaten sandwich in front of him. There were two other sandwiches on the table along with several bags of chips. The white bag that the food presumably had once been in said "Whitt's Barbecue" in brown letters.

Seeing him, Hooper ripped off his earpieces and stood. Bo thought he could make out the sound of Whitesnake's "Here I Go Again" before Hooper clicked his phone and the music ended. "Mr. Haynes."

"Hooper."

Bo sat down and gestured at the sack and sandwiches. "Lunch?"

"Yes, please grab a pork sandwich. Whitt's is my favorite barbecue joint in town."

Bo smiled and snatched one of the sandwiches. He was famished and ate half of it before he opened his mouth to talk again. He had to admit that the pork was fantastic. "Before we start, I have to know one thing."

"Albert," Hooper said. "My first name is Albert. You know . . . like Fat Albert."

"Hey, hey, hey." Bo mimicked the cartoon character, but neither of them laughed. "I'll stick with Hooper."

"Good."

"Tell me about Zannick."

The investigator stuck a chip in his mouth and grabbed a remote control from the table. He clicked it, and a movie projector screen began to drop from the wall closest to them.

Bo frowned at the screen and then swept his eyes around the plush conference room. "If you don't mind me asking, how does a private investigator afford digs like this? I know it ain't from being an Uber driver."

"My parents died rich and left me a boatload of money," Hooper said, taking a bite of his sandwich.

"Then why the hell did you choose to be a private dick."

He smiled and spoke with his mouth full. "Because I'm good at it."

55

Two hours later, as he drove his "leased" Explorer over the Tennessee River Bridge and hopped on I-565 toward Huntsville, Bo had to agree that Albert Hooper was a very good investigator. Bo's brain was still buzzing with the information that Hooper had displayed on his projector in a detailed PowerPoint presentation.

Michael Zannick had grown up in Boston, Massachusetts, the only son of Henry and Patricia Zannick. Henry Zannick was a professor of mathematics at Boston University, and Patricia worked in marketing for the New England Patriots. Michael attended elementary and middle school in the Boston neighborhood of Charlestown and graduated from Charlestown High School in May of 1996. Thereafter, he obtained a full scholarship to the Massachusetts Institute of Technology, where he went on to graduate with honors in 2000 with a degree in computer science. Zannick worked in computer design with several companies in the Boston area until 2005, when he became one of the earliest investors in the social media phenomenon known as Facebook, which had been founded by a Harvard University student named Mark Zuckerberg. By 2010, Zannick, who also invested in Twitter and Instagram, had accumulated a net worth of close to $100 million. He bought his parents a historic three-story brownstone in Charlestown and himself a palatial mansion and a thousand acres in the Berkshires.

On October 1, 2013, his parents were killed in a plane crash off the coast of Cape Cod. The airplane was a private twin-engine plane that Michael had sent to fly his mother and father to the cape for a family vacation that ended in tragedy. Two months later, after selling his mansion and his parents' home in Charlestown, Zannick moved to Pulaski, Tennessee. He bought a hundred acres on Highway 31, and within a year, moved into a six-thousand-square-foot home, complete with a man-made lake, swimming pool, and even a zip line through the woods in back. Hooper showed Bo pictures that he'd snapped of the mansion with his drone last month. During construction, Zannick rented a home on Jefferson Street in downtown Pulaski. In his first six months as a resident of Giles County, Zannick formed Z Bank, a new lending institution, with the help of local attorney Butch Renfroe. He also bought several properties along College Street and three thousand acres of farmland off Highway 64 comprising seven different tracts.

Bo reviewed the tracts with Hooper, noticing that the only property Zannick hadn't bought was Walton Farm.

Zannick was known to be in negotiations with Hoshima Automotive, an up-and-coming Japanese auto manufacturer, to construct and operate a manufacturing plant on fifteen hundred of the contiguous acres on Highway 64. The plant would assemble the Hoshima Family Wagon minivan and a new midsize pickup truck that Hoshima was calling the Bobcat.

The Hoshima deal stalled when, in November of 2014, Michael Zannick was charged with the forcible rape of fifteen-year-old Amanda Burks.

As for family beyond parents, Zannick's best friend throughout elementary, middle, and high school was a male named Finnegan McElwain Pusser. Finn was born in Dublin, Ireland, and he and his parents moved to Boston when Finn was in the third grade. Three years later, Finn's mother and father died in a car accident. After their funerals, and at Michael's urging, the Zannicks adopted the boy.

Finn Pusser graduated with Michael in the Charlestown High class of 1996, but there was no record of him going to any college. He enlisted in the navy in 1997 and received a general discharge in 2003.

From 2008 to October 2013, Finn worked exclusively for Michael Zannick in "security," based on reports from field hands who worked at the house in the Berkshires. When Zannick moved to Pulaski in December 2013, Pusser didn't come with him. Only when Zannick bought and reopened the Sundowners Club did Pusser move to Pulaski to run the exotic dance club for his adopted brother.

Zannick had no known living relatives other than Pusser. According to Hooper's extensive review of the yearbooks at both Charlestown High and MIT, Zannick had no college or high school classmates who lived within a hundred miles.

With respect to medical history, Zannick had cleft-lip-repair surgery at Massachusetts General Hospital in 1985. There were no other known surgeries or medical conditions.

Zannick donated over a million dollars to Martin Methodist College and more than a hundred thousand to the First United Methodist Church. He sat on the board of directors of the college, the Southern Regional Tennessee Health System, and the local Boys & Girls Club. When asked in an interview for the Martin Methodist College newspaper why he had left the Berkshires to come to Pulaski, Zannick confided that "I just couldn't live where my parents had died. I felt responsible and wanted to move as far away as possible and start a completely new and different life."

Bo had memorized the quote from Hooper's presentation because it was the only evidence he had of why Michael Zannick had come to Pulaski.

The Zannick story was interesting and tragic, and Hooper had done more than what Bo had asked.

But at the end of the day, there was no link to the murder of Butch Renfroe.

Which puts me right back at square one, Bo thought, feeling his spirits begin to sink as he entered the Huntsville city limits.

56

Bo's mood improved dramatically when he parked at Baskin-Robbins off Airport Road in Huntsville and saw T. J. and Lila waiting for him at one of the tables. Though it wasn't his weekend, Ezra and Juanita had relented and let him see the children since he was passing through town.

Once they had made their orders and had their ice cream cones, Lila leaned forward in her chair. "How's your case going, Daddy?" she asked, smiling at him with her mother's eyes.

"Good, honey," Bo said, but he knew that wasn't true.

"We're proud of you, Dad," T. J. said, licking his sugar cone of pralines and cream. "Opening your office back up and practicing law again. You know, we've been thinking . . ." He trailed off, and Bo saw Lila punch her brother's shoulder.

"Ask him," she pressed.

"Ask me what?" Bo said, moving his eyes from his fourteen-year-old daughter to his seventeen-year-old son. "Ask me what?" he repeated.

"Dad, what would you say if . . . maybe . . . I don't know . . ."

"Spit it out, Thomas Jackson."

"Can we move back to Pulaski?" Lila blurted the question.

Bo wrinkled up his face. It was the last thing he had expected to hear.

"I miss my friends, Daddy."

Bo scratched the back of his neck. "Well . . . haven't you made new friends?"

"Sure, but we lived in Pulaski for a long time. I miss Kara and Ellery and Hunter."

Bo smiled, remembering the clique of girls who used to come over to the house on Flower Street and stay up all night watching those High School Musical Disney movies. Then he turned to his son. "T. J., could you really leave your teammates at Huntsville High?"

The boy sighed and looked more like he was twenty-five than seventeen. "It would be hard, Dad, but I miss my friends from Pulaski too." He lowered his voice. "Mom was the one who hated it. Mom and Mammy and Pops. We always loved the town."

Bo sighed. "There are a whole lot more black folks in Huntsville."

"That doesn't matter," Lila said. "You and Momma taught us to treat everybody the same. Black, white, or purple."

Bo chuckled. "That's true, honey, but sometimes the rest of the world doesn't act like it should."

She frowned. "Pulaski is home, Daddy." She paused. "And even though Mommy didn't like it, I have more memories of her there than here. All I remember about here is her getting shot." The girl's lip began to tremble, and Bo saw that T. J. had looked away, not able to take the pain of his sister's tears. Bo leaned in and hugged his daughter's neck. "I miss her too, baby." Then, feeling his son's hand on his own neck, Bo put his arm around T. J. and brought them in for a group hug. "I love you guys. I'm sorry I've made such a mess of things."

After they finally had all let go of the embrace, Lila spoke again. "Will you think about it, Daddy?"

Bo set his jaw and gave a firm nod. "Yes, I will."

57

At 8:00 p.m., Bo drove the leased Explorer into the dealership lot at Terry Grimes Ford/Buick. He cut the ignition and walked through the double doors in front.

Before he'd even finished his first step inside, he heard a voice to his left and a man rushing toward him with a stack of papers. "Mr. Haynes, I'm Chase Robinson. Mr. Grimes had to leave, but I have all your paperwork—"

"Save it, Chase," Bo said, talking loud enough for the other patrons in the display area to hear him. "The brakes were loose, the tires slipped all over the road, and the damn thing wouldn't start after my meeting in Decatur. I wouldn't wish this piece of junk on my worst enemy."

"But, Mr. Haynes. You leased the car."

Bo smiled. "No, I didn't. You see my signature on any of those documents?"

Chase gazed at the documents, his face turning red. "But you told Mr. Grimes . . ."

Bo slapped the kid on the shoulder. "Tell him I changed my mind."

———

In the parking lot three minutes later, Bo climbed into the passenger-side cab of Booker T. Rowe's Ford F-150 pickup truck.

"You're having a hell of a few days, cousin," Booker T. said.

"Wide ass open," Bo whispered, closing his eyes and leaning his head against the window seal. The adrenaline had started to wear off.

58

They decided to meet at Hitt's Place on Bennett Drive. Terry liked coming to the bar with some of his younger sales managers because he enjoyed ogling the young college tail that fraternized here. Lou Horn looked like a square peg in a round hole in the place, which, at 8:00 p.m., was about half-full but would be packed as the night grew later.

"So what does he have on us?" Lou asked, taking a sip of Coors Light from a bottle. The bar advertised itself as having the coldest beer in town, and as Terry lifted his own Silver Bullet to his lips, he had to admit that the suds were ice cold.

"A few strippers," Terry said. "Including Lona."

Lou laughed. "She was always your favorite."

"Shut up."

Lou took another swallow of beer and exhaled. "Well, old buddy, if that's all Bo's got, he's got nothing. No way a couple of strippers are going to bring us down in a he-said-she-said contest." He frowned. "I'm a lot more worried about Zannick. He has you on tape confessing to the whole operation." He slapped his hand on the bar. "I still can't believe you did that, Terry."

Terry shook his head. "I've always had a big mouth," he said. "It's why I'm a good salesman."

Lou sighed. "I was so close on Thursday to being rid of Zannick. Sack had agreed to the dismissal, and all that was left was for Page to sign off on it."

"And Bo came in and ruined everything."

Lou drained his beer and held it to the bartender, who replaced it with a full one. "Yep."

For several minutes, the two men drank in silence. On the television screen, baseball highlights were being shown, but neither man paid any attention to them. Lou finally blurted out what both of them were thinking.

"The tape is bad . . . but do you really think Zannick could bring forward the witness he promised?" Lou paused and spoke just above a whisper. "The one who could truly break us."

Terry took a long sip of beer and let out a ragged breath. He was dog tired, and his brain hurt from the stress of his earlier confrontation with Bocephus Haynes. "I don't know, Lou, but I'll tell you this. I've learned to never underestimate Michael Zannick."

59

The arraignment of Helen Evangeline Lewis lasted all of fifteen minutes.

"On the charge of capital murder, how does the defendant plead?" Judge Susan Connelly asked as a full gallery of press from across the state of Tennessee leaned forward in their seats.

Helen let out a deep breath and spoke in a sharp voice that could be heard in the balcony. "Not guilty."

"Very well," Connelly said, gazing down at something on her desk and rubbing her chin. "The court enters the defendant's plea of not guilty and sets this case for trial on October 14, 2015."

PART FOUR

60

On the Sunday afternoon before trial, the consultation room at the Giles County Jail felt even more stuffy and claustrophobic than usual. Part of that was on account of the air-conditioning going out on Friday and still having not been repaired. Early October could be stifling hot in southeast Tennessee, and this year's edition was no exception, with temperatures hovering in the high eighties. Of course, the other reason was the dire feeling emanating from the two occupants of the closely confined space.

"So . . . we're screwed, I guess," Helen said, her tone a mixture of defeat and exhaustion. In the months since the arraignment, the General had lost weight, and her always pale skin appeared ghostly to Bo. Their meetings, which in the weeks between the preliminary hearing and the arraignment had been daily, stretched out to once a week, and Bo found his client to be withdrawing more and more into herself. Outside of Bo himself, Helen's only visitor had been her longtime friend Danny Cothren, an English teacher at Giles County High. Danny had reported to Bo that, by late August, Helen would barely say a word during his visits. "I'm worried, Bo," Danny had said. "It's not like Helen to give up. She's a fighter."

Things got even worse when, on September 17, 2015, the rape charge against Michael Zannick was dismissed pursuant to the same sweetheart plea agreement that Sack Glover had tried to push past

Judge Page in June. This time, it wasn't Sack who proposed the deal but Assistant District Attorney General Gloria Sanchez, who purported to Page that the state didn't feel there was enough evidence to warrant a conviction for either forcible or statutory rape. Over Bo's futile objections, Page entered the deal.

"Gloria's made her bed," Helen said when Bo informed her of the news. "She believes I'll be convicted. I suspect that Sack promised her that she would be retained as an assistant prosecutor when he wins the election in November if she would submit the Zannick deal to Page." She chuckled. "The ironic thing is that Gloria never believed in Mandy's case." Helen gazed at Bo with sad eyes. "She was telling Page the truth when she broke down her opinion of the case." After standing and walking to the door of the consultation room, Helen knocked twice and then leaned her forehead against the metal. "You should make your bed, too, Bo," Helen added. "I'm a lost cause. Withdraw now, and I'll pay you what I owe you. I'm sure I can get Dick Selby to take my case. No one can captain a sinking ship better than Dick."

"Absolutely not, General. I'm in this until the end," Bo said, but he was disheartened at the quit he saw in his client. When he came back the following day to alert Helen that he'd filed a civil lawsuit against Zannick for sexual assault, Helen didn't even smile.

"He'll buy his way out of that, Bo."

"No, he won't. Lona won't allow it."

She shook her head. "At the end of the day, everyone has a price. Lona and Mandy Burks are good but damaged people, and if they can recover a hefty sum and avoid the stress and uncertainty of a trial, they'd be fools not to settle." She paused and smiled at him. "Bo, you yourself will eventually advise Lona to take the money and run."

He didn't argue. Instead, he hung his head. "And Zannick will skate."

Now, a month later and twenty-four hours from the start of her trial, there was a question on the table. Bo gazed at his rail-thin client, trying to think of the most positive way he could answer her without lying to her. "No," Bo finally said. "I wouldn't say that we are screwed. We just—"

"Don't have any facts to back up any of our alternative theories," Helen interrupted, raising her eyebrows in challenge. "Right?"

"Right," Bo conceded. "Hooper is still digging. You've read his reports on Butch, Terry Grimes, and Lou Horn, haven't you?"

"Yes, and it's all fascinating. Just like his treatise on Zannick. But I can't connect the dots to Butch's murder."

Bo sighed. "Neither can I."

"Then we're screwed, Counselor."

"They still have to prove their case," Bo said. "They have the burden of proving beyond a reasonable doubt that one of the most prominent citizens in this county—a public servant for two decades, a woman who has brought numerous killers to justice as the district attorney general—brutally murdered her husband in cold blood." Bo paused. "They'll have to do that without a murder weapon, as none has been located, and without any eyewitness to the crime. All they will bring to court is circumstantial evidence."

Helen gave a weak smile. "I like it, but save the theatrics for your opening statement."

"That *is* my opening statement. No murder weapon. No eyewitness. No murder."

She shook her head. "You know damn well that a jury can still convict on circumstantial evidence. Now, in addition to Ms. Spencer seeing me at the house, my fingerprints being confirmed at the murder scene, and the mountain of motive they have against me for wanting to keep Butch from disclosing the abortion, they have Dr. Ward from the crime lab to testify that the blood droplets found in my Crown Vic match Butch's type. Ward will also testify that the hair found on

Butch's couch and on his damn robe matches the sample I provided." She paused. "How do we counter that?"

Bo gazed down at the concrete floor. "We don't."

"More like we can't. We live in the world of *CSI New York* and *CSI Miami* and *CSI New Orleans*, and Sack is going to turn that damn courtroom into *CSI Pulaski* and have that jury eating out of his hand."

Bo had no answer to this. The General was right. It was the problem with having a lawyer as good as she was becoming a client. No amount of bullshit he slung at this juncture could cover up the fact that they were pigs heading to slaughter. "I'm sorry, General. I've done my best."

"I know that, Bo, and I appreciate it. You didn't make these facts."

A hollow concession, and Bo took it as such. "I'll see you at the courthouse tomorrow morning at eight thirty."

Bo stood and walked to the door. "I want you to remember something, General."

"What's that?"

"My record in that courtroom over there is seventy-seven wins and one loss, and my only defeat was to my client in this case."

She stood and walked toward him. After giving him a quick hug, she whispered, "Thank you, Bo."

He bit his lip and managed a nod. Then he left the jail.

———

Back at the office, Bo paced around the long conference room table.

Lona stood against the far wall with her arms crossed. Since the arraignment of Helen Lewis, and despite the building being under construction for a month to repair the damage done by the fire, the law firm had opened ten additional files, eight of which were personal injury cases. Two of those, in addition to the Jess Reynolds matter, had reached six-figure settlements.

Bocephus Haynes had resurrected his law firm, and consistent with his daughter's wishes, he'd bought a house in downtown Pulaski about two blocks from their old house. Next week, he would stand before Judge Woodruff and plead his case that his kids belonged with him in Pulaski.

Regardless of whether he won next week or not, he'd been given a chance at redemption by General Helen Lewis. She'd literally breathed life back into his corpse when she asked him to represent her in this case.

I have to win, Bo thought, continuing to pace. "Did you have any luck with Darla Ford?" he asked Lona.

"None. She hung up the phone as soon as I said my name."

"Damnit," Bo said.

"What about the subpoenas we served on Grimes Ford/Buick?" Lona asked.

In the days after the arraignment, Bo had subpoenaed all video footage from the dealership for the night of Butch's murder. In Terry's written statement to the police, he said he had worked until 11:00 p.m. The video, however, showed him leaving in his Ford Expedition at 10:30 p.m. It wasn't much of a lie, but it did leave thirty minutes unaccounted for as Terry's wife's statement didn't have him arriving home until 11:15.

Lona sighed. "Bo, I waited a long time to present this, possibly because I know you probably don't want to hear it, but what about Booker T. Rowe? He had to be one of the last people to see Butch alive, and he had a lot of motive to want him dead."

"Booker T. says the last time he saw Butch was at the Hickory House Restaurant at 7:30 p.m. on the night of April 1. He'd finished eating and spoke to Butch as he was leaving."

"He also poured a beer over Butch's head. And Sandy Duncan, the waitress who was serving both of them, told you that Booker T. was drunk as a skunk and threatened Butch."

"All he said was that Butch would be sorry for not giving him an extension on his loan."

"That's a threat, Bo."

Now it was Bo who sighed. "Look, I've done my due diligence, and Booker T. is clean."

"What about the dark-colored Ford truck that Bonita Spencer saw ambling down Pecan Grove Drive during the time of the murder? What kind of truck does Booker T. drive?"

Bo laughed. "Lona, Ms. Spencer said that the Ford truck in question had a Confederate flag on the back window. I know for a fact that Booker T.'s vehicle does not fly the Stars and Bars." He paused. "Have you lost your mind?"

"Ms. Spencer said she couldn't make out the flag decal that well. Maybe she was mistaken. What if your cousin decided to make good on his promise that Sandy Duncan overheard at the Hickory House? What if, after driving by Butch's house, he went inside and shot him two times? Have you considered that?"

Bo peered up at the ceiling and ground his teeth together. "Yes."

"And?"

"Booker T. Rowe is six feet six and weighs over three hundred pounds. How could he have snuck up on Butch's house without being seen?"

"He could have approached on foot from the clearing in back of Butch's house, entered the same open door that the General did, and left the scene."

"Impossible," Bo said.

"Really?"

"Really."

"Well, what does your cousin say?"

"He says he wasn't there. That he left the restaurant and went home."

She crossed her arms. "What home? He'd been evicted from his farm by Butch Renfroe and Z Bank a month earlier."

"He was squatting on his property illegally."

"Uh-huh. Well then, what else did he do illegally that night?"

"He says he went straight to his farm, got drunk, and passed out."

"But he has no one to support that." She paused. "So let's recap. He has no alibi. A dumpster full of motive. And he owns the same make of truck that Bonita Spencer saw the night of the murder."

"He doesn't own a .44 Magnum."

"Wouldn't need one. He could've used the General's." She slapped her hands together. "Bo, you're biased because Booker T. is your cousin. That prejudice may cost the General her life."

"I believe him," Bo said, finally removing his gaze from the ceiling and looking at her.

For almost a minute, there was silence. Lona walked to the door and stepped in the opening to the hallway. She peered back at him with eyes that radiated intensity. "Face the facts, Bo. We're fifteen hours away from trial, and our best alternative theory is that Booker T. Rowe killed Butch. He had motive, means, and opportunity, which are the three things you keep harping on that we need." She paused. "You have to call him as a witness, even if he's hostile."

"I can't," Bo said.

"You must," Lona said. "It's the best chance the General has, and you owe it to her to put it out there." She paused. "Bo, you're a good man and a great lawyer. You know I'm right. *You know it.*"

61

An hour later, Bo turned up the gravel driveway to Walton Farm. He was now driving a silver Chevy Tahoe with black rims, which he'd purchased from the Howard Bentley dealership in Fayetteville a couple of days after his Sequoia had exploded. He liked the SUV, and he'd received the blessing of T. J., who said it was "badass." But as he slowly meandered up the path toward the "Big House," Bo was thinking about another truck that came into view when he crested the hill.

Booker T. Rowe's black Ford F-150 was parked by the barn. Bo cut the ignition and hopped out of his vehicle, walking toward his cousin's truck with equal parts dread and desperation. He inspected the front and side windows and walked around to the back. Feeling his heartbeat racing, Bo snapped several photographs of the decal he saw from a number of different angles. Then, walking back one hundred paces, he took a few more pictures. This would be the approximate distance from Bonita Spencer's window. *Close enough,* Bo thought.

"What are you doing, cuz?" Booker T. hollered from the front porch. Then he trudged down the steps and approached with a weary smile.

Sighing, Bo pulled a piece of paper out of his pocket. Lona had filed the subpoena thirty minutes earlier, and Bo was damned if he was going to let anyone serve it but himself.

"What's this?" Booker T. said, taking the document as Bo handed it up to him. The big man had completely sweat through his khaki work shirt that displayed the name and logo "Rowe Farms, LLC." He read the top of the document and quickly scanned it. "You're serious?"

"I have to subpoena you, even if we decide not to call you as a witness."

"Why would you call me to the stand?"

Bo decided not to sugarcoat what was happening. "To show an alternative theory for the murder."

Booker T. smirked. "Your alternative theory is me."

"You had the motive, means, and opportunity." Bo hated himself for repeating the phrase Lona had used, but his assistant had been right.

Booker T. made a tight smile with his mouth. "I can't believe that you'd do this to me. After putting me back in business." He stuck his chest out. "I've gotten all of my customers back and even added a few. I'm rolling again, and I think I may have convinced Thelma to give me another chance. Jarvis is talking to me again, telling me all about the football scholarship offers he's collecting, and Antonio is starting to ride a bicycle. Thelma sent me some video of it, saying that she was looking forward to their visit next weekend." He reached out and pushed Bo so hard that Bo almost fell down. "I've even figured out what you should do with this place." He held his arms out, gesturing toward the farmland beyond. "You know the Big Oak Ranch that John Croyle runs over in Rainbow City, Alabama?"

Bo nodded. John Croyle had been a few years ahead of him at Alabama and was an All-American defensive end on Coach Bryant's 1973 National Championship team.

"Well, how does the Roosevelt Haynes Farm for Boys and Girls sound?" Booker T.'s voice was now shaking with emotion. "The property is so big we could divide the land into a boys' part and a girls' section and put a community center in between."

Bo felt his eyes begin to burn with tears. Before he could respond, "That's perfect," Booker T. pushed him again and rocked him off balance. "Why you goin' do this to me, Bo? I'm the only family you've got."

"I have a duty to my client, and I'm out of time."

"I didn't kill him, Bo. You know that I'm not capable of that."

Bo didn't respond. Instead he hung his head. "I'm sorry." Bo started to walk away, but Booker T. yelled behind him.

"You know what you are, Bocephus. An Uncle Tom. You love being rich and playing the white man's game. What did you help me for? Build old Booker T. up so you can tear me down? That it? Are you sick like that? Well, fuck you!"

Bo reached his Tahoe and climbed inside.

"You hear me, cousin. You can go to hell! You can—"

The sound of the door slamming shut mercifully drowned out his cousin's screams.

———

Ten minutes later, Bo sat in Bonita Spencer's living room on Pecan Grove Drive. "Could this have been the decal you saw on the Ford truck that was driving slowly down the street the night of April 1, 2015?" he asked, holding his breath for the answer as she went through the photographs on his phone. He had held off as long as he possibly could to have this interview, but now he was out of time.

Bonita took her glasses off and brought her face to within a couple of inches of the phone. Then she put her glasses back on and held the device as far from her as she could. "Well, I'll be."

Bo's chest constricted. "You'll be what?"

"Damned, Mr. Haynes," she said, looking at him with a smile. "That *is* the truck I saw. I thought it was the Confederate flag on the back, but the background wasn't red. It was gray like this. And it wasn't an *X* that I saw. The decal was crooked, so it looked like an *X*, but it wasn't." She paused and placed her hands over her eyes. "How could I ever confuse a symbol like the Confederate flag with that?" she said, pointing at the picture as Bocephus Haynes's mouth went dry.

"I don't know, ma'am," he managed as he gazed at the photograph of the back window of Booker T. Rowe's truck, which didn't have a Confederate flag emblazoned on it but rather the universal symbol of Christianity.

The sign of the cross.

62

How could I have been so stupid? Bo thought as he drove the back roads of Giles County, finally pulling into the parking lot of the Bickland Creek Baptist Church. For forty years, his uncle Booker T. Rowe Sr. had been the pastor of this small congregation. And though Booker T. Sr. had passed away nearly a decade ago, Booker T. Jr. was still a regular attendee, and to show his pride in the church his father had founded, he'd stuck an emblem on the back of his Ford F-150 truck.

The sign had a gray background with a blue cross. Along both lines of the cross were the initials BCBC in white. Up close, it was easy to see the letters, but from a hundred paces away, they could easily be mistaken for the stars of the states of the Confederacy. And since Bo's cousin had attached the sticker at a slight angle, it did look a bit like an *X*, especially when peering at it from the side.

"Unbelievable," Bo whispered as he exited the Tahoe and walked toward the front door of the tiny chapel. As he had expected, the door was open. Though the storage area in back of the church was locked up, the main sanctuary was always open for those who needed to talk with God. That had been Booker T. Sr.'s rule, and the new pastor was following suit.

Bo sat on the second pew from the front, where he'd spent every Sunday of his childhood that he could remember. He gazed up at the pulpit and past it to the large wooden cross that adorned the far wall.

If Bonita Spencer was correct about the truck, then Booker T. had lied to him about not going to Butch Renfroe's house on the night of the murder. *That doesn't mean he killed Butch.* Bo's thoughts were quick to counter the suggestion, but the nausea he felt growing in his stomach was thick and palpable. Booker T. clearly had motive. And Bonita Spencer was now set to testify that she had seen his pickup truck driving past Butch's house during the time frame that the murder had been committed with plenty of time for Booker T. to park, go to the back of the house, and do the deed.

And with Helen's .44 Magnum revolver being left behind in the house, Booker T. would have had the means to kill Butch in the way opined by County Coroner Melvin Ragland.

———

For the next couple of hours, Bocephus Haynes sat in the second pew of the Bickland Creek Baptist Church. He thought about the case and tortured himself by going over the facts one more time.

Most of all, he prayed.

For guidance.

For strength.

For the courage to do what he believed was right.

God, please help me.

63

When Helen Lewis was escorted into the courtroom the next morning, she was wearing her customary black suit and black heels. As she heard the sound of her shoes clicking on the floor, she remembered knowing that the sound struck fear into the heart of many a defense attorney. Now she was the one who felt fear, and the outfit, her uniform, made her think of an officer putting on his dress blues before sticking a rifle in his mouth.

She met her attorney's eye, and Bo Haynes nodded at her with a look of confidence on his smooth face. She knew her chances of victory were slim, but she was glad Bo was here.

"Ready?" Bo asked.

"As I'll ever be."

"Remember, General. These first couple of days—"

"—are going to be awful. I know. They'll bring the hammer today and hope they pound us so hard the jury can't think of anything but my guilt. I know. I've been on that side of the table for a long time."

Bo started to say more, but then Sundance Cassidy entered the courtroom followed by the Honorable Susan Connelly. "Here we go," he whispered. And then, even though she was ready for them, Helen still felt a charge of adrenaline when Sundance said the two words that announced the start of trial.

"ALL RISE!"

64

Abortion.

If there was one word that dominated jury selection, it was *abortion*. Sack Glover mentioned it at least fifty times during his presentation, and Bo had to question the panel of forty-two people whether they could be fair and impartial to the General if the evidence showed that she had had an abortion.

The majority of the panel said they could, but Bo knew that most people weren't brave enough to tell a judge that they couldn't be fair because of a belief. And there were a few souls who actually would lie about it so that they could stay on a jury and use their prejudice and bias against the defendant. He had seen it happen.

Through it all, Helen kept her face and demeanor stoic and professional. By 4:00 p.m., the twelve individuals who would decide the case were seated in the jury box.

There were ten white men forty years of age or older, a white woman in her seventies, and another white woman in her thirties.

Sack Glover's dream, Bo thought, sizing them up and knowing that many times a case was lost before it started if you got a bad jury. However, every single one of these folks had voted for Helen Lewis each time she had run for district attorney general, though most of those times Helen had run unopposed.

That at least means there's a chance, he thought, but after Judge Connelly adjourned for the day, saying that opening statements would begin in the morning, he peered at his client, who was not having any of his optimism.

"Best go pick out my coffin," she said.

65

The state's case was well organized and methodical, and it seemed, at least by the end of the day on Thursday, October 17, 2015, rock solid. Sack Glover rolled out the same evidence that he had used at the preliminary hearing but with the added bonus of proving that the blood particles in Helen's car matched Butch's blood type and that hair matching the sample provided by Helen was discovered on the victim's couch and robe. It was indeed *CSI Pulaski,* as Helen had called it, and when Dr. Malacuy Ward from the state forensics lab in Nashville was finished testifying, all the jurors were giving Helen the stink eye.

Once opening statements were delivered Tuesday morning, Sack had started his case with Gloria Sanchez's testimony and Butch's signed press release, both of which taken together confirmed that Helen had threatened to kill Butch if he revealed the abortion she had had in 1977. Bo objected to the press release as hearsay, but Judge Connelly let it come in when Sack said he wasn't offering the letter for the truth but rather to show the victim's state of mind. The prosecution's next witness was County Coroner Melvin Ragland, who testified that the cause of death was two gunshot wounds from a .44 Magnum and placed the time of death between 9:00 p.m. and midnight on April 1.

The state's final witness on Tuesday was Bonita Spencer, who established the defendant's presence in the victim's home at near nine or ten at night on April 1, 2015. When asked whether he wanted to cross-examine Ms. Spencer, Bo hesitated, glancing behind him to Lona, who glared at him with disapproving eyes, and then to Helen, who nodded.

"Your Honor, at this time we'd ask that we be allowed to defer cross-examination of this witness." Bo was hoping to wait as long as possible to telegraph Booker T. as the defense's alternative theory. Generally speaking, it wasn't wise to waste the opportunity to cross-examine a witness, but Bo believed that the evidence of Booker T.'s truck being seen by Ms. Spencer would be equally as effective if presented as part of the defense case. *And I owe it to Booker T. to hold out as long as possible.*

This was the compromise he'd reached after his prayer session at the Bickland Creek Baptist Church on Sunday night, and Helen, who didn't think the theory was that strong—*"just because we can place Booker T.'s truck on the street doesn't put him in the house"*—agreed with the plan.

"Any objection?" Connelly snapped the question at Sack Glover, who gazed wide eyed at the judge and then at Bo.

"Uhhh, no, Your Honor," he finally said, shaking his head as if he didn't understand the maneuver.

"OK, Mr. Haynes. I'll allow it."

Bo kept his outside demeanor neutral, but inside a deep sense of relief washed over him. He'd bought himself some time.

———

First up on Wednesday morning for the state was Doug Brinkley, who testified to the General's target shooting with her .44 revolver the night of the murder. Sack then buried Terry Grimes in the middle of his case, with the county commissioner testifying to finding Butch lying on his couch at a little after 10:00 a.m. on April 2, 2015. Terry cried during his testimony when he described seeing his longtime friend's body disfigured by bruises and bullet holes.

Sack finished with the overwhelming physical evidence, calling Chief Deputy Frannie Storm to testify as to the fingerprint evidence, placing the General's prints all over the victim's house.

He finished on Thursday with Dr. Ward and the DNA.

The only points that Bo scored on cross-examination were getting Frannie Storm to concede that no .44 Magnum revolver was ever found at the victim's home and that there was no eyewitness to the murder.

At 4:45 p.m. on Thursday, after Dr. Ward left the stand, Sack Glover stood and cleared his throat. "Your Honor, the state rests."

Once the jury had been ushered out of the courtroom, Judge Connelly peered over the bench at Bo. "Mr. Haynes, do you know how long your case will be?"

What case? I have no case. Instead of saying that, Bo said, in candor, "Judge, I don't know. I'm going to have to speak with my client and make some decisions on that tonight."

Connelly shrugged, but she was obviously irritated. "Mr. Haynes, I hate leaving the jury hanging as to whether they're going to have to come back for another week. I'd appreciate a heads-up in the morning."

"Yes, Your Honor."

66

In the jail, Bo and Helen gazed at each other with blank, punch-drunk stares. "Any thoughts on tomorrow?" Bo asked.

"Call me and then rest."

"What about Booker T.?"

"I can't let you do that, Bo. We both know that Booker T. didn't kill Butch."

"Do we? Bonita Spencer will place Booker T.'s truck on Butch's street at approximately 10:15 p.m., and he had an altercation with the victim a few hours before the murder."

"Bo, come on. It's weak."

"It's all we've got."

She waved him off. "Get some rest. We've already rehearsed my direct examination enough."

That was true. Each night during the trial, Bo had taken Helen through a mock examination, doing his part and then also pretending to cross-examine her.

"OK."

"Bo?"

He turned at the door.

"No matter what happens tomorrow, I don't want you to feel any guilt about it. I know you've done your best for me." She shook her head. "For whatever reason, the deck seems stacked. From the minute I was arrested, I've never stood a chance. It's like someone's been out there playing me like a violin from the word *go*."

Bo didn't know what to say. Regardless of the General's words, if he lost this case, he was going to feel guilty for the rest of his life.

67

When he arrived at the office, Bo set his briefcase down and grabbed a beer out of the minifridge. It wasn't until after he'd taken his first sip that he saw the Post-it note stuck to the monitor of Lona's computer. He got up and snatched the note, reading it out loud.

"Bo, if you want to win this case, meet me at your father's grave at 9:30 p.m."

He read and reread the note, not recognizing the handwriting. Then he took his phone out and checked the time: 8:00 p.m. Lona had sent him a text at 7:00 p.m. saying she was heading home and asking if he needed anything for the morning. Bo had responded back, No.

The note must have been left between 7:00 and 8:00.

He didn't want to go, but he knew he had no choice. Beggars couldn't be choosers.

He drained the rest of his beer in one gulp and headed for the door. He'd grab a bite to eat at Legends and then head to the cemetery.

It was against the law to visit a graveyard at night, but that had never stopped Bo before.

68

Ennis Petrie was waiting on him when he reached the headstone.

"This better be good," Bo said, peering at the grave and taking a beer out of the six-pack he'd bought at Walmart on West College Street. He took a long sip. In the light from the three-quarters moon above, he could barely make out the name: Andrew Davis Walton. The last time he'd been here was a few weeks after Jazz's death. He'd poured gasoline on himself and lit a match, coming inches from setting himself on fire. After a few tense seconds, he'd decided against suicide, realizing that he couldn't quit on his children.

"It is," Ennis said.

"Why here?" Bo asked, gazing with contempt at his biological father's name.

"I didn't want to be seen out in public or with you in your office. Especially if Michael Zannick has one of his goons following you. And . . ." He looked at the headstone. ". . . I've always been a big fan of irony. It's fitting that I do my good deed in front of the grave of the man who ruined my life and yours."

Bo forced himself to remain calm. "Haven't heard from you since you saved my dog." Bo paused. "Thank you for that."

"Thank you for not mentioning my presence. Is Finn Pusser still in jail?"

Bo shook his head. "No, he's out on probation, but Frannie promises me that they're watching him like a hawk. They could never prove his involvement in the car bombs, so all they got him on was simple assault." Bo paused. "Where've you been?"

"Around," Ennis said. "There hasn't been any reason to see you." He paused. "Until now."

"Why now?"

"Because I can't wait any longer."

Bo squinted at the former lawman and set the remainder of the six-pack on the ground at Ennis's feet. "Beer?"

Ennis took one and popped the top.

"OK," Bo said. "Enlighten me."

"When I was in prison, the only regular visitor I had was Finn Pusser."

"You've told me this before, Ennis. Finn said that Zannick wanted information on some townspeople, and you dished about the prostitution ring."

"I didn't tell you everything," Ennis said, sipping his beer.

"What didn't you tell me?"

"The real reason that I never told the General I was investigating the ring."

Bo felt the hairs on his arm begin to prickle. "What was the reason?"

"I didn't tell her . . . because I became a client of the ring."

"You?" Bo felt his heartbeat pick up speed.

"Me."

"I . . . I don't know what to say. Tell me."

"Not much to tell. I paid for a couple of encounters with a stripper named Tammie Gentry."

Bo felt an icy chill on the back of his neck. "Who did you pay?"

Ennis looked him in the eye. "Butch Renfroe once. Lou Horn another time." He paused. "I told Finn about my participation when he visited me in jail, and I think he got one of those guys—Terry would be my bet because he's a loudmouth—admitting on tape to the scheme after being confronted with it." He paused. "I also bet it was Butch who kept the paper trail of the scheme."

"The computer," Bo said out loud. "Butch's laptop was stolen the night of the murder. The prosecution has argued that Helen was trying to get rid of any evidence of her abortion, but it could just as easily be Lou Horn or Terry Grimes disposing of the evidence of the prostitution ring."

"Bingo," Ennis said. "And Terry Grimes is a neighbor and the first person to see Butch dead. Who's to say he wasn't the last person to see him alive?"

Bo took a long sip of beer, thinking the problem through in his mind. Finally, he sat on the cool grass below the grave and chuckled bitterly. "This is all fantastic, Ennis, it really is, but what am I gonna do? Are you willing to take the stand and confess to prostitution? Frannie is liable to send you right back to prison." He drained the rest of his beer. "And even if you did take the stand, your story only implicates Lou. Terry Grimes skates free, and Terry is who we need to nail. He's the link to Butch's murder, not Lou."

Bo stood up, taking the six-pack with him. "The General is right. We're screwed."

"I know how you can prove Terry's involvement."

"How, Sheriff, because your confession ain't enough. Darla Ford was a stripper at the Sundowners, and I know she participated in the scheme, but she'll take the Fifth if I subpoena her. And Lona Burks, who can link Terry to the ring, would be torn apart on cross with her criminal record and drug history. And Terry isn't going to confess if I recall him, is he?"

"Bo, you shouldn't need any of that."

"Why?" Bo asked, the exasperation in his voice palpable.

"Because I bet Butch's lawyer would have all of this information."

"His *lawyer*? What the hell are you talking about?"

"Butch and Helen got divorced in 1995. Helen represented herself, but Butch had one of his cronies represent him."

Bo cocked his head at the other man. "You talking about Ray Ray?"

Ennis nodded. "Ray Ray is your ace in the hole."

Bo's exasperation turned to anger. "Ennis, you know as well as I do that Ray Ray is dead. I can't call him to the stand."

"Don't you lawyers keep *files* on clients?"

Bo felt another chill on his neck. "You think Ray Ray might have mentioned something about this in his file?"

"Think about it, Bo. He was representing Butch in a divorce, and a money and property settlement could have been greatly impacted if Helen ever got wind of any side money Butch was making running whores."

Bo blinked his eyes and gazed at his father's headstone. Not too far from this very spot was the grave of Raymond Pickalew. "His file?" Bo asked.

"Do you know where Ray Ray's files went after he died?"

Bo thought about it for a half second, and then his face broke into a grin. "I believe I do."

69

Bo dialed the number the second he got back to his car. *Please answer . . .*

The call was picked up on the third ring. "Hello, Bo? Is that you?"

Bo closed his eyes and said a prayer of gratitude. "My believer. Have I got a favor to ask of you."

———

During his own trial for the murder of Andy Walton four years earlier, Bo had taken to calling Rick Drake his "believer" because of the kid's earnest presentation in front of the jury. Now thirty-one years old and on the cusp of closing the offices of McMurtrie & Drake in Tuscaloosa so that he could return to his hometown of Henshaw, Alabama, Rick sounded excited to hear Bo's voice.

"Been following the trial, Bo. Whatever you need, name it."

"Do you remember what happened to all of Ray Ray Pickalew's client files after he was killed?"

Silence for five seconds. "Not off the top of my head, but I'm pretty sure I've got some notes about wrapping up Ray Ray's estate on our computers here at the office. The Professor was the executor of Ray Ray's estate. Can I check and get back to you?"

"Yeah, but go fast, dog. The clock is running out on us here."

———

Thirty minutes later, Rick called back with the answer. "All the files are in a storage facility in Meridianville. Landwehr Mini-Storage is the name."

Bo sighed with relief. "Meridianville is only an hour away."

"Are you looking for the General's ex-husband's file?"

"Yeah. I think there might be something in there we can use."

"What about the attorney-client privilege?"

"Butch is dead," Bo said, "and I wasn't his lawyer. I need to see that file."

There was silence on the line, and then Rick spoke into the phone. "Bo, I have a pretrial conference tomorrow in Tuscaloosa, or I'd go to Meridianville myself and try to help you find that file."

"No worries, I've got someone to help. Thanks, Rick. I really appreciate this."

———

For ten seconds, Bo tried to breathe, wondering if it was possible that Ray Ray Pickalew might save his ass one more time from the grave. Then he placed his last call of the night.

"Hooper," the voice answered, loud and alert.

"You out Uber driving?"

"Not tonight."

"Good. I need your help with something, and it's an emergency." For the next fifteen minutes, Bo explained what he wanted and provided the combination and passwords that the private investigator would need to get into the unit. When he finished, Bo let the investigator know the stakes. "No pressure, but the whole case rides on this." He hung up the phone before the other man could answer.

70

Bo arrived at the courthouse the next morning at 8:30 a.m. He was wired on adrenaline and caffeine. He called Hooper from his parking space, and the investigator was inside the storage facility in Meridianville. There were, by his estimation, at least five hundred file jackets to go through. "I've already been through half of them, but it may take me a while longer to know whether Renfroe is here."

"We don't have a while, dog. I'm going to call the General as my first witness, and if I haven't heard from you by noon, I'll have to go in a different direction." Bo cringed at the prospect of recalling Bonita Spencer to place his cousin's truck on Pecan Grove Drive and ending the case by putting Booker T. Rowe on the stand.

"You'll hear from me by noon," Hooper said. And the phone clicked dead in Bo's hand. He gazed at the architectural beauty of the Giles County Courthouse and took in a deep breath. As he exhaled, he said a silent prayer.

Please God, let me be on my game today. Please . . .

71

The courtroom was standing room only. All rows of the main floor were occupied, and the balcony was overflowing. Helen glanced behind her and moved her eyes around the gallery. She saw a few smiles mixed with several hard stares. Mostly she observed curiosity in people's faces. The way folks looked at a movie screen when they weren't sure what was about to happen. Or the fixed gaze a farmer gave a stray dog who had ambled onto his property.

"ALL RISE!" the bailiff bellowed, looking as buffed and resplendent as ever. Helen almost smiled. How many times had she heard Sundance say those words over the years? Helen's stomach clenched as she waited for any acknowledgment from her old friend, but none came. He had turned to watch his boss enter the room.

The Honorable Susan Connelly walked toward the bench with her head down, focused on the path in front of her. A soldier doing her duty. It had been her demeanor all week. She took her seat and looked out at the mass of humanity that had come to see this, the presumed last day of trial. Leaning forward, she spoke into the microphone in a voice hoarse with fatigue and the beginnings of a bad cold.

"Before I bring in the jury, I want to remind the spectators today, and especially you members of the press corps, that I expect absolute quiet while the witness or witnesses, whatever the case may be, testify today. Turn your cellular phones off or put them on silent mode. If I hear a phone ringing, the owner will be held in contempt and placed in a jail cell for the night." She paused and glared out at the crowd. Then she turned to Sundance. "Escort the jury in."

Seconds later, the group of men and women who would decide this case walked toward their seats. Once they were in place, Judge Connelly lowered her bifocals and gazed at the prosecution. "General, are you ready to proceed?"

As she had the first four days, Helen flinched and had to stop herself from responding.

"Yes, Your Honor," Sack Glover said, running a hand through his thick red hair. "The state is ready."

"And the defendant?" Connelly had made a point not to look at Helen all week, but this time she did. Her eyes were creased with worry and a twinge of fear.

"Yes, Your Honor," Bo's deep voice rang out, and Connelly moved her eyes to him.

"Then call your next witness."

"Your Honor, we call the defendant to the stand."

Though the crowd of spectators had clearly expected this development—that was why most of them were here—there was still a collective sucking in of air.

Helen stood and walked toward the witness stand. For almost thirty years, she had questioned people who had sat in this very box. Murderers. Rapists. Drunk drivers. Eyewitnesses. Medical examiners. Victims and their family members. Every type of person from every conceivable walk of life.

Now, she took her place in the box.

"State your name for the record."

Helen cleared her throat and lowered her mouth toward the microphone. "Helen Evangeline Lewis."

"And please tell the jury what you do for a living."

"I am the district attorney general for the Twenty-Second Judicial Circuit."

"General Lewis . . ." Bocephus Haynes's voice rose to the back of the courtroom, and even Helen herself felt the hair on her arms and neck begin to tingle.

". . . on the night of April 1, 2015, did you kill Frederick Alan Renfroe?"

"No," Helen said, speaking as firm as she knew how to speak. "I did not."

"Did you threaten Mr. Renfroe earlier that day, in this very courtroom, that you would kill him if he revealed a secret that the two of you had shared since 1977?"

Helen looked directly at the jury. "Yes, I did."

"And what was that secret?"

"In December 1977, I told Butch that I had aborted our child. I told him that I didn't want to have children because I wasn't ready."

"And did he promise to keep the abortion secret?"

"He did." Helen knew the prosecution could object to Butch's comments to her as hearsay, but why would they? All of this abortion talk was fanning the flames of their case.

"But on April 1, 2015, he threatened to disclose this secret to your opponent in next month's election for district attorney general, Mr. Sack Glover?" Bo gestured with his right arm to Sack.

"Yes."

"He also said that he had drafted a press release that he would send to the local papers and television stations, correct?"

"Yes, he did."

"And you threatened to kill him?"

"Yes. I was upset. He'd promised never to say anything."

"General Lewis, did you go to Doug Brinkley's shooting range that night after work?"

"I did. When I'm stressed out, I like to shoot guns. My favorite gun to shoot is my .44, and that's what I was using that night."

"How long were you at the range?"

"A little over an hour. I thought it would calm me down."

"Did it?"

Helen shook her head. "No. If anything, I was madder."

"What happened next?"

Helen took in a deep breath, and her exhale was audible on the microphone. Then she spoke in a matter-of-fact tone. "I drove to Butch's house on Pecan Grove Drive. I had been there once before, right after he moved in about a year earlier, to look at the place on his invitation. I parked on the curb and walked around to the back of the house."

"Why?"

"Because I knew the door would be unlocked—when we were married, Butch never locked the doors—and I wanted to surprise him."

"Were you intending to kill him?"

"Absolutely not," she said.

"What was your intention?"

Helen gritted her teeth. "Honestly, I wanted to beat his lying ass."

There were actually a couple of laughs from the gallery and one snicker from a juror in the back row. Helen watched as Bo paused and gazed at Sack Glover with a look of satisfaction. *A laughing jury doesn't convict,* she'd always heard.

"What happened when you walked inside?"

"Butch was sitting on the couch getting drunk. I approached him and said that I felt there was only one way to solve the problem he had presented." Helen's hands began to shake, and she held them together in her lap.

"What did he do?"

"He started to cry, the pansy, and then he began to take another sip from his drink."

Again, there was a smattering of guffaws from the packed courtroom, and Bo paused before asking his next question. "What did you do next, General?"

"I hit him in the face with the butt end of my revolver."

297

"The .44?"

Helen nodded. "Yes. I hit him three times before he grabbed my arm and knocked the gun free. He pushed me away and told me to leave. When I tried to get my gun back, he said that he'd bring it to me the next day."

"What happened next?"

"I left."

Bo gazed out at the packed gallery and looked up into the balcony, which was also full. "General Lewis, did you ever once fire your revolver while you were in Butch Renfroe's house on Pecan Grove Drive?"

"No, I did not."

"General Lewis, does it surprise you that your fingerprints were found in Butch Renfroe's house and on his clothing?"

"No. I beat the crap out of him in his house. I would have expected that."

More laughter, this time from higher up in the balcony.

"And would it surprise you if microscopic blood droplets of Butch's were found in your car?"

"Same answer. I'm surprised they didn't find more."

"General Lewis, when you left Butch Renfroe's house on Pecan Grove Drive, what time was it?"

"Approximately 10:00 p.m."

"Did you have your revolver with you when you left?"

"No. The last time I saw my .44 was on the floor of Butch's den."

Bo gave a curt nod and waited a good three seconds so that everyone in the courtroom could take in what they'd just heard. Then he spoke. "No further questions."

———

"Cross-examination, Mr. Glover?" Judge Connelly asked, and Helen almost smiled at her old friend's failure to use the "General" title. Sack

298

Glover clearly noticed the omission, as his face turned a dark shade of red. *Mad lawyers make stupid mistakes,* Helen thought, wondering how Sack was going to begin. *I admitted everything and gave a plausible explanation for how the physical evidence could be present without me killing Butch.*

"Ms. Lewis . . ." Sack clearly took pleasure in not calling Helen by her title, even more so after Judge Connelly's similar slight of him. "In December 1977, you had an abortion, didn't you?"

Sack was looking at the jury as he asked the question, clearly hoping to gauge their reaction when Helen said yes.

"I told Butch I aborted our child."

Sack turned his head toward her and blinked. "Yes, we know that, General, and that was because you did, in fact, have an abortion in December 1977, correct?"

Helen had waited seven months for this question, hoping that it wouldn't come in so direct a manner. She had written Bo's questions for her on this topic, but she had no control over the prosecutors. She had known, as soon as the letter written by Butch was leaked to the press, that she'd eventually have to face the music. Better right here, right now, in front of the jury that would decide this case in a standing-room-only courtroom.

"Judge, would you please instruct the defendant to answer the question?"

Helen gazed up at Susan Connelly, and Her Honor peered down at her with concerned eyes. "General Lewis, you must answer. Did you have an abortion in December 1977?"

Helen released a sob and then covered her mouth. Slowly, she turned back to face the jury and told them a secret she'd been keeping for thirty-eight years.

"No," Helen said.

There was an audible gasp from the gallery. One of the spectators yelled, "Oh my God!"

"Order!" Judge Connelly bellowed, banging her gavel. "I'll have order in this court." But Her Honor likewise looked flustered. "Go ahead, Mr. Glover."

"Excuse me," Sack said, grabbing his collar and trying to keep his composure. "Let me ask it again. Ms. Lewis, did you or did you not have an abortion in December 1977?"

Helen cleared her throat and spoke into the microphone. "I did not have an abortion."

Sack's mouth hung open, and he made the fatal mistake of any cross-examination. He asked a question to which he didn't know the answer. "What happened then?"

"I told Butch that I had an abortion, and then I left school after my first semester of my third year of law school. I had more than enough credits to graduate, so I left. After traveling to New York and Las Vegas, I went to Los Angeles, California, and had the baby at a hospital there on June 16, 1978." Her lip began to tremble, but she finished. "I immediately gave my child up for adoption."

The blood appeared to have drained from Sack Glover's face, he was so pale. Now that he had stepped in it, he knew there was no turning back. "Why did you lie to Butch?"

"Because I was raped after the Alabama-Tennessee football game in October 1977, and I was afraid the baby would not be Butch's."

Silence permeated every inch of the circuit courtroom. Helen had been to the morgue at the hospital countless times, and the overwhelming sense of quiet in that place of death was what the courtroom felt like to her now. *An apt analogy,* she thought.

A lie she had been perpetuating for almost forty years had just died.

"Did you press charges against the rapist?" Sack finally asked. His voice was so high it sounded as if Helen's high heel was scrunching his balls.

"No. He used a date rape drug." She sighed. "I didn't think anyone would believe me." She paused and made eye contact with as many

300

jurors as she could. "That's why I went on to become a cop and later the district attorney general of this county." She paused. "I wanted to make sure what happened to me never happened to anyone else."

Sack took a couple of steps backward, and the back of his knees hit the prosecution table, nearly causing him to stumble. Helen could tell he wanted to ask another question, but he was terrified of losing any more ground.

"You lied to your ex-husband, didn't you, Ms. Lewis?"

Helen scowled back at the prosecutor. "And he lied to me."

Sack turned his head upward to Judge Connelly. "No further questions, Your Honor."

"No redirect," Bo said.

"The witness is excused," Judge Connelly said.

As Helen left the witness chair and returned to her seat, Bo watched her with shock and wonder.

"At this time, we're going to take a short recess," Judge Connelly said. "I think everyone could use a break."

After the jury filed out, Bo turned to his client, but Helen had her face in her hands. She tried to stifle her anguish but wasn't very successful. Bo looked beyond the table to the gallery and caught Lona Burks's eye on the front row. He motioned her over. "Can you . . ." Bo trailed off and gestured to the General.

"Yes," Lona said, putting her arm around Helen. She looked at Bo and mouthed the words, *That was incredible.*

"*I know*," Bo mouthed back.

Patting the General on the back, he grabbed his phone and made a beeline for the door, glancing at the screen. He had no text messages and no missed calls. "Damnit," he whispered under his breath. The General's testimony had been the high-water mark for the defense team, but they still needed an alternative theory, and they were out of time. If his private investigator hadn't found anything, Bo knew he had no choice but to call Ms. Spencer and Booker T.

Where the hell are you, Hooper? Bo thought, barreling out the double doors and almost colliding with a man heading in the opposite direction. Blinking his eyes, Bo could have kissed the man when he recognized him.

Albert Hooper was carrying a file jacket under his arm.

"Is that it?" Bo asked.

Hooper nodded.

"And?"

The plump investigator smiled from ear to ear. "I think you're going to love it."

72

"Your Honor, the defendant calls Mr. Terry Grimes to the stand," Bo said, his voice firm and authoritative though his heart was pounding in his chest. There were times in trial when a lawyer had to trust his gut and take a risk, and this was one of those times. As Grimes strode back into the courtroom to take his place in the witness chair, Bo gazed up at the balcony, noticing a clean-shaven man with a crew cut looking over the railing with keen interest. Ennis Petrie, the former high sheriff of Giles County, Tennessee, peered at Bo with eyes that glowered with intensity and held his right thumb up. Bo gave him a curt nod. Then he focused on the witness.

Terrence Robert Grimes wore a light gray suit, white shirt, and dark blue tie. His salt-and-pepper hair was combed in a neat part, and he spoke in a soft, deliberate tone. After once again being sworn in by Sundance, he looked at Bo with blank eyes.

"Mr. Grimes, you're a county commissioner, isn't that right, sir?"

"That's right."

"And you've been a county commissioner for going on twenty-two years, right?"

"Correct."

"Butch Renfroe was your friend and neighbor, right?"

"Yes, sir, he was."

"And it was you that discovered Butch's dead body the morning of April 2, 2015?"

"Yes, sir."

Robert Bailey

Bo walked to the edge of the jury railing and made eye contact with several of the jurors. Then he glared across the courtroom at the witness. "Mr. Grimes, isn't it true that you and the victim, Butch Renfroe, were once investigated by the former sheriff of this county, Ennis Petrie, for being involved in a prostitution ring?"

"Objection!" Sack Glover had almost leaped out of his chair. "This question is irrelevant and preposterous."

Bo didn't hesitate with his response and looked right at the jury when he gave it. "Your Honor, this is at the very heart of the defense's theory of the case, and I'm entitled to a thorough and sifting cross-examination."

"I'm going to allow it," Connelly said, peering over the bench at Grimes. "Answer the question, Mr. Grimes."

"I've never been charged with prostitution of any kind."

"Not charged, sir. Investigated. Were you ever investigated by the sheriff's office for prostitution?"

"No, I was not."

Bo gave a look of incredulity. Then he went over to the defense table and grabbed the ancient file jacket with the label "Renfroe, File #95-0047" on the manila tab. "Mr. Grimes, isn't it true that for two decades you and Butch Renfroe and Lou Horn were engaged in a prostitution ring that you ran out of the Sundowners Club on Highway 64?"

"That's a lie," Grimes said, spittle flying out of his mouth when he spoke.

"And occasionally, every so often, y'all would use the old Sands Motor Hotel for a few of these soirees, wouldn't you?"

Grimes's face became ashen as Bo slowly removed a videotape from one of the folders of the file jacket. He didn't answer the question, but Bo didn't care.

"And on some of these occasions, you and Butch liked to videotape these encounters, didn't you?"

"I don't know what you're talking about," Grimes said. His voice had become weak.

"Mr. Grimes, would it surprise you to know that Butch had given a few of the tapes to his lawyer, Raymond Pickalew, for safekeeping?" He held up the tape in his hand for Grimes and the jury to see.

When Bo turned back to the witness, Terry was looking at the videotape like it might be a poisonous snake.

"Mr. Grimes," Bo began, not waiting for an answer. He approached the stand and held the tape in front of him. "I'm going to ask you again. Were you a part of a prostitution ring with Butch Renfroe and Lou Horn?"

"Objection, Your Honor," Sack said. "Again, Judge, this is completely irrelevant."

"Overruled. Answer the question, Terry."

Terry Grimes bit his lip and gazed down at the podium. When he spoke, his voice was a low squeak. "I plead the Fifth."

A loud rustling went up from the gallery, and Bo could smell blood in the water. "Mr. Grimes, did a man named Michael Zannick ever threaten to go public with his knowledge of this prostitution scheme if the rape charges brought by General Lewis against him weren't dropped?"

Grimes cleared his throat and then croaked into the microphone, "I plead the Fifth."

Bo looked at the jury. "Mr. Grimes, where is the computer you stole from Butch Renfroe's house?"

"Objection, Your Honor. Lack of foundation!" Sack howled.

"Overruled," Judge Connelly said.

Terry Grimes had started to cry. "I plead the Fifth," he said.

73

Terry Grimes was taken into police custody immediately after being excused from the stand.

"Judge, I'd ask for a mistrial," Sack Glover pleaded. "The questioning of Mr. Grimes by Mr. Haynes was reckless and improper."

"Denied," Connelly said. "Call your next witness, Mr. Haynes."

"Your Honor, the defense rests."

———

Two hours later, after closing arguments were delivered by both sides and the jury instructions were read by Judge Connelly, the jury was given the case.

They were out all of eight minutes before knocking on the deliberation room door and announcing they'd reached a unanimous verdict.

———

Once the jury was back in the courtroom, Judge Connelly asked the parties to stand and then addressed the foreperson. "Has the jury reached its verdict?"

"Yes, Your Honor," the foreman said, clearing his throat. "We the jury, on the charge of first-degree murder, find the defendant . . . not guilty."

———

Bo closed his eyes and then felt hands and arms wrapping around him. "You did it, Bo. You did it." It was Lona Burks. His strawberry-blonde assistant had tears in her eyes. Bo hugged her back and walked across the courtroom. He extended his hand to Sack Glover, but the prosecutor wouldn't take it. "I'm going to write you up for this, Bo. Get ready for a third suspension."

"Go for it," Bo said, looking past the prosecutor to Sheriff Hank Springfield, who did shake his hand.

"Congratulations, Bo," Hank said.

Bo strode back to the defense table, hoping to embrace his client, but General Lewis was nowhere to be found. "Where'd she go?" Bo asked Lona.

Lona pointed toward the double doors. "She's gone."

74

Six hours after the not-guilty verdict was rendered, Chief Frannie Storm and a team of sheriff's deputies located the computer stolen from Butch Renfroe's house in the attic of a hunting cabin that Terry Grimes owned in Elkton, Tennessee. Though an attempt to erase the information on the computer had been made, an IT specialist inspected the computer and was able to recover several of the files, including a tape of Terry and Lou Horn having sex with several women in a hotel room and an Excel spreadsheet saved under the name "Ring" with a list of names and payments.

Grimes was arrested on charges of first-degree murder, burglary, and prostitution. Horn was charged with prostitution.

75

Bocephus Haynes celebrated his first trial victory in five years by splitting a six-pack of beer with Albert Hooper. After both men were sufficiently buzzed, Hooper said he wanted to see what was on the infamous VHS tape that Bo had dangled in front of the jury several hours earlier.

"Wait a minute, dog. Are you telling me that you haven't watched the tape yet?"

"I didn't have time. I just saw the folder labeled 'Friday afternoon, Sands Hotel.'"

"Do you have a VCR?"

Hooper giggled and went to his car, returning with an actual VCR. He hooked it up to the TV in Bo's office and pushed the tape in the slot. "Ready?"

"Where in the hell did you get a VCR?"

"I borrowed it from the Giles County Library this afternoon so we could watch the tape."

For a moment the room was silent, and then Bo grumbled, "Play the damn thing."

Hooper pressed "Play," and for a split second, there was an image of a naked Terry Grimes on the screen. Then snow filled the screen followed by the familiar jingle of "I'm Alright" by the great Kenny Loggins and images of a golf course.

"You've got to be kidding me," Bo said, grabbing the sides of his face with his hands.

"You were about to play *Caddyshack* for the jury this afternoon," Hooper said.

After a three-second pause, the room broke up in raucous laughter.

76

An hour later, Bo drove up the long and winding road leading to the "Big House" at Walton Farm. He parked next to his cousin's truck, glancing at the decal of the cross on the back window and shaking his head. Then he stepped out into the cool autumn night and gazed up at the porch. He carried a bottle of Bombay gin in his right hand and walked toward the house, feeling a bit unsteady on his feet after the three beers he'd consumed at the office with Hooper. The fatigue and stress from the trial had also begun to set in, and his legs felt like cement blocks.

Booker T. Rowe was sitting on the steps of the porch, and for a few seconds, Bo stood in front of him, saying nothing. Then finally, Bo took a seat beside him. He unscrewed the top on the bottle of gin and took a sip, closing his eyes as the alcohol warmed his throat and belly. Then he extended the bottle to his cousin. Keeping his eyes shut, he held his breath until he felt the container being removed from his fingers.

He turned and gazed at Booker T., who hesitated before taking a long sip. Then the big man's mouth formed a tight grin. "Congratulations."

Both men now peered forward. The glow from the half moon above shone on the cornfields that had recently been harvested. "Thanks," Bo said.

For at least a minute, the only sounds came from the wind rustling through the trees to the north. There were many things Bo wanted to ask his cousin, but none of them seemed all that important right now. Eventually, he stood and stretched his tired arms over his head. Then he took a couple of steps forward, moving his eyes around the thousand acres that had defined much of his life. "The Roosevelt Haynes Farm for Boys and Girls," he said out loud. He turned to look at his cousin.

Booker T. Rowe's face loosened, and he gave a tentative nod.

Bo returned the gesture and looked back at the land. "I like it."

77

Helen Lewis sipped from a pint of Jack Daniel's and gazed down at the small headstone, which read: FREDERICK ALAN "BUTCH" RENFROE. BORN JANUARY 15, 1950; DIED APRIL 1, 2015.

"I'm sorry, Butch," she said for at least the hundredth time since her arrival in the cemetery. Immediately after the verdict was read, she had walked down the hallway to the district attorney general's office and grabbed a file from the cabinet. Then she'd walked to the basement of the courthouse and sat on the floor of the janitor's closet and cried. By the time she had left the building, it was almost dark and after closing time.

She'd taken a cab to a liquor store, bought the pint, and then had the cabbie drop her off two blocks from the graveyard.

Helen had been sitting in the damp grass in front of her ex-husband's grave ever since.

"Tell me something," a familiar voice said from behind her.

Helen made no move to turn around. She was too tired, too drunk. Besides, she'd heard that voice for twenty years. "Thank you for your help, Ennis."

Ennis Petrie took a seat next to her. "Congratulations, General."

Helen wiped tears from her eyes. Finally, she sighed. "You know I killed him, don't you?"

He nodded. "Yes."

"Why?"

"Because the person whose name is on this file tab"—he pointed at the manila folder lying in the grass between them—"paid me one hundred thousand dollars to kill Butch." He paused. "But when I went inside his house the night of April 1, he was already dead."

Helen glanced at the file and then looked at Ennis. "You've known all along."

He nodded.

"Where's my gun?"

The former sheriff squinted at her. "I think you'll eventually figure that out."

Helen peered back at her dead ex-husband's grave. "What about Grimes?"

Ennis snorted. "My theory is that he came over and discovered the body the next day and decided to steal the computer because he knew it would be searched and he'd be implicated in crimes. It never made sense to me that Grimes would come over at night and kill Butch. I've known Terry a long time, and that's not his style." Ennis paused. "Now, would he seize an opportunity to get rid of evidence to save his own hide?" The former sheriff snickered. "Absolutely." He paused. "You gonna let Grimes take the rap for Butch's murder?"

Helen gave a weary smile. "If I'm elected to another term in a few weeks, I'll make sure he's only convicted of burglary and prostitution." She ran her hands over her face. "Even if Sack wins, I doubt he's stupid enough to try the murder case again against Grimes. A deal will be reached. I guarantee it."

For several minutes, the two former colleagues sat beside each other in the shadowy cemetery, lost in their respective thoughts. Finally, Helen broke the silence.

"Everything happened exactly as I said it did this afternoon," Helen said, talking as much to herself as she was to him. "I went over there to kick Butch's ass. I beat him with the revolver, and he took it away from me." She shivered. "But I didn't walk away. I tried to wrestle the gun back from him, and it went off. When I stepped away, he was bleeding from his chest." She wiped her eyes. "I knew it was a kill shot, and so did Butch." Helen gazed at Ennis. "He asked me to finish him off. Begged me to do it."

"So you did."

She nodded. "I was in shock afterward and must have blacked out or something. I didn't remember leaving the gun at the house. I didn't even realize it was gone until I checked my glove compartment the next day." She hesitated. "Ennis, if you knew that I did it, why didn't you leave my .44 at Butch's house? Or at least put it somewhere that the sheriff's office could find it? That would have made my conviction a slam dunk."

Ennis stood and stuck his hands in the pockets of his jeans. "No comment."

Helen gazed up at him. "OK, forget the gun. Why did you help Bo during the investigation and trial of the case?"

He let out a ragged breath. "Because I believe that good people make terrible mistakes in this world. I . . . made an awful one that I'm still paying for. I didn't want you to have to go through that."

"Why?"

Ennis looked down at her with kind eyes. "Something tells me that you've been paying for something else for a long time."

She nodded. "Since 1977."

EPILOGUE

1

A week after the trial of Helen Lewis had concluded, Bocephus Haynes stood before Judge Lucas Woodruff in the circuit court of Madison County, Alabama, and made his case to be awarded full custody of his children.

"Your Honor, I have bought a house in downtown Pulaski, I have a law practice that's doing pretty well, and I've kept my nose clean." Bo gestured behind him where T. J. and Lila sat side by side in the first row of the gallery. T. J. had his arm around his sister, and both kids had anxious looks plastered to their faces. Each of them had already testified to wanting to live with their father in Pulaski. "I've made arrangements to reenroll T. J. and Lila in the Giles County School System, and they can start next week." Bo paused. "Your Honor, I've made a lot of mistakes in my life, and I've paid dearly for them." He stopped and had to keep his voice from shaking as he finished. "I want my family back, Your Honor. I need them, and they need me."

Ezra Henderson's response was short, bitter, and to the point. "Judge, this man's record speaks for itself. He's a criminal, and just because he's managed to stay out of trouble for six months doesn't mean he's ready to be responsible for my daughter's children and my grandchildren. Bocephus Haynes is a dangerous human being, and those kids are better off with their grandmother and me."

After a five-minute recess, where Bo, T. J., and Lila paced the floors of the hallway outside the courtroom, Woodruff reconvened and made his decision.

"After consideration of the arguments made by counsel, the wishes of the children, and the statements given by Mr. Haynes and Mr. Henderson, it is the ruling of this court that custody of Lila Michelle Haynes and Thomas Jackson Haynes be awarded to . . ." He paused and smiled. ". . . their father, Bocephus Aurulius Haynes."

———

In the aftermath of Woodruff's ruling, Bo hoped for some kind of reconciliation with Ezra, but the old man fled the courthouse before Bo could talk to him. Juanita Henderson, however, stayed behind and gave Bo a kiss on the cheek. "Take care of my grandchildren, Bo."

"Yes, ma'am," he said. Then he turned to his kids, both of whom were smiling ear to ear. "Well . . . are you guys ready to go home?"

———

That night, in their new house on Jefferson Street in downtown Pulaski, Bo kissed his daughter on the cheek while tucking her into bed. "Do you like your room?"

"I love it," Lila said, hugging his neck tight. "Hey, Daddy," she whispered in his ear.

"Yeah, baby."

"Thank you."

"For what?"

Lila's eyes glistened in the faint light from the moon, which shone down through her window. "For not giving up on us."

Bo bit his lip hard as he reflected on the long road he'd taken to get to this point. The pain. The obstacles. The loss. He saw fleeting images of Jazz and Tom McMurtrie in his mind and then a five-year-old boy on a suffocatingly hot August day who saw something no child should ever have to witness.

What was it that made a person not quit? Was it God? The human spirit?

Or could it be the people who came along in your life and who taught you to endure the pain . . . the obstacles . . . and the loss and keep going? For Bo, there had been three such people.

Coach Paul "Bear" Bryant, who had taught him the value of a strong work ethic and that the lessons of winning on the football field carried over to life.

Professor Thomas Jackson McMurtrie, who had shown him, through his words and his actions, how to practice law and, more importantly, how to face adversity.

And Jasmine Henderson Haynes, who had granted him the most ethereal of gifts: a wondrous love, acceptance, and . . . two priceless and precious gifts.

Now, as he gazed across the bedroom at one of those bequests, Bo blinked back tears of gratitude. Then he whispered, "I love you, Lila."

"I love you too, Daddy."

2

On November 6, 2015, the people of the Twenty-Second Judicial Circuit voted to reelect Helen Evangeline Lewis to a record fourth term as district attorney general. A victory party was thrown at Giles County

High School chaperoned by Danny Cothren, and over one hundred people came to give their best wishes to the General.

The next morning, Gloria Sanchez reported to work, fully expecting to be fired. Instead, she found fifteen case files on her desk. Before she could even sit down, Helen bellowed from her office, "Gloria, I'm way behind, and I need you to come in here and give me summations on every file that I put on your desk. There's a settlement docket in front of Page this afternoon, and I want to be ready."

Gloria tiptoed through the opening to Helen's door and stood in front of her. "I still have a job?" she asked.

"Did I stutter? I need those summations," Helen snapped. "Chop chop."

"Why?" Gloria asked, unable to contain her curiosity. "I testified against you in your trial, and I dismissed the rape charges against Michael Zannick. Why aren't you firing me?"

"Because doing those things took guts. You had to make difficult choices, and you didn't shy away from them. You made a decision and stood by it." Helen paused. "Besides, as I said, I'm six months behind, and who else is going to catch me up? I doubt Sack Glover is going to offer his help."

"Th-thank you, General," Gloria said.

Helen gave her a look. "Don't make me regret this."

―――

A week later, the civil lawsuit filed by Mandy Burks went to early mediation. After eight hours of negotiations, Mandy, with her mother's blessing, agreed to accept the sum of $1.5 million in full settlement of all claims against Michael Zannick. After the paperwork finalizing the agreement had been executed by all parties, Bo called Helen and delivered the news.

"Zannick buys his peace," Helen said, her voice tinged with bitterness.

"And skates clean," Bo added. "After everything."

———

Within twenty-four hours of the execution of the settlement documents and the contemporaneous dismissal of Mandy Burks's civil lawsuit against Michael Zannick, the deal with Hoshima was announced. A thousand more jobs were coming to the town of Pulaski.

That night, Michael Zannick had a huge party at his mansion off Highway 31 and invited the entire town.

Helen didn't show up until the end. When she did, she asked for a word in private.

He invited her into his study, and Helen sat in a rocking chair and gazed at him. "I'd like to know what you did with my gun."

He smiled. "Ahh, General Lewis. I wondered when you would put two and two together."

"It's the only thing that makes sense."

Zannick reached into a drawer and pulled out the .44. He admired the weapon and then slid it across the coffee table that separated their chairs to Helen.

"After I was acquitted, I went back and looked at your file, Michael. One of the things we have to prove on a statutory rape charge is the defendant's birth date. It's a part of the predicate. You have to be shown to be over eighteen while the victim must be under eighteen."

"And what is my birth date, General?"

"June 16, 1978."

"And where was I born?"

"Los Angeles, California," Helen said, her voice soft and wan.

He smiled. "And who was my mother, General?"

"Patricia Zannick. She—"

"—and Henry Zannick adopted me at five years old. After I'd been through three sets of foster parents." He paused. "But whose womb did I come out of?"

"Mine," Helen said.

Zannick started to clap his hands. "Very good, Mother. I was beginning to believe you were never going to figure it out. Bravo."

"Is that why you came to Pulaski? To play games with me?" Helen felt the beginning drumbeats of a budding rage forming under the surface of her being. She remembered thinking early on after her arrest that someone was playing her like a violin.

Someone was . . .

Zannick shook his head. "I came here to get even."

"Did you?"

"No." Zannick stood and walked to the window, leaning his forearm against the sill. "I thought I had, but I was mistaken."

"How so?"

"Well, I thought I'd become the most powerful person in my parents' hometown and that I'd framed my mother for my father's murder." He paused, chuckling. "That would have been a worthy effort."

"If that was your aim, then why didn't you leave my gun somewhere that it could be found?" She gestured at the weapon on the table. "Discovery of the murder weapon would have cinched the prosecution's case."

Zannick continued to gaze out the window. "Because my goal wasn't simply to win. I wanted you to suffer." He turned toward her. "Butch was worthless. Orchestrating his killing could be considered mercy." He hesitated. "But you're strong. I was going to hold out and see what you and your excellent attorney came up with. Then, at the last second, I planned to have the gun conveniently be found and pull the rug out from underneath you." He grinned. "That would have been the ultimate revenge."

"You're a sociopath," Helen said as the anger that she'd initially felt deep in her subconscious spewed to the surface. "Why didn't you do it?"

"Because I wasn't expecting to hear that my real father was a rapist." He said the words as if he were somehow irritated with her for upsetting his plans, and Helen couldn't contain her rage any longer.

She reached forward and snatched the revolver from the table. "Your father was just like you," she said, checking to see how many rounds were left in the chamber and pointing the weapon at her son.

Zannick's face went ashen. "You killed Butch," he said. "I didn't set you up. You did it. *You killed him.*"

Helen said nothing and cocked the pistol.

"So . . . ," Zannick started, struggling to find his voice. "You gonna kill me too?"

Helen stuck out her jaw and gripped tight to the gun. "You raped Mandy Burks and got off scot-free. Exactly like your father did."

"Go ahead then. Put me out of my misery. But before you do, you should know the Burks girl set me up. She and her boyfriend were the only two high school kids who came to that party, and she was the aggressor." Zannick paused. "She lied to you and to her momma, and now she's a millionaire."

"You raped her, and you should've been punished for it."

"Based on the check I wrote, I'd say she made out pretty good in the deal."

"You're a monster," Helen said, hovering her finger over the trigger.

"I'm your son."

Helen continued to hover her finger over the trigger. Then, keeping her eyes on Zannick the whole time, she lowered her weapon and returned the revolver to her pocket. Seconds later, she was heading for the door.

"Come on, Momma," Zannick teased, but his voice was shaking with nervous energy. "Stick around. Shouldn't we catch up? Don't you want to know why I tracked you down?"

Helen Evangeline Lewis turned and peered at him. "There'll be enough time for that in the future."

Then she walked out the door without looking back.

ACKNOWLEDGMENTS

My wife, Dixie, is always my first reader, and my stories would have never been published without her help and encouragement.

Our children—Jimmy, Bobby, and Allie—are my inspiration and joy.

My mother, Beth Bailey, is a constant source of love, support, and assistance. She is also one of my earliest readers, and I value her critique.

My agent, Liza Fleissig, has been my wingman on this writing journey, and she continues to help me achieve my dreams. I am eternally grateful for her persistence.

My developmental editor, Clarence Haynes, offered insights, ideas, and advice that improved my story and characters. Clarence is a phenomenal editor, and I'm blessed to have him on my team.

Megha Parekh, my editor with Thomas & Mercer, was a calm and steady presence, and her encouragement and support were much appreciated on this journey.

To my entire editing and marketing team at Thomas & Mercer, thank you for your continued support. I'm so proud and honored to call you my publisher.

My friend and law school classmate, Judge Will Powell, was an early reader, and I leaned on him again for advice with respect to criminal law matters.

Thank you to my friends Bill Fowler, Rick Onkey, Mark Wittschen, and Steve Shames for being early readers and for providing me with support and encouragement.

My brother, Bo Bailey, was also an early reader, and I am grateful for his help.

My father-in-law, Dr. Jim Davis, continues to be my proofreader with respect to firearms, and his positive influence is much appreciated.

My friends Tom Castelli and Kristen Kyle-Castelli were instrumental in helping me understand Tennessee criminal law.

My friends Joe and Foncie Bullard from Point Clear, Alabama, have provided tremendous support, and I'm so grateful for their help, encouragement, and friendship.

A special thanks to everyone at my law firm, Lanier Ford Shaver & Payne, PC. I am so grateful for the support and encouragement of my colleagues.

My friend Danny Ray Cobb, to whom I dedicated this book, passed away in January 2019. When you are trying to achieve your dreams, you remember the folks who were with you in the beginning. Danny Ray was my first fan in Pulaski and organized my initial event at the Giles County Public Library. Thank you, Danny Ray, for everything.

ABOUT THE AUTHOR

Photo © 2012 Dixie Bailey

Robert Bailey is the bestselling and award-winning author of the McMurtrie and Drake Legal Thrillers series, which includes *The Final Reckoning, The Last Trial, Between Black and White,* and *The Professor. Legacy of Lies* is his fifth novel. For the past twenty years, Bailey has been a civil defense trial lawyer in his hometown of Huntsville, Alabama, where he lives with his wife and three children. For more information, please visit www.robertbaileybooks.com.